FACE
TO
FACE

Elinor Norton had risked everything for this man—her marriage, her good name, her lost chance of happiness. Now in the great dining room of this isolated mansion, she sat facing Blair Leighton, gazing at the handsome features she knew so well.

"Tell me it's not true what they say. Tell me it isn't," she demanded.

And in answer she saw the mocking light in his eyes, the sardonic turn of his mouth, the terrible coldness.

And suddenly she knew she was the prisoner not of love—but of hate. . . .

THE STATE VS. ELINOR NORTON

Mary Roberts Rinehart

A DELL BOOK

Published by
DELL PUBLISHING CO., INC.
750 Third Avenue
New York, New York 10017

Reprinted by arrangement with
Holt, Rinehart and Winston, Inc.
New York, New York
Printed in Canada
Previous Dell Editions #R107, 8248
New Dell Edition
First printing—July 1971

1

I had anticipated some profound change in her when they brought her into the dock. It seemed incredible that so much living, such passionate love and later such violence of fear and despair could have left her without visible scars; that the long loneliness of the past few years, broken only by that man's returns to her—and God knows how he had returned, time after time—should have left only a rather pitiful look of patience and waiting.

Even there in that dock, and surrounded by the panoply of the law, she had that look, as though she waited for something. Or somebody. Yet for what could she wait? Or for whom? Old Caroline was dead. Even Isabel Curtis had turned against her, and while I had counted for a great deal in her life, I had never been a vital factor.

"Why is it," she had asked me once, "that when I care so much for you, I cannot care enough?"

"We can't control those things, Elinor. They are or they aren't."

Perhaps she waited for an end of waiting, as though any decision would be better than none. People have killed themselves for such a reason; for certainty as against uncertainty, an end on the rocks rather than endless drifting. She would not take her life. She considered that weakness. But she would let these people take it for her if they so decided.

"What does it matter?" she had said to Shirley Johnson. "I did it, and one way or another I shall have to pay for it. That's not only man's law, Shirley."

Which was in its way an echo of old Caroline herself, creature of her world and high-church Episcopalian as she was, but with the ghost of John Calvin at her elbow all her

5

days. To the end of her life she had believed that all mankind was conceived in depravity and raised in corruption; that even her daughter Elinor was the seed of sin, and that the cry of vengeance in Deuteronomy was the authentic voice of God. . . .

The courtroom had been very still when she entered, and after the first shock of seeing her again, and there, I had plenty of time to watch her. She was quiet, entirely self-possessed. When she glanced over the room and saw me I thought her face lightened for a moment; as though we looked at each other, not across a crowded court but across the years. Then the look of patient endurance returned. I doubt if she so much as saw the grave faces of the ranchers and their wives, the local gentry, the battery of cameras and the small army of reporters, sent to that remote town from hither and yon.

But after that one glance at me she seemed to forget me. Like the crowd, I did not matter. Clearly, to her this was her own personal problem, one which she could share with no one, unless perhaps with that cold Jehovah of her mother's.

She was, I saw, carefully dressed, and I surmised that the Mayhew girls, her cousins, had sent her the rather too smart black clothes she was wearing. As though they had said, *She simply has to look decent. After all, she is a Somers, and a cousin. And the newspapers will be taking pictures of her. It won't do for her to be shabby.*

Perhaps I am unfair to them. They had envied her her beauty and the dramatic intensity of her life, but they were not malicious. And from wherever they came, she had accepted the clothes, the small black hat, the black suit with its white blouse, the shoes which were rather large on her small feet. She had always been proud of her feet. I can remember once sitting on the beach with her at Newport and saying that her feet were like a baby's, all white above and pink below. She had been pleased about that.

She had accepted the clothes. I could see her in the cell at the jail, and a matron bringing in the boxes. Could see

6

her patiently and quietly trying on the suit, maybe borrowing some sewing things and altering it. She had always been expert with a needle. Trying on the shoes too, and sliding her feet about in them. The matron standing by, and Elinor sliding her feet about in those pumps, and even smiling faintly. She would have smiled if they came from the Mayhews. They had always hated her small feet, those cousins; her small feet, and her delicate hands and her lovely face. Hated the way she held her head, too; like a young French marquise of the old régime.

She wore the string of pearls her mother had given her at her marriage, a short string but very good indeed. She had saved them from the wreck, somehow. I know now, of course, that she had hidden them, for during the trial there was that story of Leighton on that last day hunting for something. Tearing the house wide open, even lifting the carpets, and even ransacking that secret drawer in her desk. But she never told what he had wanted. It was too sordid. It debased the thing for which she had sacrificed so much. She had never really felt debased until at the very end.

Dearest Carroll, she had written me only a few months before. *Do try to understand me and not mind too much. Carroll, I don't want you to come here again. How dreadful that sounds, written to my oldest friend! But I can see that things here only worry you, and I am really all right. We are anxious, naturally, but we have enough money to carry on with. Not too much, of course, but we can manage to get along. We shall not need any more help.*

It was the "we" in that letter which had angered me, not its other contents. As though I had ever worried about Blair Leighton! What was Leighton to me? And whatever she might write or say, I knew by that time that she had chosen a lonely road, and that he would travel only a part of the way with her. It did not help that she had scratched out the "we" in two places and had written "I" instead. I knew that she was only trying to save that last and final blow to my pride of which her marriage had been the first.

I had known nothing of the tragedy until after her arrest

the following morning. They had come for her with a car, and she had said little or nothing on the way in. It was a cold day, and she sat huddled in that old fur coat of Ada Mayhew's, beside the sheriff. She had seemed not so much dazed as thoughtful; as though she were still trying to think out something vitally important. And they had treated her well at the jail.

She had stopped on the pavement and taken a final look about her. Then very quietly she went in, and the sheriff was calling to somebody. "Joe?"

"Yes, sir."

"I want this little lady to be comfortable."

"All right. I guess we can take care of her."

The jail was modern and clean. They put her in a room with a bed, a table and two chairs. The man called Joe brought her some magazines and turned on the steam heat. Then the sheriff came back and asked her if she wished to notify anyone.

"Notify?"

"Your friends. They'll want to know."

"Thank you. But this must be my affair. I did it, you know."

He looked shocked, and went away quickly.

It had all seemed quite simple to her. In such a way had she lived her life. In such a way had she been driven to do what she had done. It was her life and her responsibility. She could look neither behind her nor ahead. And she wanted no help. For her it was the end.

It had not been the end, however. If she knew about it she must have been astounded at the sensation which followed. Shirley Johnson, old Caroline's attorney, was on his way West to assist in preparing her defense. The press was covering the story from every angle, and was only kept out of the house at the ranch by main force. Old photographs had been resurrected and published, of her coming-out, of the ballroom at Sherry's where her first ball took place, even of her marriage to Lloyd Norton; this last showing her, small and exquisite in satin and old lace, standing

8

beside Norton and looking rather frozen, while surrounding them were a dozen bridesmaids and a row of none too steady ushers with white gardenias on their lapels.

I saw that picture just before the trial, and was almost startled to find myself in that row, and determinedly smiling into the camera. God knows I had not felt like smiling.

Through it all she sat quietly in her cell. Sometimes she sewed or read, but often she merely sat and thought. She asked for no newspapers, for public opinion meant nothing to her, sitting there alone. What mattered desperately to her was that she should herself understand what had happened, and why. Perhaps now at last she could see. For three years Blair Leighton's big hulking body had stood between her and the world. She had never seen past it. Now the spell was over. She was determined to be honest, to discard all the small hypocrisies and even the unconscious defenses she had built through those years to justify herself. She would even be fair to Lloyd Norton, perhaps for the first time. As for me, I doubt if she thought of me at all. This was between the three of them, Lloyd and Blair and herself.

And only she was left to be honest. She was left, there in her cell with her two ghosts.

The matron coming in in the mornings with a smile. "And how did you sleep last night?"

"I slept a little, thank you."

"Maybe I'd better ask the doctor for a bromide."

"Please don't bother. I'm all right."

And so another night, alone with her two ghosts: the one the man she had married, the other the man she had loved and killed.

This is not the story of Elinor's crime. It is not even the story of her trial, the vast machinery for which was in course of preparation during those endless days and nights of hers; the great portable switchboard being installed, with its almost 200 wires; the press tables being introduced into the courtroom, and additional space being made for the stenographers; the arrangements for flashlight pictures; hotel rooms reserved for the trained seals of the writing profession, who were coming to interpret what they saw and heard.

Yet it is, in a way, the story of both. Why must we always begin with our crimes? Surely it is what leads to them that is important; the slow inevitable course of events, the building toward tragedy, not away from it. What I am doing now is what Elinor wanted to do on the stand and what she was unable to do, to fill in the background; to take, in effect, that dozen awful hours or so while the jury is out and the reporters are playing poker in hotel bedrooms, and, beginning at the beginning, to build toward the end. To be the counsel for the defense.

Nobody knew that story, even when the trial was over. She had wanted to tell it, or such part of it as she might; and for days the press, gathering together in hallways and in the speakeasy across the street, had had a story among themselves that she had wanted no defense, and that for the past week or two her local attorney and Shirley Johnson had been fighting her to keep her off the stand, and wringing their hands over her attitude.

It was true.

"I want to tell the story," she said to Shirley. "The whole story. I don't much care what happens to me, but there are one or two people who still care for me, and they have a right to know."

"You'll never get a chance to tell the whole story, Elinor."

"It isn't so long, really."

"Don't you understand?" he said savagely. "They'll get you up and drag one incriminating thing after another out of you. That's what they're there for."

"But I am making no defense."

"For God's sake, Elinor! What am I here for?"

He tried to tell her what was coming; the prosecution watching the press and feeding it so that public opinion would be against her before the trial began; the press itself, taking commonplace and familiar things with which everyone is familiar, and thus stressing the close relationship of the crime to the everyday life of its readers; ferreting out commonplace facts, too, which the prosecution had overlooked, and again bringing the crime home in familiar guise, for example, to every woman who owns a sewing table. Elinor's antique sewing table had been found upset on the floor.

Nothing at all of the last few years. Nothing at all really about Elinor, except that rather exotic setting of her earlier life. And now the woman, sitting in her cell with her two ghosts; or in a crowded courtroom, facing with a queer young dignity a battery of cameras and flashlights. The public which crowded the courtroom that day and saw her enter, slender, proud and still lovely, had picked her up on the day when they opened their morning newspapers and saw her name in the headlines. True, some of them may have remembered her début, and later her marriage. But there have been other fashionable débuts, other smart marriages. To them she began to exist on the day when she felt that her life had ended.

They knew her name, of course, or if they did not the press enlightened them. The daughter of a former Ambassador, born and reared to wealth, educated at one of the best of the schools for the daughters of such families and finished in Switzerland, so that she had always put my schoolboy French to shame: this was Elinor as they knew her. Among the old photographs which had been discovered and published there had been one of the big sailing yacht, long since rotting in a basin along the Massachusetts coast; and another of her mother in the dress she wore when she was presented at the Court of St. James's, long white satin train, heavy drapery about the hips, and the inevitable three feathers in her hair.

It was a background which was glamorous and dramatic against the monotony of their own hard-working lives.

But of this woman I have called Elinor Norton they knew nothing whatever. They had picked her up, press and peo-

11

ple, when on a cold and stormy night on a remote ranch in Montana she had killed Blair Leighton with Lloyd Norton's service automatic.

2

Caroline Somers, Elinor's mother, was one of my earliest recollections. Her big summer house was next to our own cottage, a few miles from Newport, and I was afraid of her, always.

She was one of those thick-bodied women of the nineties with surprisingly slender legs and ankles, a fact which I discovered one day to my own cost. I had moved a chair from which she had risen, only to see her attempt to sit down again on it, and to sprawl on the floor. It remains an indelible picture, that sudden destruction of majesty; Caroline on the floor, barrel-bodied as usual, but with those surprisingly slender legs exposed. And Caroline, when she could speak, ordering me out of her house. "Now leave this house and don't come back," she said. "Do you understand?"

I ran. I was 10 at the time, and it was two years before Caroline asked me back. To a children's party, that was, on Elinor's birthday; Elinor in white organdie, holding a prim little bunch of flowers, and with that look of breeding which Caroline lacked, but which the Newport cousins, the Mayhews, both had to a lesser degree.

But for those two summers of my exile I was a lonely boy, and for days on end I would wander about within a small radius of my own, of which the big house was the center. A hideous center, I realized now, with its huge bulk, its corner tower, its wide painted verandas with their rows of rocking chairs, and its mid-Victorian furnishings. I shall

12

never forget what in my childhood was called the long par-
lor but later on became, by a shift in terminology but no
other change, the drawing-room.

It had, I imagine, been furnished with all the discarded
elegances of the New York house, and it overcame me—
rather as did old Caroline—by sheer weight. Buhl and
ormolu chests and cabinets, heavy plush-covered chairs and
sofas, unimportant oil paintings in important gilt frames,
all were crowded together into an impressive and hideous
whole. There was, I remember, an enormous French gilt
clock on the mantelpiece, surmounted by an equally enormous French gilt angel playing a harp. Compared with that
room the chintz and wicker of the small living-room at our
own cottage seemed poor and shabby.

On the second floor a tower alcove opened out of Caroline's bedroom, and it was there that she spent much of her
time. At her desk, with her back turned to the windows,
writing her innumerable letters and notes, auditing her
household bills, calling to account one after the other the
small army of servants. I never saw her look at the sea.
When she went out she was hatted and veiled against the
sun, and from my hiding-place outside the cutting-garden
I have seen her, still hatted and veiled and gloved, with a
pair of shears and a basket, delicately snipping flowers for
the house.

She terrified me. I moved on one such occasion, and she
looked in my direction and called sharply, "Who's there?"

But while she was feeling for her lorgnette—she would
not use glasses—I ran wildly.

Elinor she saw at stated intervals; in the morning when,
neatly starched and ironed, she was brought to the tower
bedroom before being taken to the beach; and in the late
afternoon before her bread-and-milk supper. But this second appearance was not inevitable. There were many guests
in the house. Caroline had quarreled with Newport and set
up on her own some 15 miles away, and in one way or another she managed to secure a good many visiting notables.

I can see all this now, but then I only knew that for some

13

reason or other my own people in their small cottage were not on Caroline's list. To her dying day my mother resented Caroline Somers. Shut out as she was from that glamorous world, I realize now that she used my sharp young eyes to picture it to her.

"You say they have *two* men in the dining-room besides the butler? Good heavens, what does she find for all those servants to do?"

Or: "What does her maid wear, Carroll?"

"I don't know. Black, I think, mostly."

She would sigh. "You would think, John," she would say to my father, "that with a maid to look after her she might look better dressed. She's positively dowdy."

She would run her hands over her own pretty hair, with a certain complacency. But even then I knew that Katie, coming down from the upstairs in a fresh white apron to serve the dinner, represented failure to her.

She deeply resented my exile, and when the invitation to the party came there was a bitter conflict over it.

"Let him go if he wants to," said my father.

"Let him crawl in and lick her hand, like a whipped dog?" said my mother, holding her chin high.

But I went. I would have gone if they had locked me up. Absurd to say that I was in love with Elinor then, but she represented something, something small and exquisite, set in a world so far from my own that she had all the charm of the unattainable. I went, and I took all my spending money for the summer so that I might carry with me a present for her. It was a heart-shaped gold locket on a chain set with an infinitesimal turquoise, and containing an almost microscopic photograph, a reduced snapshot of us both.

Elinor hung it around her neck, but Caroline scowled.

"Does your mother know you bought that?"

"No. No, ma'am."

"I hope not," she said, and promptly forgot me.

I believe that later on she ordered Elinor to give it back to me, but she never did.

This is no boy and girl story. I have pictured Caroline

14

Somers because she played her own part in Elinor's story, and I have pictured the small boy who for two long summers drew his furtive circle about that gray and monstrous house, the vegetable garden, the maze—yes, Caroline had planted a maze—the pond which at low tide was a salt water marsh, and then along the beach. But I have not pictured Elinor.

She, too, was a lonely child. Her mother was in her late 40's when she was born, and with the perspective of maturity I still wonder at that child-bearing. What impulse sent Howard Somers back to his wife after years of more agreeable associations no one can know, but Caroline's latent Calvinism prevented her escaping its result. She bore his child in indignation and revolt.

I have tried to forgive her. She was too old to be a mother, too far from her own youth. Perhaps also some of her resentment against her husband entered into it. She had hated him for years. I have only a vague picture of him in my mind, a thin elderly man with a jaunty air and a carnation always in his buttonhole. But I recall distinctly a summer evening when our Katie with a flaming face rushed into the house and said he had insulted her on the beach.

He died not long after that. There was a rumor that he had died in the apartment of some woman or other, but the newspapers conveniently altered that to his club. Caroline never forgave him that final *faux pas*.

But at last she was free. Free and ambitious. During the years which followed she encouraged less and less the young people in the neighborhood, for Elinor was definitely headed now toward Newport and a début later on. Caroline was renewing old acquaintanceships there and forgetting old enmities. She still stubbornly stuck to her carriage, and our sailing or bathing plans were often ruthlessly disrupted so that, carefully chaperoned, Elinor might drive away in the carriage with its two big bays. One of the under-footmen became a groom then, and in a flattish silk hat to match the coachman's and tight doeskin breeches sat on the box beside him.

15

But Katie brought in stories that Elinor loathed Newport and all it meant, that she frequently rebelled, and that she cried herself to sleep sometimes. Katie was an invincible romanticist, and one day she found me shaving in the bathroom and planted herself in the doorway: "She's off again today, Mr. Carroll."

"Off again, on again, gone again," I said, through the lather. "Who's off again, Katie?"

"Miss Elinor. And if you ask me, she'd rather stay and sail with you than go to a dozen Newports."

"Get on with you, Katie; you and your Irish tongue!"

"It's true, Mr. Carroll. Delia over there's been saying it right along. And she was crying before she went."

I spent that day on the beach, overwhelmed with joy and despair. True, with the mixture of the sentimental and the practical which is 19, I returned to eat a substantial luncheon at noon. But I ate gloomily and absently, under Katie's eyes, and the despair was real enough. By that time I was frantically in love with Elinor Somers, with the frantic love of the age when long years loom ahead before that love can be anything but ridiculous. I can remember counting the years on my fingers: four years at college, four more to be able to support a wife. And always there was Caroline, Caroline now interested in Elinor for her own purposes, buying her clothes carefully, standing off like a showman to judge the effect. I had seen her once, when Elinor was brought down to exhibit a new dress.

Caroline had lifted her lorgnette. "Turn around."

And the look she gave her, long and concentrated, was the look of a showman. It was fixed, not on the dress, but on Elinor in it. And Elinor flushed. "Is it all right, Mother?"

"It suits you," said Caroline. "Draw it in a little under the arms, Hawkins."

Hawkins held it, tentatively, and so revealed more clearly the line of Elinor's small firm breasts. Caroline nodded. "Like that," she said, and lowered her lorgnette.

I saw Elinor's glance at me, and I felt ashamed for her. But she said nothing. Long years had taught her to say nothing at such times. She went out however with her head high, and she did not come down again.

I was tolerated at the big house by that time. I imagine Caroline had found even her own fierce will daunted by my persistence, so that it was easier to endure me than to keep me away. And why should she fear me? She knew her world well, did Caroline. She had seen boy and girl affairs before, and soon now Elinor would be making that celebrated début of hers, meeting men, entering into a sophisticated and glittering society which made an art of living luxuriously and of playing extravagantly.

I am even not at all sure that Caroline did not know that Elinor met me on the beach, the night after Katie had spoken to me. Like most heavy women she walked lightly, and I saw a white dress near the boathouse while Elinor was crying in my arms. For that is what happened. Taken all in all, it was a queer little scene.

"I'm sorry you care for me, Carroll," she said gravely. "You see, I'm different. I'm not what you think I am at all. I don't care for anybody; not for anybody, anywhere."

It was then that she began to cry. If I had been older I might have understood; the fierce repression of all those years, the frozen emotions, perhaps—almost certainly—a yearning toward her mother and a bitter disappointment there. And a resulting fear of love of any sort. "I don't love anybody. I can't, Carroll."

It shows Caroline's complete control of herself and of the situation, that she left us there and went away. Still noiselessly.

A long way, all this, from that scene in the courtroom. Two children weeping together on a beach under a young moon, the one because she could not care and the other because he cared so desperately. Not so far, after all, for Elinor revealed that night the submission which was to bring about her marriage three years later: "I can't fight her, Carroll. She's so strong. Nobody knows how strong she is."

"You'll have to live your own life. She can't live it for you."

"Not live it," she said with conviction, "but she'll arrange it. Watch and see."

"You mean, she'll marry you to someone you don't care about?"

"Not necessarily. She would probably make me think I care! She's perfectly capable of that."

Yet it is indicative of our youth and its inherent light-heartedness that a few minutes later we were dancing together on the sand while I whistled a tune. Two children dancing on the beach under a young moon.

3

I suppose Lloyd Norton was somewhere in the offing during those summers. I have a mental picture of a tall and very thin youth, with a sallow skin and a weak mouth, but whether I ever saw him or have reconstructed the boy since from the man he became, I do not know. When I did meet him he made little or no impression on me. He had an indolent manner and a considerable assurance; very probably I remember that because I had neither. And he had a drawl which could be rather offensive, and an exaggerated courtesy toward women which seemed to me even then to have something of contempt in it.

The news, in my senior year at college, that Elinor was engaged to him hit me hard. I wrote her the desperate letter of a heartsick boy; that she had destroyed my faith in all women forever, and I even intimated that my life had no longer any value for me and that at any time I might end it! I believe her mother got it, for there was no answer.

She had come out the winter before in New York; the usual ball at Sherry's, the usual stag line, the usual truckload of flowers to be sent half withered the next morning

18

to hospitals, the usual photographs in the papers. It was a famous ball, even for those days just before the war, when there was still a Four Hundred in New York, when women still wore real jewels, and when sumptuous eating and drinking were no small part of social life. Caroline, according to the papers the next day, wore her famous tiara that night, and received her guests in the small Louis XIII ballroom. And Elinor, of course, was in white.

I knew she was in white, because I was in the crowd on the pavement when she arrived that night, and I walked all the way to the Brooklyn Bridge later and stood for a long time gazing at the water below. But it looked cold and a long way down, so I stopped somewhere for a sandwich and a cup of coffee. After all, she was only remote then, not lost.

Nevertheless, I was losing her. The next morning I studied the photographs in the papers, but the Elinor who looked out from them was not quite the Elinor of Seaview. She looked older, for one thing, and I thought disillusioned and not too happy. There was very little there of my old playmate of the sands.

Years later she told me something of that winter. "It was horrible," she said. "I was so nervous, and I felt so alone. The other girls had been brought up together, but you know how Caroline did." Her mother was Caroline to her by that time. "She took me away from them all, and then shoved me back too late. I was always an outsider, and if you think that girls are not cruel, then you just don't know."

But she went through it, of course, and turned out pretty successfully, according to Caroline's ideas; plenty of invitations that winter, enough of what were beginning to be called heavy suitors, a good many expensive clothes, and her room filled with cotillion favors. Caroline watched her cards and carefully edited her lists, but there was one ball given by a newcomer where the favors were over-elaborate. That eliminated the newcomer thereafter, but years later I was to see on Elinor's little pine bureau a gold-stoppered scent-bottle which had been one of them.

We were separated, there in New York, only by Central Park. Nevertheless, a whole world lay between us, that gap between upper Fifth Avenue and the West Seventies which is the social Rubicon. Mother, I think, was vaguely jealous when I came home for my winter holidays: "Where have you been, Carroll?"

"Just taking a walk."

She knew well enough, poor Mother, where I had been; walking past that tall narrow house across the Park, with its boxwoods in jars flanking the entrance door, its man in livery inside, and upstairs in the drawing-room which ran across the front of the house old Caroline, perhaps at the tea table, and Elinor somewhere near.

Mother would pretend not to know, of course. She would put on a cheerful smile, run her hands over her pretty hair. "I suppose you're hungry, then. There's lamb stew for dinner. You like that." And the fact is that I did.

I know very little of Elinor's inner life that winter, what she thought, what she felt. There must have been times when escape, any escape, would have been welcome; but she was caught in Caroline's treadmill. She had her own maid, slept until noon, lunched out or gave a lunch party, went in Caroline's second motor—she had finally bought a car—with a footman beside the chauffeur to innumerable teas, rested an hour, dressed, dined out, and danced until morning. At the dances Caroline sat rigidly in her chair against the wall in the chaperon line, and watched her with her steady appraising gaze.

But the first stirring of her dormant instincts seems to have occurred at that time. Very faint it was, for a woman who was later on to throw herself away with such passionate recklessness. She told me about it the following summer, in answer to a question of mine.

"There was one man I liked, or might have liked. But he really wasn't anybody. I knew it was no good from the start, and, of course, Mother eliminated him."

"You mean," I said unsteadily, "that you fell in love with him?"

20

"Something of the sort. Don't look like that, Carroll! It's not a tragedy."

I gathered from her voice, however, that this affair, so lightly touched on, had gone deeper than she cared to acknowledge. She was silent for a moment or two.

"He was very good-looking, and he was very gentle, for such a big person," she added. *Gentle* seemed to me then an odd and unflattering word as applied to any man, but I can see now what she meant. Some big men are very tender with women, and God knows Elinor had had little tenderness. She never told me his name, but I know it was not Blair Leighton. Nevertheless, I am certain that she never quite forgot him. He was the first man to rouse her romantic imagination. I never had done so.

To be fair to Caroline Somers, she did not care whether Elinor married money or not. She was not mercenary. What she intended was that Elinor should marry properly, into her own group, her own social order. Probably we are the last nation in the world to set store by such matters; we are extremely class-conscious, and Caroline represented to the extreme her generation. Family, birth, and manners were her gods. If she made an art of the running of her houses, in New York and at Seaview, it was because her houses were the setting where she exhibited these qualities and received only those who likewise possessed them.

So she had eliminated this man. On certain afternoons she and Elinor were at home. A footman stood at the front door, another in the back hall received the men's hats, showed the women to the small room where Caroline's maid took their wraps. Upstairs the butler announced the guests; Caroline herself poured her tea, and people came and went, talked, laughed, flirted. She had no difficulty in eliminating this man.

"But I still don't see how she did it, Elinor."

"She simply told the footman to say we were not receiving," Elinor said, in a slightly flattened voice. "He could hear the people in the drawing-room, of course, so he knew what it meant."

21

She never saw him again.

I do not believe that she had cared very greatly for him, but his going left her feeling rather alone. She was listless, and Caroline grew fretful. She had brought out a beautiful daughter, had spent hours sitting on hard ballroom chairs when she had wanted to be in bed, and here was Elinor apparently about to go over into her second season without even a proposal, so far as she knew.

It was during Lent that she spoke to her. "I've done my best for you," she said. "You've met every eligible man in New York and some from Europe. And you have moped about and made no effort whatever."

"I haven't really cared to, Mother."

"Cared? What has that to do with it? You can frolic and play with that boy at Seaview all summer. You're lively enough then. You're not by any chance imagining that you care for Carroll Warner, are you?"

"I'm not in love with him, if that's what you mean."

It was characteristic of Caroline that she did not mention the other man.

I have no idea that she, Caroline, particularly cared for Lloyd Norton. Indeed the time was to come when she actively disliked him. But, although no one knew this but Caroline herself, she was coming close to the end of her financial resources; and another winter of trying to make a good marriage for Elinor would be highly expensive.

When he offered himself she took him. I say that almost literally, for he went to Caroline first. To Elinor I know he meant nothing more nor less than escape. Not an unpleasant escape, at that. He had been about all that winter. He had not particularly courted Elinor, but he had seen her with considerable regularity. Once accustomed to his drawl, to his rather exaggerated good manners and his tall thin immaculately dressed figure, Elinor rather liked him. Perhaps he was vaguely reminiscent of her father, who had in his easy-going way been indulgent to her.

But when I met her one day that spring on the street, she was rather vague about her engagement: "In love with

22

him? How sentimental you are, Carroll!"

"But look here," I said doggedly, "you must care for him if you are going to marry him. That's only—well, that's only decent."

"I like him. And I'll make him a good wife, Carroll. Don't worry about that."

"Who's worrying about that? Will he make you a good husband? That's what matters."

She did not answer at once. Then she shrugged her shoulders. "Why not?" she said. "He has been everywhere and done everything. I believe that sort settles down into marriage very comfortably."

"And that's what you think of him? Elinor, that's wrong."

"It's not wrong in the least," she said evenly. "I'm facing facts, that's all. I'm fond of him, too. Don't forget that."

I carried that away with me, to brood over for the next few months. Norton had lived and wanted to settle down, but Elinor had never lived at all. There was a profound injustice in that situation. I was not sure but that there was a profound immorality as well.

I was fretful and morose all that spring. Caroline, true to her tradition, had carried Elinor abroad to Paris for her trousseau and to London to be presented, and the town seemed empty to me and life very stale.

Mother, I know, was worried. "You shouldn't read so late at night, Carroll."

"I get plenty of sleep, Mother."

That was the spring of 1913. Children playing in Central Park, the tall house closed and a caretaker in charge, an increasing feeling of tension in Europe; and in Paris Caroline selecting Elinor's trousseau; spending more than she should on extravagant undergarments, negligees, dresses of every sort, God knows what. Elinor standing by, slim and proud and apathetic. A Belgian lacemaker mending Caroline's old lace for the wedding gown. Endless fittings for this and that, and Caroline watching through her lorgnette: "Draw it in a little under the arms, madame."

It was in London that Elinor first met Blair Leighton. He

seems to have made little or no impression on her, save that he danced well. She was presented at court in due time, after rehearsing her curtsies at the American Embassy under the tutelage of the Ambassadress and practicing stepping backward without falling over her train; and finally with shaking knees finding herself confronting their two resplendent majesties. When it was over she was hurried to a photographer's, and Mother at once seized the picture she sent me and had it framed in silver.

It still sits on our piano. I did not want it myself. I was carrying about with me a small snapshot of her taken on the float at Seaview; that was my Elinor, not this doll with her long train and the three Prince of Wales feathers in her hair.

It was early July when Caroline brought her home to be married. The arrival at Seaview took on something of the aspect of a Roman triumphal procession. I was young enough and bitter enough to call it that, with Elinor the captive chained to the wheel of Caroline's chariot, and the loot following in what Katie estimated at a dozen trunks.

4

It was shortly before her marriage that Caroline presented Elinor with the pearls. They were her own, given her by Howard Somers in atonement for that *faux pas* which had been Elinor. If Caroline had had any humor she might have seen a bit of comedy in her gift of them at that time; as if with one stroke she was erasing both Howard and his mistake from the record.

She had no humor, however. "Every bride should have pearls," she said in her prosaic manner. "And you need something at your neck."

Elinor herself was listless and tired. Once or twice early in the summer we rode together, Elinor on her big horse, I on a livery hack with a hard mouth and a tendency to bolt. There was no chance to talk then. But several times she went out again with me on my yawl; she was a good sailor, and she had that capacity for long silences which sailing requires; a sort of catlike content on her part; curled up forward on the hot deck and apparently not even thinking. But I remember one or two things that she said.

"It's a queer thing, this getting married."

"It's a darned serious thing."

"I suppose it is. One minute you belong to yourself, and the next—well, you don't."

"I thought that was all over," I said, steadying my voice. "I thought marriage wasn't possessive any more."

"That's not Mother's idea!"

I wondered then what sort of talk had gone on between mother and daughter, since the engagement. I could guess some of it. Norton was a man of his particular world, neither better nor worse, and I could see Caroline stating flatly that a wife's duty lay in subservience to her husband, and more or less that she belonged to him, while he belonged to himself. It was the unquestioning creed of women of her generation, and she herself had lived it. . . . Elinor was, in other words, to be married and to stay married; to give all of herself and to take what she got. My blood boiled, but there was nothing to say, and then a wind came up and we were pretty busy until we got in.

That was practically all, except one day when we had been swimming, and I had beaten her to the raft. She pulled herself up, her dark hair wet and outlining that lovely small head of hers, and sat down beside me on the warm boards: "I'm going to miss all this, Carroll."

"I hope to God you do!"

She looked at me as though I had surprised her. "I thought you were over that boy and girl stuff, Carroll."

"Not necessarily. Maybe you've grown up, and I haven't."

"But you will, you know."

"Oh, sure I will."

"You don't really mind, do you?"

It was so absurd, put that way, that I almost laughed. But I was feeling very young and tragic, and I wanted to hurt her. "Not any more than losing my right leg."

She laughed at that. "And it's such a long and handsome leg," she said. "Such a good swimming leg, too. Poor Carroll!"

I saw less and less of her as the time drew near for the wedding. There were parties of all sorts, and Caroline's house was full of guests. There was one incongruous figure among them, a quiet-faced woman in black habit and veil, with a silver cross on her breast, and I often saw her walking quietly in the garden. She was Caroline's sister-in-law Henrietta and a member of an Episcopalian sisterhood. Above her bands her handsome face was calm, but her eyes were clear and searching.

And one day I happened to overhear a conversation between the two women. I had been shown into the drawing-room and then apparently forgotten in the general excitement. Not a surprising thing, considering the serio-comic nuisance I must have been even to the servants; and the sisters were on the veranda.

"It isn't even a good marriage, in your sense of the word," Sister Henrietta was saying.

"He has enough."

"Enough perhaps, if she cared for him. She doesn't, Caroline. And hasn't he lived pretty hard? It seems a pity. She's so lovely."

"She has no attraction for men," Caroline said brutally.

"She is very young. Give her time." And Henrietta added in her quiet voice, "She has never had a great deal of affection. You know that. She'll make a compensation some day. If not now, later."

But Caroline brushed that aside. "As to his living hard, that is odd coming from you! You lived your life as you wanted to for a good many years."

"And have since repented," said Sister Henrietta softly.

That was only a day or so before the wedding, and on the last night I did a rather foolish thing. Caroline had insisted on quiet that final evening, and so I made once more my old furtive circle about that vast house, stealing along outside the vegetable garden, beyond the ridiculous maze skirting the far side of the pond, and then along the beach.

On the beach I found Elinor. She was sitting alone, and she had been crying. I do not recall that we said much of anything, but for a long time she sat with her head on my shoulder, and my arms about her. It was then that she said what I have quoted earlier.

"Why is it that, when I care so much for you, I can't care enough, Carroll dear?"

"We can't control those things, Elinor," I said huskily. "They are or they aren't."

"But I do care. Terribly. I always have."

I wish to God I had believed her that night, had run off with her. At least I would have tried to make her happy. But I did not believe her. I felt that she was only frightened, and that I was simply someone rather dear and familiar who demanded nothing of her.

She was married the next day, at high noon.

Whatever was lacking in that marriage, it was not expense or care for detail. Trust Caroline for that. There was a special train from New York for guests, and another special which carried the caterer's men and supplies. Up from the city, too, came case after case of old Howard Somers's finest vintage champagnes, selected by himself long before from the cellars of Rheims and Epernay; his old Bourbon and his Liqueur Scotch. And on the day of the wedding his library became a bar, with all the proper fittings save the mirror.

Caroline had had a vast marquee erected just off the front terrace, and floored it for dancing later on. The walls were concealed behind trellises covered with climbing roses, and luncheon was to be served there before the dancing began. So elaborate indeed was all this preparation that the ceremony itself shrank to comparative unimportance; and my

27

own clearest recollection of the day was of taking the car to Newport and trying to sober up some of the ushers so that they could get to the church.

Somewhere, however, between the stationing of detectives to watch the wedding presents and the seating of vast numbers of important people at luncheon, Elinor was married. Frozen of face and very pale, she dragged her long satin train up the aisle of the church; met Lloyd and his best man, faced the Bishop and the local rector—for Caroline meant this marriage to stick—and became the Elinor Norton of this narrative.

I saw very little of her after that; at the bride's table, but hidden from me by the flowers which covered it, and on the stairway later on, throwing her bouquet of white orchids to her bridesmaids waiting below. Then she was gone, and it ended, that marriage, in being the sort of carousal which must have made old Howard turn over in his grave at its sheer waste of good liquor; with two or three of the ushers going swimming in their morning clothes, and one at least turning up at the raft in the bay with his top hat still on his head. Long after Lloyd and Elinor had started on their wedding journey, to Europe, the noise kept up.

I went through it all slightly dazed. I was an usher, and I remember that the Mayhew girls were among the bridesmaids, and that I took Elizabeth Mayhew down the aisle.

"What on earth makes you tremble?" she said.

"First experience," I told her. "Knees shaking too. May flop at any moment."

"Well, don't flop on *me*."

I had not wanted to be an usher, but Elinor had insisted on it. I thought Lloyd Norton was not greatly pleased. He was not jealous of me, heaven knows. I was only a youngster to him. But I can see, looking at that old photograph, that he may have resented my youth. All the others were older men, and most of them in that picture are looking with worldly and rather dissipated eyes over the heads of the bridesmaids and into Caroline's garden. Or perhaps I have imagined all that. What was I to him but a raw college youth, still uncertain in manner and awkward in my new morning clothes? I doubt if he even knew, or at least remembered, my last name. I was Carroll to everyone about, and he had called me that from the beginning, in that patronizing drawl of his which always made me feel young and of no importance.

"Why Carroll?"

"He is my oldest friend."

"I thought the ushers were *my* perquisite!"

"You can have all the others."

"All right. Carroll it is. Better give me his initials. He'll get a cigarette case out of it, anyhow."

He was like that. He was not so much amiable as he was too indolent or too self-indulgent to make an issue of most things, and there must have been other weaknesses in him too. Certainly when the time came a stronger man could have done something, made a fight, met his emergency. There was something lacking, some quality of vitality missing. He was no coward; his war record later on shows that. But for all that there was something effeminate about him, for want of a better word. He was as sensuous as a woman, liking the feel of soft fabrics and the exotic odors of perfume, liking soft lights and rather delicate food, and with an eye for what attracted him rather than the fine or the beautiful.

This is my judgment today, the judgment of a man who is trying to be fair. He had no passions, I think, but a sort of sensuality, not exigent but obvious enough even to my youth and inexperience. It was furtive, not robust like Blair's later on. And it never drove him; he would make no sacrifices for it.

It was into those hands, well manicured and well shaped but rather soft, that Caroline delivered Elinor that day. Weak rather than vicious, and Elinor still unformed, a bit of soft and lovely clay to be molded by the first hands that touched her. She was just 19.

5

How much comes back to me that I had thought was forgotten! My father's extra-hearty manner to me that night; he offered me a cigar, I remember, his first concession to the fact that I had attained a certain maturity. My mother, looking at me furtively. She was rather upset, poor woman, on her own account.

"When I saw that she had actually seven other coffee sets—"

"She'll turn it back and get something else," said my father comfortably.

"It was engraved with her monogram. And all the others were engraved! Carroll, you're not eating."

But I remember something else. Father had suggested a game of chess, but I had begged off and gone to the beach. The tide was low, and I wandered along on the hard wet strip where all sorts of small living things washed out of the sea lay helpless and dying. Often Elinor and I had thrown them back, and so now I stooped occasionally and did the same thing. I was electrified when a girl spoke to me out of the darkness.

"Kind-hearted, aren't you?"

I turned. There was a girl lying on the dry sand beyond me, and I moved over to her.

"Who are you? Do I know you?"

"You do now. But I know you. You're the boy friend, aren't you?"

The phrase was a new one then, and I stiffened.

"You might as well sit down and talk to me," she went on. "Misery loves company, and you see—I'm the girl friend. And don't get that wrong, either. You don't know me and I don't give a damn what you think. I may be a bit of

30

a fool, but I'm still virtuous!" She laughed, not very pleasantly, and I was stunned into silence. One has to remember that this was just before the war, and that such utter frankness as was Isabel Curtis's that night was beyond my experience.

"What on earth are you doing here?"

"The same thing you are doing. Saying good-bye."

I could see her more clearly by that time, and from her voice rather than her speech I realized that here was no girl who had been a part of Lloyd Norton's buried and secret life. That was verified by her next speech.

"Keep a sharp eye out for Caroline," she said. "She's a born snooper. Well, things look rather empty tonight, eh?"

"I'm not making any fuss about it."

"But I am. I've been making the devil of a row, all to myself. I knew it had to come, so I thought I'd do it properly on the scene of the crime." She paused, but I was too astonished to think of anything to say. "I'm not complaining, you see. I did it myself. I was engaged to him and I broke it off. But—"

"Why did you break it off?"

"Because I want a man when I marry. I know Lloyd Norton in and out, and he's weak. Weak and selfish. I cared for him before I found that out. That's all." She drew a long breath. "Well, that's over," she said. "Tomorrow I'll be a good bit more than resigned. I'll be relieved. This is the worst time, of course."

She heaved herself out of the sand, and I saw that she was a tall slim girl, in a long cape or wrap of some sort over an evening dress. She looked down at it.

"I quit a party," she said. "How's that for a broken heart? And now I'm going back and enjoy myself." She put her hand on my arm. "Don't nurse it. Forget it. There are plenty of other girls. Me, for instance!"

She left abruptly, picking her way over the sand, and soon after I saw the lights of a car go on up the road, and heard her motor starting. She took the way toward Newport.

I tried to follow this advice of hers that summer, but it was pretty hard. She had the distractions of the life of organized play, of course. I did not even know her name then, but I knew that Newport was very gay that year, and once in a group picture taken on a yacht I saw her. Her name, it appeared, was Isabel Curtis, and she was smiling. But I had no such distractions, and it was useless to try to forget Elinor with my boat moored just off the pier and the raft rising and falling, day and night, in that eternal monotonous inevitable rolling of the sea.

Things were better in the autumn. I went into my father's law offices in New York and began to make friends. What with school and college I had pretty much to begin all over, but a single man not unpersonable can always find a place, and I went about rather a lot. Not in Elinor's crowd, of course. That was the small intimate group which clung together in a defensive alliance against the proletariat, entertained largely in its own houses, lunched occasionally at Delmonico's, and largely attempted to ignore the bustling hardworking world around it.

They never knew I existed. My mother, I think, was hurt for me; but my own group pleased me. The men did things, had ideas; and the women as often as not did better things and had better ideas.

It was interesting, but it was not living. I was 22, and if the real passions come only in later years, the emotional disturbances of late adolescence can be highly painful. All the fall I was in a state of unstable equilibrium, in which now and then I brooded over the possibility of suicide. Not, I am sure, that I would ever have carried it through, but my morbid imagination committed me to a dozen deaths. Never in all of them, however, did I see myself as extinguished. Rather I was always somewhere close at hand, and Elinor grief-stricken and remorseful at my grave.

I made no effort to fight this state of mind. I had framed the snapshot of Elinor on the float, and it stood on my desk. I would go out and dance half the night, and then come home and sit in front of it, and contemplate the least painful method of extinction. But by Christmas nature had commenced to take its course. Then, just before the New Year, the Nortons came home again.

I was hardly rational for the next few days. Somehow I had thought that Elinor would call me up at once. When a week had gone by and I had had no message I finally took my courage in my hands and telephoned her at their apartment. "Hello, Elinor."

"Oh, hello. It's Carroll, isn't it?"

There was the gulf, in that sentence. It was healthy. It put me where I belonged. But it hurt damnably. Even her invitation to tea the next day, still in that cool and impersonal voice, did not help greatly.

I went. All that mattered was that after months of starvation I was to see her again, to revive old memories, to claim that bit of her which had been mine. I discovered that I had lost even that. She was very kind, in an elderly sister sort of way, but she was too quiet, too composed. The old frankness was gone.

"I'm so glad to get back. I was frightfully homesick."

"You stayed a long time."

She glanced at me quickly. "It takes time to get adjusted," she said, with that new maturity of hers. "And then Lloyd wanted to stay. He likes Europe."

Watching her, I decided that she did not look happy. She seemed suppressed and even, in a breathless sort of way, uneasy. I have wondered since if Norton knew she had asked me that day.

"Elinor," I said impulsively, "you're happy, aren't you? It's—all right?"

"Of course it's all right. Please don't go on worrying about me, Carroll."

"He's kind to you?"

"Certainly he is kind. What do you think I married? A monster?"

That lessened the tension somewhat, for she laughed a little. After that we talked, or I did. I gave her the small gossip of Seaview, even told her about the silk hat and the float. But when that was over there was a distressing silence. And I was not too tactful when I broke it: "It's no good, Elinor, is it?"

"What's no good?"

"Our trying to make talk, like this. We can't go back, and all we have between us is a few memories. Rather tragic, isn't it?"

"Perhaps we're lucky to have those."

The next minute she was up, insisting that I see the apartment and the old furniture they had picked up in Europe. I made the rounds with her. Here and there as we moved about I saw her smooth a cushion, straighten this and that, and I saw in what she did that finicking fastidiousness of Norton's. Not as though she had acquired it, but as though it had been imposed on her. I could see no other change in her, however.

Except that she did not look happy, he had put no mark on her whatever. He never did, in one sense of the word.

I do not remember much about the apartment. Years later I was to see the furnishings transplanted to another life, another world; was to hear her playing her Bechstein piano against a silence and a darkness outside that was like something tangible, as solid as a wall; was to hear of the small sewing-table in her blue and silver boudoir that day as playing its small part in her ultimate tragedy. But of that afternoon I can recall only one thing, and that is seeing her hesitate before a door, and then throwing it open.

"This is our bedroom," she said. "Lloyd's dressing-room is beyond."

I glanced in. There were the two beds with their silk covers and their daylight air of never having been slept in; and on her toilet table the ivory brushes and other things which had been one of her wedding gifts. I turned away, but not before I had seen another thing which surprised me. Beside the toilet table was a small cabinet with glass doors, and in it row after row of scent bottles, all apparently in use.

"You've rather gone in for perfumes, haven't you?"

She colored slightly. Never had I known her to use scent at all, but here she was, surrounded like a cocotte with every sort of foreign stuff. "Lloyd likes them, and they're cheap in Paris," was all she said.

I saw her only occasionally after that. So far as I could discover, her life that winter differed little from her life the year before. At night they dined out or gave a dinner. In the afternoons she went about, or received callers. In the mornings she slept. Caroline was on the Riviera, her job done and her house closed.

"It isn't a normal life," I said once, rather roughly. "Don't you get any exercise?"

"I dance a good bit."

"Good God, that's not what I mean. A stuffy ballroom and heels like that! Don't you walk?"

"I've tried it, but I'm really not up to it. I can't be out late at night and then walk the next morning."

"You might try getting to bed at a decent hour now and then."

But she only smiled. "You haven't changed, have you?"

"I never change. You'll find that out some day. And I wish to heaven you'd stop scenting yourself like a prostitute."

"That's extremely rude, Carroll. A little change would do you good."

I do not know what the scent was, nor does it matter. But now and then since that day I have in some unlikely place, a theater or an elevator, got a whiff of that same scent. I may not recognize it consciously, but at once I am back with Elinor again, and she is looking up at me with anger and surprise.

For that one mark Norton had put on her. He liked his women scented, and she was scented.

I saw her once or twice again. Once at a dinner, where she was uncomfortable in a dress obviously cut too low, and was continually pulling at its shoulder straps. It was characteristic of Lloyd Norton that he felt it necessary to explain why they were there, in a house not so exclusive as usual.

"Fine fellow," he said of the host. "Business associate of mine, you know."

But the following summer in August the war broke out in Europe, and I went over with one of the early ambulance corps. One way and another I was there until we went in in the spring of 1917, and then I only came back to get some training, and to return as a second lieutenant of a machine gun company. We saw a good bit of fighting, and although I got a piece of shrapnel in the leg toward the end of the war and was back shortly after the Armistice, I was away from home for more than four years.

I grew up in those four years. There were times when Elinor ceased to be an obsession, and became a gentle memory in that welter of cruelty and sudden death. Perhaps in my own way I enjoyed the war. It was my first and perhaps my only chance at dramatic living. It was carefree too, after its fashion. One followed orders or passed them on down the line. When I got leave I was neither better nor worse than the rest. If I was trying to bury the ghost of a girl at such times, probably the others, too, had their ghosts to bury; dead men they had known, or women they had loved.

But if I had grown up, so had Elinor. I had not seen her since my return. Her New York apartment was closed, and she was not at Seaview. It was not until early in February that I met her one day in a train. Both of us were on our way to Newport News, she to meet Norton and I to meet one of the men from our office, both returning on the same transport. I saw at once that she had changed. She was as beautiful as ever; more so, rather; in some fashion she seemed to have ripened, and her eyes had a new luminous quality which puzzled me.

I had not been with her five minutes, however, before I knew she was frightened. Badly frightened.

6

No one, so far as I know, has yet written the story of the weak men who went to the war; not the cowards, but the fastidiously sensuous types to whom even killing or death was less horrible than the stench of filthy trenches, the personal uncleanliness, and the general squalor of the whole miserable business.

They could dramatize themselves in the big moments, but big moments were very few. Between were the long stretches of time when they tried to adapt themselves to such living conditions as they had never conceived could exist; but the raw human animal, which in most men is thinly veneered, was in them overlaid with layer on layer of civilization. Often they fought like demons, because in fighting they escaped out of their own particular hell. Then they went back, to vermin and foul odors, to the close bodily contact of other men, equally offensive and always inescapable. They had no privacy and none of the essential decencies of living, and the neuroses they developed were the results, not of fear but of disgust.

The men of this sort who remained with the army of occupation had time to make their readjustment. Germany was clean, orderly, and in time even friendly. But Lloyd Norton like myself was shot back among the first returning troops, still sullen and still bitter.

Certainly he was bitter enough. He had hated not only the war and all that it connoted. He had loathed the sheer democracy of the army life. A firm believer in caste and himself a Brahman, by a chaotic reversal of all that he had ever known he found himself taking orders from the Untouchables; new officers, recruited for ability and not for social standing. Months later he spoke of it to me: "Do you know who was my commanding officer at one time? My grocer, by God!"

This was the man Elinor was on her way to meet that day; a man dislocated and unnerved, his superiority destroyed, his senses and his nerves alike outraged, and—although I did not know that then—suspicion flaming in him like a torch.

I happened on her unexpectedly in the train; and for all my conviction that I had put her away for good, my heart missed a beat when I saw her. That was a warning, and for a moment I was undecided whether to speak to her or not. She was sitting alone, staring out the window, and her face looked strained and set.

But when she saw me she smiled. "Why Carroll!" she said. "After all these years! Come and sit with me. I hear that it was you who won the war!"

"Of course. They'd have had a hard time without me," I told her gravely. "What are you doing here?"

"I'm meeting Lloyd." She gave me a quick glance. "And I believe I'm a little nervous, Carroll. You see, it's so long, and so many things have happened."

She was more than a little nervous. I saw that at once. Her lips were shaking.

"That's silly, Elinor. He's done a fine job and now he's coming home, and damned glad he's doing it. What is there to be uneasy about?"

She seemed to be turning about, looking at it carefully, measuring it against some hidden thing in her mind. Or perhaps she was merely trying to think of Lloyd in this new guise of the conquering hero coming home. Whatever it was she leaned back and relaxed a little.

"You're a great comfort to me, Carroll," she said. "Of course, he'll be glad to get back. You see, his letters have been rather queer; but then he's been through a lot. He did awfully well, you know, Carroll."

I did know and said so; and she grew more talkative after that, and seemed happier. He would need nice living again, and some gaiety. He must be made to forget the war. She

38

hoped he would be demobilized soon. Then she meant to rally his friends around him, and there was the theater. He had always liked the theater. And having thus as it were charted her course, she turned at last and looked at me.

"You've actually grown, Carroll! You were always big, but you look bigger than ever. And now tell me about yourself."

But what was there to tell her? That I had tried to bury her ghost in ways that would have hurt her; and that I had not succeeded? That I had gone forward to do reckless things because I had lost her? Or that a silly little picture of her, now stained and dirty, had been a part of my fighting equipment?

"It's either too big or too little a story to tell, Elinor. It would take a month, or two minutes."

She did not insist. Caroline, it appeared, was not well, and had stayed at Seaview all that winter. She herself had worked very hard, for the Red Cross. Did I think she looked tired, she inquired anxiously. She had felt rather strained. "Women had all the work and worry of war, and men had all the excitement."

She was merely talking, not thinking of what she said. It seemed that she had been staying for some time with a young woman named Isabel Curtis. Did I remember her? She had been at the wedding. She had taken an apartment in Washington, and it was usually full of people.

"All sorts and all nationalities," she put it, and then suddenly lapsed into silence. When she spoke again it was to inquire for my mother, and if Katie was still with us; and when we approached Newport News it was to ask me not to be with her when she met Norton.

"It's silly, of course," she said, with her nervous smile. "But—I suppose it's the strain—his letters have been suspicious, if that's the word. He seems to think all sorts of things; in spite of the fact that I've been with Mother right along, and he knows it."

"Except this winter," I said.

She looked at me quickly. "Of course, the past few

weeks—" she said. And then rather abruptly added that she must clean up for our arrival, and left for the washroom.

Probably the only time men are intuitive about women is when they are in love with them. Then they develop a sixth sense of some sort. They are like bats who fly blind in the day, but at night develop an awareness of the nearness of things. That day I knew that Elinor was near to trouble of some sort, and that it related to her husband. There were other women around us, gaily talking. They, too, carried small vanity bags to the washroom, preparing themselves for reunion. Among them all only Elinor, I felt, was girding herself for battle.

When she came back I questioned her. "See here," I said. "What do you mean by letters being suspicious? He's certainly never been jealous of me."

"I don't know. At least I'm not certain."

"Not certain of what?" I insisted stubbornly.

And finally she told me. She was afraid she had put a note meant for someone else into a letter to him. It was a childish thing to have done, if she had done it. Not that there was any harm in the note, but he might think there was. There was something feverish in that explanation, and I spent a miserable ten minutes until the train drew in. She tried to talk, but I had little to say. It was not that I was afraid of Norton; I never thought of him. I was furiously and unreasonably jealous—jealous and afraid. As we sat there too, I became aware that, unscented before, the air about her now was heavy with that subtle exotic perfume which I had noticed once before.

I realized then how frightened she was. Already, before his arrival, she was in effect promising him to be good; making her small gesture of submission to him.

When we got out of the train she was holding her head high, and wearing a determined smile.

I met my man, radiantly glad to be at home again and loudly demanding a drink, and it was not until we were in the train that I saw Lloyd Norton and Elinor. They were

40

still on the platform, and neither of them had seen me. He looked older and too fine-drawn, like a man in the last stages of nervous strain, and he was frowning with irritation. "I told you the damned train would be crowded," he was saying. "Why on earth couldn't your mother have sent a car?"

"Mother's ill. And I've written you, Lloyd; I've been staying in Washington with Isabel Curtis," she explained patiently.

He turned and looked at her. "That strumpet!" he said, and grinned unpleasantly.

I suppose I should have seen then his emotional unbalance, but all I was aware of was a sudden and furious anger. I flung myself out of my seat and made for the train platform, and I have no idea what might have happened had not Elinor seen me first. She made a small gesture, and I stopped and pulled myself together, but not entirely in time. Norton had seen me, and was staring at me fixedly.

"Well!" he said. "So you're here too! Quite a welcome for the returning hero!"

"Sorry," I said rather shortly. "I came to meet one of our men. But I'm glad you're back safely."

"That remains to be seen," he said, and flicked a glance at his wife.

I pondered the situation as the long train slowly made its way to Washington. Even without another man in the picture, it seemed filled with wretched potentialities. We knew less then than we do now of war neuroses, but Norton was certainly not normal. It was not only his irritability. A jerky incoördination in his movements as he stood on the platform had alarmed me.

Not all of us had returned from France filled with joyful anticipation; I knew that. Some of us had dreaded the readjustments, sentimental and otherwise. Some had resented the return to the old rut from which the war had liberated them. Others were unwilling once more to do their own thinking and providing, after having had it done for them for so long. And still others had been permanently dislocated, either by shock or long tension, and would never again adjust themselves to the world about them.

It was in this last class that I placed Norton that day. And if to this situation there were added another man the thing was dynamite and I knew it. That was because of a certain quality in Norton himself. Older than either Elinor or myself, he had outlived all his illusions before he ever married; but to be fair to him, his cynicism up to this time had been an indulgent one. His philosophy had been neither to trust nor to suspect, but to live fastidiously and with an eye to his own comfort. Emotion, being uncomfortable, had not entered into it. Yet it was always his uncanny ability to sit outside and comprehend the emotions of other people.

It was Isabel Curtis who put that into words later on. "He's as mean as the devil and as detached as God," was what she said.

If Elinor had fallen in love, as I suspected, he would not be long in finding it out. And in his present condition he could make her life actual hell. Indeed, my anxiety for her was so great that day in the train that at last I got up and went back to their car. I did not go farther than the door, however, and neither of them saw me. They were sitting side by side, but Elinor was rigidly staring out the window and Norton was as rigidly gazing straight ahead of him at nothing.

While I stood there she evidently made another effort, for she turned with that determined smile of hers and said something to him. Whatever it was he ignored it, and I shall never forget the look on her face when she turned back to the window.

I was like a crazy man the rest of the way. Martin, the clerk from the office whom I had met at the transport, had fortunately found his drink somewhere and gone to sleep, for I was not rational. The thought of abandoning Elinor to that sullen brute was more than misery. It was torture.

It was a curious trip. We had only day coaches to Washington, and across from me the elderly general of a division was snoring heavily while a group of his aides had turned

42

over one of the seats and was playing red dog on top of his suitcase. Those wives of officers who had met their husbands were trying to bridge the gulf of months or years, and scraps of their talk came to my ears.

"He's awfully like you. Everyone says so."

"Everything is so expensive. And as for rents—!"

Except for Martin and the sleeping general, and here and there a man obviously still detached and bewildered, the train seemed filled with joyous and expectant masculine youth. Women, drink, and food vied in their talk with ribald memories, and in our car only the women and the sleeping general prevented their raising their voices in song. Among them I felt old and tired.

The arrival of the transport at Newport News had been unexpected, and no crowd met the train at Washington. Some of the enthusiasm died on that discovery, after the wild excitement of New York over the earlier returning men; but there was confusion enough, and I was some time in discovering Elinor and Norton. When I did he was giving his bags to a porter and demanding a taxi, and I had a moment with her.

"Everything all right?" I asked.

"Yes. Please go on."

"You're staying here?"

"Only overnight, at the Shoreham."

"I'll see Isabel Curtis if you like, and if you need me—"

"Please!"

I had only time to stoop over my own bag when he turned. Luckily he did not see me.

Martin went on alone, rather grumbling, to New York that day, and I went to the Willard. It was four o'clock by that time, and after some difficulty I located Isabel Curtis's apartment by telephone and found her in.

"What!" she said. "The swain of the sands! Do I remember? Shall I ever forget it? I practically offered myself to you, didn't I? And you refused me."

She could see me at once; better than later on, since there would be people dropping in for cocktails after five;

"people," as I discovered later on, being largely men of all ages, uniforms, and nationalities. She was alone, however, when I got there, and we examined each other rather critically but smilingly.

"Bigger and better," was her verdict. "And what a mess I was that night! Shall we have a drink to our memories?"

I liked her on sight. She was frank and direct, if rather staccato, and she looked like a practical young woman with a considerable amount of good sense. Later on I was to know her well, to find her playing her own part in Elinor's catastrophe. But not an unfriendly part, even at the end. She was bitter at times, but often she was wise and always she was honest. A tall fair girl, not beautiful and with a rather husky voice, but attractive to most men, I imagine.

"I want to talk," I said. "Let's postpone the drink."

"And the memories?"

"No. As a matter of fact, they brought me here."

I thought I saw a flicker of caution in her face, but she smiled. "Don't tell me that I made a real impression on you that night."

"Something you said did. About Lloyd Norton."

Then I told her. Whatever her faults were—and I dare say they were plenty—she was fond of Elinor. But as she listened, turning over a square emerald on her finger, I began to wonder whether like myself she had ever forgotten that early love affair. There was a conflict in her of some sort.

"Just what are you afraid of?" she asked me finally. "He's not crazy, is he?"

"No. But he's not normal. Elinor is afraid of him; I could see that."

"He'll never hurt her," she said, almost with contempt. "He hasn't the courage. I don't mean physical courage. Moral. He hasn't that. And I don't think she's afraid of him. Not that way, anyhow."

"Then in what way?"

"I'm afraid I can't say anything more than that. I shouldn't have said anything at all. And don't think what

44

you are thinking. Elinor's straight, you know. She's so straight that it hurts! I'll tell Lloyd that if you like. At least," she added with a half smile, "he knows I'm always honest with him. He hates me for it, of course."

In the end she did talk, however. My anxiety must have been contagious. Elinor had fallen deeply in love with a man she had met in Washington, although the phrase "in love" did not suit Isabel.

"It's not what I call love at all," she said. "It's pure infatuation with her. She's entirely mad about him, although she'd die rather than acknowledge it. But it's the fact, nevertheless. And you're right in one thing: it's going to raise a merry little hell if Lloyd learns about it. It will hit him in one place where he is vulnerable, in his pride."

Then she told me who it was: Blair Leighton, the man Elinor had met in England the year she was presented. She herself had nothing against him, unless it was a certain arrogance of good looks and a too great popularity with women. She didn't know whether Leighton was hit or not, but Elinor was, badly.

"She has fought it, you know. She hates the whole idea, really. And lately she has taken to slipping around to St. John's and praying over it! She doesn't know I know that."

"How many people know about it?"

She shrugged her shoulders. "Elinor and Blair Leighton. At least I suppose he sees it. He isn't blind. And I know it, although I'm not supposed to. I'm neither blind nor deaf. Nobody else, so far as I know."

We were sitting in a small end room of the apartment. The apartment was very large, and through double doors the room opened into a succession of reception rooms with parquet floors. Isabel had risen and was standing by the fire. Now there was the sound of footsteps far off, the quiet ones of her butler, the firm and heavy tread of someone else.

She glanced up quickly. "Here he comes now," she said. "British. Good-looking, popular, and very cocksure of himself. For God's sake play up!"

Then the butler's voice announced Colonel Leighton,

and I was confronting a man taller than myself, blond and smiling. Looking back, it is hard to detach the Blair Leighton I knew later from this slim, youngish, and clear-skinned Englishman, left over from some mission which I have forgotten; erect from long wearing of a uniform, although he was in civilian dress, broad of shoulder and lean of flank, and with the candid blue eyes which usually hide considerable shrewdness behind their ingenuousness.

Isabel had presented him and then disappeared, and he stood smiling in front of the fire. "Captain Warner? Then you are the friend of a friend of mine."

"Who is that?"

"Elinor Norton."

"An old friend," I said, as easily as I could. "I have known her since she was a child."

Isabel came back then, followed by a man with a tray of cocktails; and soon other men began to come in and even a woman or two. I found myself watching Leighton as he moved about. Evidently he was popular. He was "Blair" to most of them, and while he was both hearty and amusing with the men, he was different with the women. He had a very definite technique with them, hardly so much a tenderness as a suggestion of it.

"What do you think of him?" Isabel asked, under cover of the crowd.

"He knows his way round with women," I said watching him.

She considered that for a moment. "Yes and no. That is, men like him too. Of course, women adore him."

"But you don't think he is in love with Elinor?"

She shrugged her shoulders. "I imagine he is a little in love with a good many women. But we can't talk here. Won't you stay to dinner? We'll be alone. I have a chaperon of sorts, but she's in bed with a cold."

But I was too uneasy to stay. The voices had risen until the noise rasped my nerves like a file, and to a man accustomed to the open air for more than four years the atmosphere was stifling. I declined, and the last picture I saw before I left was Blair Leighton, bending solicitously over a girl in mourning who looked frightened and out of place in that crowd.

I walked back to the hotel. It was as cold and raw as only Washington can be in winter, and it took me back to the wet dreariness of France; to some of the helplessness every man over there felt now and then, that helplessness which he translates into terms of fatalism. But so apprehensive was I that night that I remained in my room and even dined there, so as to be close to the telephone.

And the dénouement which came the next morning was absurd to the point of the ridiculous.

7

Even today I do not know what precipitated that situation. Normal men, I imagine, came home to their wives after the war like tired children to a mother. But I believe that while Norton was certainly not normal, his attack on her that first night of his return had been mental rather than physical; that the jeering, jibing brute which is in all men when their pride is assailed had kept them apart while lashing her into desperation.

The result in any case was the same. Some time toward morning he fell into an exhausted sleep, and she slipped out of the hotel and walked the streets until ten o'clock. I myself, having slept badly, was roused by the telephone at that hour, to hear Elinor's voice at the other end of the wire.

"I must see you, Carroll. And I haven't much time."

"Where are you?"

"Downstairs. I'm coming up."

"You can't do that, Elinor. I'm not even dressed. I'll be down there in five minutes. Where are you?"

But she would not let me go down. We might be seen, she said, and she closed the discussion by hanging up the receiver. I was as angry as only a man can be when caught at his worst by a woman he loves; but I put on slippers and a dressing-gown, and had just time to run a brush over my hair when she rapped at the door. It was absolute insanity, and I told her so without admitting her.

"I refuse to look like a fool, Elinor," I said, "or let you look like something worse. Go down to the desk and ask for a sitting-room, and let me know where to find you."

Then I saw her face, and I simply opened the door wide and took her in. There was nothing else to do.

"I've left Lloyd, Carroll," she said. "And I want some money. I'll have to get away from here."

"Where do you want to go?"

"To Mother's, I suppose," she said listlessly. "I don't believe she'll let me stay, but where else have I to go?"

My first reaction was one of impatience; to tell her that she had gone stubbornly into this marriage and that it was her job to put it through. I felt sorry for Norton too, returning from one hell to face another. At the time I saw nothing to the situation except the revolt of an infatuated woman against a husband she had never loved. I tried to tell her something of all this, but she paid no attention. Instead she seemed to be listening for some sound from the hall.

"You can give me some money, can't you?" she insisted. "I'll send it back. I must go away. I simply can't go on with it, Carroll. I drive him wild, and I can't help it. I think he must hate me, hate me terribly."

"You haven't told him anything to—well, to upset him?"

"Told him what?" Then her eyes fell. "No," she said. "What has that to do with it? I've done nothing wrong."

And of all absurd and tragi-comic things to happen, Norton chose that moment to walk into the room. To save my soul I cannot even now help admiring him for the way he

48

came in, and for the manner in which he carried off a situation which belonged in a farce. If he was pale, he was entirely composed.

"Sorry, old man," he said to me. "There's a maid in the hall, and I didn't want Elinor to jump out the window!" He took out an immaculate handkerchief and passed it over his face and I saw that, cool as the room was, he was sweating.

"Don't think I misunderstand this," he went on. "But my wife cannot be seen coming alone out of another man's room at this hour of the morning, and so I am here." He had not so much as glanced at Elinor. Now he turned to her, still composed, still with considerable dignity; but it was to me he spoke. "As a matter of fact, I am here to apologize to my wife for driving her to another man's room, if not to his arms." He went over and put a hand on her shoulder. "I'm sorry, Elinor, and I'm sorry before a witness!" He smiled faintly. "Is that good enough, or shall I swear to do better before a notary?"

She looked up at him like some hypnotized creature. There had been something vital and living in her before he came. Now it died. I remember that she had a sable scarf twisted around her neck and that she put up a hand and loosened it, as if it choked her. Otherwise she did not move.

"What about it? Are we going to forget it and start again?"

She saw what was happening to her, but he had left her helpless. She could not leave him now. Whether he had cruelly and willfully closed her one avenue of escape or whether he really meant what he said, the effect was the same. She nodded.

"I'll try," she said quietly. "I shouldn't have done it, of course. I'll do my best, Lloyd."

He patted her shoulder and turned to me, smiling. "Well, that's that," he said. "Sorry to have intruded this domestic situation on you, Warner, but I didn't select Elinor's confidant." And he added, this time without a smile, "This coming back from a war plays hob with a man's nerves."

It was by way of being an apology, and if he was acting

it was good acting. He put his handkerchief away, whipped a glance around my untidy room, and picked up his service cap—he was still in uniform. "I dare say you'll want your breakfast. And need it!" he said.

Then he opened the door for Elinor, made a smart salute, and the next second they were both gone.

I suppose I should have known then what her life from that time on was to be, the continual driving her to desperation, always followed by his facile and apparently sincere regret, so that she could never leave him. I suppose I should have recognized that he himself was being scourged by the twin devils of mental and physical impotence, augmented by pride and jealousy. I suppose I should have known, too, that he had had that incriminating line of a note meant for Leighton, although he had no clue to the identity of the man.

But that morning I saw in him only a certain gallantry and a real remorse. Like the fool I was, I trusted her to him. They left for New York late in the afternoon, Elinor going back to their apartment, and he to camp pending demobilization. But I stayed over in Washington for a few days. There were some wires to pull to get Martin out of the service, and I picked up some war acquaintances of my own and went about a little.

Incidentally I discovered that a good many people knew Leighton, and that most of them liked him. Now and then a man would indicate that his good manners covered a fairly physical animal, or would wonder why he stayed on in America; but that was all. He was of a respectable upper middle class family, had been a wanderer in queer places until the war, and evidently had an income of some sort. Now and then I saw him. Once, taking a lonely walk in Rock Creek Park, he passed me on a horse. He had an excellent seat, but he had worked his big mare until she was in a frenzy of nerves. There was a ford nearby and she slipped going into it and almost fell. He pulled her out of it skillfully enough, but he kicked her viciously after it was over. Then he recovered his good humor, and the next minute he was crossing the creek and whistling cheerily as he moved out of sight.

He had not seen me, and better men than Blair Leighton have lost their tempers over horses. Nevertheless, I felt as I went on that there were enormous potentialities both for good and evil in the man. That infernal gentleness of his to women was not entirely assumed, but as I pounded along I realized that, if Norton was a devil at times, Leighton could be a brute. The two men most close to Elinor, I thought; and what was I? Neither one nor the other. Only a commonplace individual, undistinguished in war as in peace, and now merely fearful of a tragedy in the making without doing anything about it.

Later on during that walk, when I was turning to cross the road, I saw a small sports car draw up and Isabel Curtis waving to me. "Have you seen a god going by on a big horse?" she said.

"He's about finished the horse. But he rides well."

"He does everything well, my poor friend," she retorted. "And he'll finish the horse, of course."

"What do you mean by that?"

"I don't think he likes to leave anything unfinished," she said cryptically, and drove on.

I saw her once more before I left. We sat together at a dinner, and under cover of the talk she reverted to Elinor and Lloyd Norton. It was then that she made the statement I have quoted: that Norton was as mean as the devil and as detached as God.

"Always on the outside looking on," she explained. "Pulling strings and making people dance. He's always done that. It's easier than dancing himself, and it puts him in the superior position." She added, after a moment, "Queer that I'm still fond of him, isn't it? I dare say I wanted to make him over, and thought I could! It's like the attraction cold women have for some men."

"Have you heard from Elinor?"

"Not a word. I thought you might have. Odd, isn't it? I have a sort of conviction that she cares more for you than she realizes."

"Very odd," I said drily.

Then the terrapin came on, she exclaimed that she adored terrapin, and I had no further talk with her.

Leighton was at the dinner, being very attentive to a girl in blue; and in the procession out of the dining-room, as carefully arranged as to official rank as the procession into it, I happened to be close to him. It was the first time I had seen him in evening clothes, and he was magnificent. I had no chance to talk to him, however. We were only a short time in the smoking-room, and soon after we joined the women in the drawing-room the ranking guests were rising to go. I left Washington the next morning.

Fortunately I was busy that spring. By and large the income tax put a good many law offices on their feet, and we shared in the activity. But my people had moved up the Hudson, so that I had to take an apartment in town, and I spent a good many nights in work.

Katie had wanted to come with me.

"You'll need a woman to do your mending, Mr. Carroll," she pleaded. "And what's all this talk about a Jap? I don't trust them Orientals."

Mother was horrified, however, although Katie was a buxom 45, and so I got a Japanese servant. His name was Taki, and if he was rather better on fancy hors-d'oeuvre and cakes than on my mending and pressing, Katie never knew it. I was comfortable enough, but the apartment was lonely. I carried work home with me, but I missed my mother's gaiety and my father's substantial presence. I was under 30 even then, and there were times when the very walls of the place seemed to close in on me, as though I lived in a small vacuum. There was life all around me, but I was insulated against it.

Once more I had lost Elinor, if one may lose what one never has had. I did not see her, and her name and Norton's did not appear in the papers. All I had was that war-stained

52

snapshot of her on my desk, with her hair in wet strings and a cheerful grin on her face. But it aroused little or no feeling in me. The boy who had so slavishly loved the girl was gone, and the girl also. What we were now was man and woman, and the woman had married one man and was in love with another.

Nevertheless, I suppose that picture kept me from some of the resources of men of my age, freshly back from war and madly trying to forget it. And when to my surprise I later on received a decoration for something or other—men are rarely decorated for the things which really deserve it—I took out the back of the frame and placed my medal behind the picture. It was a mute acknowledgment of two things which had ended for me.

It was early in February when Norton returned, and in May I saw old Caroline. There had been a terrific storm along the coast, and Mother had called up and asked me if I would go to the cottage at Seaview.

"The sea has got over the wall, Carroll," she said, "and you'd better get Mr. Mortimer to see what needs to be done. If the rugs are wet they'll need drying."

The place was in great disorder when I got there. Mortimer, the caretaker for all the cottages on the beach, had lifted the rugs, but the porches needed bracing and I found seaweed and the remains of a dead fish in the garage. The ocean had subsided, but the shore where Elinor and I had spent so many hours was devastated; and it was there, sitting on a log and wrapped in a heavy coat, that I saw Caroline Somers again for the first time in years.

She was sitting erect as usual, and staring out at the sea. She sat immovable, and I had the feeling that two irresistible forces were confronting each other.

Mortimer chuckled beside me. "Probably telling the ocean what she thinks about it," he said. "Coming in on her property like that! Giving it hell, most likely."

"How is she?"

"Failing fast. She was no chicken when Miss Elinor was born. And I hear she's sick too."

"Has Miss Elinor been back lately?"

He lighted his pipe before he answered. "Now it's funny, your asking me that. She has and she hasn't. Simmons in town says he drove her out one night about a month ago, and that she's brought a bag along. But she didn't let him take it in; said she mightn't stay. In about an hour sure enough she came out and got into the car again, and told him she was taking the night boat back. She did, too. Simmons says she looked mighty bad, and she hadn't anything to say. She used to be quite a talker; friendly, you know. But she never spoke until they got back to town."

I felt myself going cold with anger. Mortimer had moved away, and I surveyed that detached and immobile figure on the beach with hatred in my heart. She still sat there, with the surf pounding only a few yards away. For many years she had lived a part of her life by that sea. It had been the background to her ambitions, her inflexibilities. It had crooned to her and fought her. It had taken her to triumphs in Europe, had carried Elinor to be educated and brought her back to be dominated, and to its requiem she herself had been widowed and finally left alone. But never before had I seen her look at it.

It did not touch me. It maddened me.

She did not hear me until I was close to her. Then she looked in my direction. Her face did not alter. She had not the remotest idea who I was. But my anger died as suddenly as it had flared. Here was no ambitious dominant woman, but an old and a sick one. A feeble one too, for now I saw that her hands—the thin, beautifully kept, but wrinkled hands of age—were resting on the handle of a stick. So little did I interest her that she was looking away again when she saw me whip off my hat. Then she studied me more carefully.

"Carroll Warner, Mrs. Somers," I said. "I've come down to see about the damage."

She nodded, without giving me her hand.

"It was a bad storm," she said. Then she eyed me. "You have changed a great deal."

54

"A good deal of time has passed."

There was an awkward pause. She had resumed her staring at the sea, and I thought I was dismissed. But suddenly she said, "Tell me. Do you see Lloyd Norton very often?"

"Not in New York." I added that I had seen him when he landed, and she listened carefully. There was another pause after that, and I thought she meant to let the matter drop. Looking back, however, I think she was fighting some sort of inward battle, between a lifelong reticence and the actual need for information.

"How did he look to you?"

"Not too well. Nervous, I thought. The war played hob with a lot of nerves, you know."

"But he was physically well?"

"I really don't know. He was thin."

"He was always thin," she said rather acidly. "That's nothing. Elinor seems to think there is something wrong with him, but if it is only nerves— Of course, it's all absurd. Men have no nerves because they have no imagination."

That was more like her. I could have argued the question, but to what good? The sum of what followed, however, has a bearing on Elinor's tragedy, and so it belongs here. For Elinor, it appeared, wanted to get Norton out of New York.

"Out of New York," she repeated. "A man whose life is New York and always has been! If you can see Lloyd Norton on a farm I cannot."

"I suppose," I said, choosing my words carefully, "Elinor really knows his condition better than anyone, including himself. The war definitely changed a good many men. I think myself that it has changed him."

"The war! I'm sick of hearing about the war. The Civil War left men behind it. Are you telling me that this war left only a million or so neurotics? Don't be an idiot." And she added, "I take it you don't see much of either of them?"

"I never see them at all."

She nodded and got up. It was startling to see the effort it cost her, although she waved away my proffered help.

Startling also to see that her once barrel-like body was thin to the point of emaciation. A woman with a blue cape over a white uniform was coming along the sands.

"My nurse," she said. "She's a nuisance and she's stupid, which is worse." She was leaning on the cane with one hand, the other unexpectedly she placed on my shoulder. "Listen, Carroll," she said, "this marriage has got to go on. I will have no scandal, and I will not countenance any divorce. I want you to tell Elinor that. My means are considerably diminished, but I am helping them now. If they break up there will be no help for either of them."

There was no time for argument. The nurse was close by that time, an intelligent, pleasant-faced woman, no longer young. I had time only for one sentence.

"You can't browbeat people into happiness."

"Happiness!" She almost snarled it. "There is no such thing. Don't be a fool. There is only duty and responsibility. If this world has gone crazy I have not. She'll stick, or I'm through."

She did not introduce me to the nurse. She turned her back on me in dismissal, took the woman's arm, and the two together slowly moved away. As they passed along the sand, carefully avoiding the wreckage of the storm, it seemed to me that just so was old Caroline passing through her life; leaving behind her all sorts of human wreckage, moving toward the sanctuary of her house and soon perhaps her grave, by the simple expedient of ignoring or avoiding the unpleasant things in her path.

8

As I went back to the cottage I was reconstructing that night visit of Elinor's, and I know now that I was fairly accurate. She had gone there out of a desperate resolve to state her case to her mother, and perhaps to stay until she could make some plans. All the way, in train and cab, she had been rehearsing her story: that Norton was drinking too much and working too little; that he was violent when he was drinking and sardonic and moody in the intervals. But there were a thousand intangibles that she could not put into words, and the one cause for divorce which her mother would recognize, infidelity, she knew was not a fact.

Never in her wildest dreams could she conceive of telling her mother that she cared for another man.

Henry, the old butler, had admitted her. There were no footmen now, and Henry was almost blind and had not recognized her at first. She stepped into the hall, and all about her was that vast house, dark and ugly. It daunted her, as it always had. Upstairs her mother was in bed in that enormous bedroom. There was a lamp beside her, the only light, and she had been reading her prayerbook. The nurse was in the adjoining tower room. She had put on a night wrapper and was at Caroline's desk, writing letters.

Elinor stood beside the bed, frightened and pale. "I want to speak to you alone, Mother."

Caroline only stared at her, but the nurse heard and closed the door. Then Caroline spoke. "About what?"

"About my marriage. About Lloyd and myself."

Caroline had raised a thin hand. "At this hour?" she said. "Have you no consideration? You come here on some foolish impulse—"

"It's not an impulse, Mother. I simply cannot go on. He loathes me, and I'm afraid. I'm afraid, Mother."

"Why should he loathe you? What have you done?"

"Nothing," Elinor said desperately. "Nothing. I swear it. But he suspects all sort of things. There is such a thing as mental cruelty, isn't there? I could go to Reno and get a divorce. He wouldn't miss me, Mother. He would really be better without me."

Caroline did not speak. She touched a small hand bell beside the bed and the nurse came in. "Call Henry," she said, "and see that Miss Elinor's room is ready for her.

And you might give her a bromide, Miss Evans. She is not quite herself tonight."

Elinor turned and went to the door. There she stopped. "This is no impulse, Mother," she said. "It has lasted for six years. I'm not a child, and I am quite myself. But I need help. I need help as I have never needed it before. If you won't even listen to me—"

"I shall listen to no talk of divorce, now or ever," said Caroline coldly, and picked up her prayerbook again.

Lighten our darkness, we beseech Thee, O Lord; and by Thy great mercy defend us from all perils and dangers of this night. She had read that prayer every night for 50 years, but she showed Elinor no mercy that night. Miss Evans had followed her into the hall, but Elinor left her there. Henry had disappeared from the lower hall, and the gaunt old house surrounded her with its ghosts. She slipped into what had been her bedroom, turned on the light and looked about her; but it brought back no gentle memories. Plenty of memories, but none of them tender. It must have been then that she picked up the gold-stoppered scent bottle, for later on when she was back in the station she found it in her hand.

This visit to her mother was her only revolt. She said later, and I believe her, that Blair Leighton had nothing to do with it. She had not seen or heard from him since they left Washington. Now and then a letter from Isabel would mention him: *Our good-looking English friend is still playing around.* Or: *Saw B.L. last night. He asked about you.* But he lived now only in her dreams. She could keep him away during the day, but at night she would dream about him and waken to find her pillow wet with tears.

Trying to analyze that later on she was troubled. "I hardly know, Carroll. He was strong and—well, I suppose gentle is the word I want. It was a sort of tenderness, and I hadn't had much of that."

Strong and tender! Well, perhaps, but he was unscrupulous and bad too. Even his strength was purely physical. He was always weak where women were concerned. Yet that

58

very weakness gave him a sort of enchantment for them. It was as though they saw his strength weakened for them, laid like a tribute at their feet. And against all this Elinor had no protection.

Through Caroline's influence Norton had been promptly demobilized, and on the surface at least he had settled down to his old life. He went to his office, came home. At night he coughed a good bit, the result of gas in France, and he would get up and take a drink, generally whisky, to stop it. By and large he was drinking secretly a great deal of whisky. I suppose it provided an escape for him, gave him back some of his old confidence. For an hour or two he was a man again, among other men. But he was not normal. The war had dislocated him. He did not fit into the old pattern. One night he told her he had not been faithful to her while in France, and justified himself by the assertion that she herself had taken a lover. She resented that furiously, but he only sneered at her. Not once, however, did he mention that scrap of paper, and she did not dare to do so.

I know very little of war neuroses, but I do know how things were between them in the spring of 1919. Somewhere back in his mind must have been a fear, unbased on fact, that his infidelity had left its mark on him. He went to various medical men, and all of them reassured him. He damned them for a lot of ignorant fools and moved his bed into his dressing-room.

Along with all this persisted his unreasoning and almost insane jealousy of Elinor.

I can understand this, as can any man. His confidence in himself was gone. He felt unable to cope with her, or with the world at large. Even the New York traffic alarmed him. I saw him myself one day waiting to cross the street, and the indecision, and even terror, of launching himself from the curb was written all over him.

The thing which precipitated the crisis the night she went to Seaview was a part of all this. Elinor had been out at a tea, and she came in to find her maid in the hall, and the sound of slamming drawers coming from her boudoir. The maid looked frightened.

"He's been calling for you, madam," she said. "I think something has happened."

What happened immediately was that Norton flung the door open and confronted her. His face was distorted with rage, and he held in his hand that absurd locket I had given her when she was 10. The desk was a small French one she had brought from home, with one of those perfectly obvious secret drawers which opens on the pushing of a button, and she had not even examined it for years. But there inside the drawer he had found the sentimental absurdities of a young girl's secret life: a dried flower or two, a fan from an early cotillion, with names scrawled over it —including mine!—and that locket.

He was blazing. He ignored the maid, or the fact that other servants were within hearing distance. He ignored the date on the locket, and that the tiny picture within it had been reduced from one of a small freckled boy and a little girl with curls. And he shouted that she was an unfaithful wife and a sentimental fool to boot.

She took it with her head high, standing before him and waiting for the inevitable cough and exhaustion. Then she said quietly, "Don't you see how I disturb you, Lloyd? It isn't that all this is unreasonable and childish. That doesn't matter. What does matter is that I make you like this."

"What do you mean by that?"

"I mean that you would be better off without me."

"To go to Carroll Warner!"

"As I have seen Carroll just twice in more than four years, that is merely ridiculous. To go to my mother."

She had been handing her wraps to her maid. Now she took them back again and began to put them on; and suddenly he was abject. He crawled, almost literally, and there was that same terror in his eyes that I had seen as he faced the traffic. For here was the real tragedy for both of them; he needed her, and she knew it. He was dependent on her, even while he hated her for it; and in all that I have written

60

here I see that which Elinor probably never did see: the terror of a man who had lived excessively and now, while still comparatively young, found himself burned out.

Nevertheless, she left the house at once, going to her mother for sanctuary rather than for help. And old Caroline sent her back to that hell on earth, and then picked up her prayerbook; to pray for mercy for herself and also for patience, I presume, with a willful silly girl who wanted to drag the Somers name into the newspapers.

That was in April, 1919. The world was still panting for breath after the furious race of the war. Short hair, short skirts, and the jazz age were still in the future; and women were still feminine and charming. I saw Elinor once or twice at that time, after my visit to Seaview, and I thought she had never looked so lovely. I remember a little dark blue velvet suit, with a hat to match, and that scrap of sable around her neck, in which she looked like all the women a man wants to care for and protect. But she was very thin that spring, and the eager look which had vitalized her earlier had entirely gone. I saw it only once that I can remember, and the occasion alarmed me.

That was on a Sunday morning in Central Park. I had gone for a walk, and suddenly I saw her ahead of me. There was no mistaking her, or the blue velvet outfit. She was walking slowly, and I accelerated my pace to catch up with her. But I never did. From where she was, the bridle path was some distance away, and a man on a horse was cantering briskly along it. He did not see her, nor did she attempt to attract his attention; but she stood stock-still and followed him with her eyes until he was out of sight.

It is small wonder that in surveying those years which led to her tragedy I always see Blair on a horse. In Washington, in New York, in Montana, he is always ahorse for me, sitting his beast with arrogant ease and surveying a world from which he meant to have only the best at the least cost to himself.

9

' It was not until the end of May that things reached a crisis for Elinor. On the surface Norton was much the same as usual; was suave before outsiders, a perfect if cynical host, took inordinate care of his appearance, dressing every night for dinner, and seemed rather better physically; but to her great relief he was still sleeping in his dressing-room. Then one night, having gone early to bed, she wakened to find him standing beside her in his pajamas, and when she turned on the light she saw that he had his army automatic in his hand.

She sat up in bed and stared at him. "What on earth is the matter?"

He looked down at the gun, and then at her. "I thought I heard someone moving in here," he said sheepishly. "It's all right. Go to sleep."

He turned and went out again, but she did not go to sleep. She sat up all night, watching the doorknob, and toward morning she saw it steathily turning. She shot out of her bed and slipped the bolt. Luckily the door into the hall was already fastened. But it is a rather dreadful picture to contemplate, each of them standing there in absolute silence, with only that bolted door between them. He was on the other side, she knew. It was a long time before he took his hand off the knob, and a still longer time before she heard him cautiously moving toward his bed again.

Mad as all this sounds I have never thought of Norton as insane, then or later. As I have said, the dislocation of the war plus his inability to compete with the post-war world had set up a definite neurosis of some sort. To this was added a new Elinor, kind and even tolerant, but with the tolerance of a woman to whom he did not greatly matter. He had never had her in any real sense, but now he had lost her. It roused in him a demoniac fury that was hardly sane, but his essential sanity was borne out by his conduct for the next few months.

However that may be, early on the next night she heard him fumbling at her door. When he found it locked he began beating on it with his hands, and Elinor caught up an armful of clothing and rushed by way of the hall to her maid's room. She had a narrow escape, for after a time she heard him following her; but she escaped by the service staircase.

"I thought of coming to you," she told me, "but it would have looked odd. And I had no money. I'd forgotten my purse. So I went to Aunt Henrietta."

There is a certain dramatic quality in that part of her story; Elinor hurling herself through the darkness in her small car toward that convent-like house where Sister Henrietta had laid aside the world and taken the perpetual vows of her order; and invading her hard-won peace with that story of human passion and despair.

She had arrived at the Compline hour, the last office of the day, and the lay sister who admitted her put her fingers to her lips. Back along the hall was the small chapel, and from it came the voices of the sisters. Like Caroline, they prayed for a quiet night. "Vouchsafe, O Lord, to keep us this night without sin." But Elinor did not go back. She was beyond prayer by that time, almost beyond hope of salvation.

She waited in the small reception room, with its case of religious and contemplative books, its smells of cooked food, of floor polish, of old upholstered furniture, of the indefinable mustiness of ancient houses in spring, and over all the faint odor of incense from the chapel.

Later she tried to tell me of that visit. "I just walked up and down," she said. "It was peaceful there, and I was wondering if Aunt Henrietta had found the answer after all.

Perhaps it wasn't any use to fight. One just escaped. Into good works," she added, as though she had been disloyal. "They work very hard."

With the end of the service the sisters dispersed. She could hear the soft swish of their voluminous black skirts, the padding of their flat soles; but no one came in to her, and so at last she went back into the chapel. It was there that Henrietta found her at last, on her knees crying as though her heart would break. And it speaks well for Henrietta that she merely knelt beside her and remained quiet, until at last Elinor moved to get up. They must have looked a strange pair, this thin elderly sister with her bands and her quiet eyes, and Elinor, expensively dressed and disheveled, with her face ravaged by distress; all the passionate vitality of the one against the calm detachment of the other.

It was in the reception room again, with Sister Henrietta's white hands folded in her lap, that Elinor told her story. Not all of it. She carefully suppressed the Washington episode and Blair Leighton. But Henrietta Somers had lived before she died to the world, and she had all of Caroline's hard common sense into the bargain.

"You are sure that is all, Elinor?"

"I've told you. I think he's crazy."

"You have done nothing to provoke all this?"

"Nothing to justify his conduct, Aunt Henrietta."

But Sister Henrietta merely sat quietly, her still handsome face quiet but watchful.

"I was never in love with him. You know that. And he knew it too. He didn't seem to care."

"Why did you come to me, Elinor? To have a place for the night? Or to tell the truth?"

"Both."

"Then tell the truth. There is somebody else. That's it?" Sister Henrietta asked, more gently.

"He only suspects. He doesn't know about it."

After that she told the whole story, blurting it out without evasion. She told about Blair Leighton, and the sheet of note paper on which she had written: *Dearest, I find I*

64

cannot ride with you today; that later she had missed it, and she was afraid she had used the other side in a letter to Lloyd. She told about her infatuation, sturdily and honestly, and Sister Henrietta listened, nodding. She was not shocked. She understood. Now and then she fingered the silver cross she wore. "One fights these things," she said. "Not alone, of course."

"Do you think I haven't fought it? I don't want to be in love with Blair," Elinor said passionately. "Why should I? It isn't even reasonable. He makes love to every woman he meets. I don't even know anything about him. It's not rational."

"It never is rational, Elinor dear. It is not even unusual. How many young women go through marriage without this happening to them? Do you think you are alone in all this?"

Nevertheless, she was uneasy, this Sister Henrietta who knew so well the world she had left. She got from Elinor finally a pretty fair picture of Leighton, of his physical size and his gentleness with women, that almost deadly combination; and she faced a picture of devastation which alarmed her. It was clear that Elinor was mad about him, with an utterly unreasoning passion; and that that night it was out of control. When at last she got Elinor up into the small whitewashed room where she was to sleep, she was utterly at a loss.

She took Elinor a glass of hot milk and waited until she had drunk it. Then she left her, on her narrow hard bed in that bare room, with only its pine dresser, a chair, a table and the crucifix on the wall; left her and went down to pray again in the chapel. And—being a practical woman also—later to go out and shut off the engine of Elinor's car.

She did not see Elinor until late the next morning. There was a rule of complete silence until nine o'clock. But she sent in a breakfast tray, and at half past nine she was astonished to see Elinor fully dressed and coming down the stairs. She was dry-eyed and quiet, with her mouth rather set.

65

"I am going back, Aunt Henrietta," she said. "Perhaps we can go away somewhere. It's New York he is fighting, really. Not me. Not even Blair. Besides, if Mother hears about this it will kill her."

Sister Henrietta was not fond of her sister-in-law, but she hesitated. "What else could I have done?" she was to ask me later, folding and unfolding her white hands. "We could not keep her; the sisterhood is very poor. And Caroline would not take her back. I knew that. I thought of you. You'd been an old friend of Elinor's, but why bring you into it?"

"Everyone seems to have thought of me," I said bitterly, "but that's as far as it got. So you sent her back to a half-crazy man who had tried to kill her!"

"What else? To this Englishman? As I gathered, he didn't even want her!"

So she went back. It must have taken courage, but she went. It was noon when she got there, and Norton had not gone to his office. He was in the living-room of the apartment, pacing the floor and smoking one cigarette after another. He stopped and stared at her.

"Where have you been?"

"With Aunt Henrietta. You can call up and ask her."

He threw away his cigarette and faced her. "See here," he said, "we'll have to come to an understanding about this. If you intend to lock me out of your room—"

"Only when you bring a gun in with you."

"I had no gun last night. I swear it. And I will never hurt you, Elinor. I'll swear that too if you like. I was all right until I found the door locked. Then I thought—well, that doesn't matter. What I want to say is this: I'm not well here. The damned town gets on my nerves. Let's get out of it and start again. Would you do that?"

"I'll do anything to help," she said simply. "You know that."

He went to her and kissed her; not the caress of a lover, but the appeal for forgiveness of a frightened boy. She knew it for what it was, and she put her arms around him

66

and held him. "We'll see this through together, Lloyd," she added.

He was eager and happy after that. The terrified servants quieted down. They lunched together. Once he reached over and touched her hand, and she could have cried for sheer pity.

Evidently the idea of getting away was not new to him. He had a dozen plans, and together that afternoon they canvassed this possibility and that: Florida and orange growing, Southern California, raising cattle in Montana. He had a small capital. For the first time he was frank with her about money, and it appeared that, even with her allowance from her mother, they had lived beyond their means for a long time.

"God," he said, "I'll be glad to pay my bills and get out! If I could find somebody to go in with me it would help."

It sounds incredible after that devastating night, but the man was like that. Unpredictable. Somewhere in this flow of talk Elinor was waiting for a chance to confess about Blair. Not all the truth, but enough to explain that note, if he had got it. She was not afraid any more. After all, she had never been unfaithful, and she wanted to start fair with him in this new life they were planning.

But the cards were stacked against her. They were still talking when the doorbell rang at five o'clock, and Blair Leighton was announced.

10

Sitting in the courtroom during those early days of the trial I was going back over all this; through the long and dreary empaneling of the jury, through the challenges of the counsel for the defense, through its final selection

and the judge's speech to them: that all of them were working toward one end, and that end was that the purposes of
justice be served. That his function was to determine the
law and theirs to decide the facts. Justice? Facts? Where
could they be made to meet, in the case of the State *versus*
Elinor Norton?

Who, for instance, was to say just why Blair Leighton
rang that doorbell and sent in his card at five o'clock of
that May day of 1919? Or that Elinor should now be sitting
in the prisoner's dock because he came then, and not a week
before or a month later? Chance, coincidence, but never
the law or justice. What law or justice would take into account the combination of relief and apprehension with
which I learned that she and Lloyd were going West? The
apprehension of the man who hopelessly cares for a woman,
and the relief of knowing that at last he has reached bed-
rock and can sink no farther.

For I had no idea then that Leighton was mixed up in
it; not until I met Norton on the street one day, looking
better than I had ever seen him, and he stopped me and
told me.

"I suppose you've heard the news?"

"I've heard rumors. That's all. Is it true?"

"Yes. Elinor and I are pulling out. Going West."

If he was watching me for any reaction I think he was
disappointed. "That's fine," I told him. "I wish to God I
could. What do you mean, West? California?"

"Montana," he said. "Sounds good, doesn't it? A man
Elinor knows is looking up a ranch for us. He's been there
before. Fellow named Leighton. Maybe you've met him."

I felt my face stiffen, but I doubt if he noticed it. There
was a little malice in his smile when he moved on, but that
was for me. He was no longer jealous of me, but he knew
well enough that I had cared for Elinor. I have wondered
since if Isabel Curtis ever told him about that night on the
beach. She was entirely capable of it.

I stood still for a minute or two. My first feeling was
one of helpless anger against Elinor herself, that her infat-

uation had carried her to such a length. After that came a premonition of tragedy, which I carried with me all that afternoon. But I did not suspect the fact, which was that Blair had fascinated Norton from the first afternoon they met, and that Elinor had found herself helpless between them.

He did it unconsciously. So far as I know he made no effort. He sat there, big and imposing, with his highball beside him, and let Norton talk. Now and then he glanced at Elinor, but only with the appreciation of his sort for a beautiful and young woman. Certainly he was not in love with her at that time. Probably he never was in love with her, in the best sense of the word, either then or later. His reaction to her was a purely physical one. He had none of the imagination which makes the lover.

To do him justice I believe that call of his that day, in spite of what Isabel had said, was without malice prepense. He had had an empty hour or so, and he was willing to fill it with a pretty woman who had been in love with him. But he found Lloyd there, enthusiastic about leaving the city, and Leighton idly suggested Montana.

The inevitability of it is shocking. For Elinor did not want Montana, and her resistance to the idea probably piqued him. He began to draw little word pictures of the life. He knew something about it. He had friends out there. He had been there himself, big game hunting, before the war.

"It's free," he said. "Big open country to ride over, and shooting of all sorts. It's a man's country, of course. Takes a man to fight it, but it can be done."

That naturally appealed to Norton, not too sure of his own manhood just then; and there were other pictures, of great droves of cattle moving up into the mountains for summer grazing, or being herded across the flats in the fall toward the shipping pens at the railroad. Prices were good at that time, and with Elinor's gaze on him he drew airy pictures of large profits.

Norton's eyes began to gleam. When he left, the two

men were engaged to lunch together the next day. When the lunch was over it was settled that Leighton, who was going West on a visit, should look over the ground; and Norton went home with a new look on his face and an armful of books on the cattle country.

Two weeks later he received a wire from Leighton. He had located a good property at a bargain and thought Norton should go out and look it over. And 24 hours after that he was on his way West, and I went home to find Taki having an attack of jitters in the hall, and saying that a Mrs. Norton was waiting for me in my living-room. I went in, to find Elinor sitting back exhaustedly in one of my big chairs.

She had taken off her hat, and my reaction to seeing her there like that, as though she belonged, should have shown me where I stood. She did not move when I went in, but smiled up at me faintly.

"Don't look so startled," she said. "I need some advice, Carroll, and where should I come but here?"

"I charge for advice, you know. Would you like a drink?"

"I'd like a cup of tea, if you don't mind. You're very comfortable here, aren't you?"

"Comfortable? Well, I suppose I am. Rather lonely at times, of course."

She thought that over for a minute or two. Then she said something which almost disarmed me. She said, "I wish I had married you, Carroll."

"Why?" I said lightly. "Because I'm comfortable here?"

"I don't know. I suppose it's because— What's that about the heathen in his blindness bowing down to wood and stone?"

"Gods. Gods of wood and stone," I explained gravely.

"I know all that," she said impatiently. "What I meant was that you wouldn't have let me do that. Or would you? Would you have just let me go on, being a fool and an idiot?"

The tea came, and it was not until Taki had gone that

either of us spoke again. Then I said, "Is it as bad as that, Elinor?"

She did not reply at once. She had none of the modern flair for self-analysis, no morbid liking for laying her soul on the dissecting table for all and sundry. Old Caroline had seen to that. But she did reply.

"It's pretty bad, Carroll," she said.

When at last she began to talk she made no defense, although I gathered that the first weeks of her marriage had been horrible to her. Like all women, she had considered sex only a part of the love life, and she had married a man who knew no love aside from passion. Not in extenuation but as a matter of fact, she implied that he was never tender with her, or gentle. "He never really loved me at all," was what she said.

Nevertheless, she had got along. She lived her own secret life of dreams, submitted to him, conformed, adjusted, for that first year. She dressed for him, scented herself to satisfy that streak of the sensuous in him, and abandoned her own friends for his. "You know, Carroll, how seldom I saw you?"

I did know. Who better?

It was when the war came and he went to France that she began to change. She felt free for the first time in her life. Not that Norton had been unkind or even domineering, like her mother. But he had been exacting, and as time went on, jealous and watchful. His going had been pure relief. She had worked very hard, and she told me—which touched me—that she had prayed daily for my safety. "And Lloyd's," she added.

Then Caroline became ill, and although she did not need Elinor or even want her about, the girl went to Seaview to be near her.

"I used to talk to your Katie about you," she said. "And I lay on the beach in the sun a good bit. You remember how we used to? And I would think that, far away across the water somewhere, you were fighting; you and Lloyd. And—don't misunderstand this, Carroll dear—that I was

71

more frightened about you than I was about him. You were my old friend, and Lloyd was—well, what was he? He didn't love me. I wanted him to be safe, of course, but I didn't much want him to come back to me. To come back, but not to me," she repeated. "How wicked that sounds!"

"Not so wicked," I told her. "You probably had plenty of company. A good many women—"

But she was on her way to a confession. She hardly heard me. What she was trying to tell me was that as she lay in the sun, peaceful at last, vital and warm and young, something had happened to her.

"It was as though I had just begun to live, Carroll. Queer, wasn't it?"

"Not so queer, my dear. Perhaps you had."

She considered that gravely, and then rather abruptly she came to Leighton. She had no idea that I knew about him. "He was—he is—very good-looking, but that hardly explains it. I've never really cared about looks in a man. But we walked and rode together and—I suppose you'll have to know the worst—he made pretty passionate love to me. You know the sort. It didn't mean much to him, I think. He had made love to so many women. But it did something rather dreadful to me. Do you remember my telling you once that I was different? That I couldn't care for anybody? Well, I'm not different, that's all. I simply went crazy about him, and I can't get over it."

There was more to it than that. Isabel Curtis had suspected her, and began to watch her. Isabel, she thought, still cherished a tenderness for Lloyd, and she loathed Blair. But one day the thing happened which had shocked her into a sort of sanity. She missed from her desk that sheet of note paper on which she had commenced the note to Leighton. She had decided not to send it, and then she missed it. She was certain that it had gone to Lloyd in France. She remembered catching up a sheet of paper to add a postscript to a letter to him, and now she was sure he had it.

"Can you wonder that I was afraid to meet him at the

train?" she asked me. "You knew I was afraid, didn't you?"

"I didn't know how much reason you had to be afraid. I don't know now."

"I'd been disloyal but not unfaithful. I suppose that's what you mean. It sounds rather stilted, but it's true. That doesn't alter the fact that I'd have run away with him in a minute if he'd asked me to. He never did. He would have had to make an honest woman of me afterward, and he would have detested that!"

The irony was new to me, coming from her. She went on, however, without bitterness. As he was, he was. She had no illusions about him; but also she had no illusions about herself. "What I am afraid of," she said, "is that he will neither take me nor leave me alone. I know that Lloyd and I can manage if Blair will only stay out of it. But I'm afraid he won't. You see, he knows I care for him. And I don't want any triangle, Carroll. I won't have a dirty, sordid affair with him, and I won't be dragged in the dirt."

"But if you are going away—"

"How do I know he won't be there? He is there now. It's strange, but he seems to have hypnotized Lloyd. I suppose because, just as a fine physical animal, he is all that Lloyd would like to be." And she added irrelevantly, "Lloyd has always thought that note was to you. He knew we used to ride together, and I had written that you were back from France. Do you mind?"

"Not too much," I observed, rather drily. "You're protecting Leighton at my expense, of course, but I can stand it."

"I'm protecting myself, Carroll." But she got up and came over to me. "I'm sorry, but I didn't know what else to do. You see, I have nobody but you. I haven't even any money! I can't run away. And if Lloyd learns now who it was I believe he will kill me."

For, it developed, she had come with more than a confession. She had brought me something to do for her. I was to induce Blair to keep away from them both! She could manage Lloyd. They might begin all over again in a

73

new environment, and she could get rid of her obsession. People got over things like that, she said. But Blair would have to go back to England, and that was where I was to come in. "If he comes back East with Lloyd," she said, twisting her wedding ring around her finger, "you could see him, couldn't you? He doesn't pay any attention to me. A man is different. He wouldn't laugh at you, Carroll."

By which I gathered that she had already made an appeal to him, and failed. Indeed, I know now that she had, way-laying him in the park to do so; and I can see him now, leaning against his horse and smiling down into her troubled eyes.

"Why worry, darling?" he had said lightly. "I may stay; I like the country out there. Or I may not. But why should that disturb you? You are a very virtuous little lady, and all virtuous little ladies are safe, aren't they?" Then he had added more soberly, "Listen, Nellie." He was the only person I ever knew who called her that. "Listen, Nellie. You've shown me where I stand, and you have nothing to be afraid of. The thing is to help that poor devil to find himself again. You and I don't count, and I'll not bother you."

"Then you *are* going to stay out there?"

"I don't know. That's the fact. But if I like it I may."

Probably he meant it at the time, but she did not believe him. He even told her of the vast size of the country, and of the unlikeliness of his getting under her feet. He might find a bit of land and raise polo ponies—some of his friends out there were doing that—but the chances were he would be far away. And in all honesty to the man I believe he meant it, although she did not. He liked his power over her, and the feeling that she was afraid to have him near; but women had always been easy for him, and he was too self-indulgent to waste time on good ones or to risk a jealous husband.

She did not tell me that day of this meeting, however. I promised to see what I could do, and she put on her hat with unsteady hands and then came over and kissed me

74

gently. "I'm not so selfish as you may think," she said. "Lloyd is going to have his chance, Carroll. I swear that. I've been to his doctor, and he is sure it is going to help."

But after she left that evening I walked the floor for a a long time. Whether Leighton stayed or went back to England, I could see no miracle for her, alone in some remote ranch house with a man who was certainly not normal, and living under conditions for which she had had no preparation whatever. She would go, I knew that. Like many another woman, she was ready to immolate herself as a sort of atonement for the sin of not loving her husband. I saw, too, what I had not seen before; that she was clinging to the idea, even holding to Norton, because she had lost confidence in herself.

That was why I was to assist in this program. I was, God helping me, to ask Blair Leighton to get out of the country; or at least to keep himself at a safe distance! I wondered rather grimly how a man set about such a business, and spent most of the night cursing myself for the fool I certainly felt myself to be.

Then, within the week, I learned that the whole affair had been taken out of my hands. Elinor had received a long telegram from Norton, telling her that the property was all that could be desired, and more or less ordering her to have her furniture packed and to come herself at once. She called me up that night when it arrived, but my father was not well and I had gone home for the weekend. What I would have done I do not know. It was all of a piece with that ringing of the doorbell. Certainly I would have tried to hold her in the East at least until she knew Leighton's plans more definitely. But how tell that to a jury?

I did not come back until the following Wednesday, for my father's condition had been rather critical. When I did come it was too late. She had persuaded herself that it would be all right.

11

I saw her only twice after that. My father's illness persisted, and I was in and out of town for the next ten days. Mother was like a distracted creature. For more than 30 years he had dominated her life—even, after his quizzical fashion, had done her thinking for her. They had always slept in the same bed. I could not remember their being separated, for a single night.

Now this solidity of union was threatened, her sense of permanence and security endangered. There were days when she looked for the first time like an old woman. I had sent up a nurse, but she was jealous of her; jealous that any woman other than herself should take care of him. "She drops asleep at night, Carroll. I found her myself, dozing beside the bed."

In the end my father sensed the situation and sent the nurse away. Mother became herself after that, bustled around, even looked better, and in the end claimed his improvement as her own work.

It was in the midst of such distractions that I saw Elinor for the first time. I found her standing in the midst of chaos, with packers all around her and a smock over her dress. She looked excited and very young.

"Let's get out of the noise," she said. "Will you give me tea somewhere? And what do you suppose I shall do with all this stuff in a ranch house?"

I saw that she did not care to raise again the issue of that visit to me, and that she avoided looking me in the eyes. But I was not to be put off.

"What about Leighton?" I asked. "Don't you think you ought to know his plans first? Did Lloyd say anything about him?"

76

"No, but Lloyd's buying the ranch alone. I don't think they are together now. Blair was going to visit some people he knew, and I suppose that's what he is doing. Please don't talk about him, Carroll," she added. "I want to forget him."

Then she left me to change her dress, and I looked about me. The packing was well under way, and as I stood in her small boudoir I saw that the cabinet was empty of its perfumes. They lay in a waste basket on the floor, to be thrown away, and it seemed to me that that small gesture of hers had its own significance. She and Lloyd were to start again on a new and sounder basis. It was even an act of self-assertion on her part.

In spite of all we could do, however, that tea stands out as a conspicuous failure. There was no going back to the tempo of the day in my apartment. Elinor talked, but not once did she revert to our earlier conversation. She made no mention of Leighton at all, and she brightly announced that she was going to raise turkeys!

Turkeys, she understood, did well out there, and brought very good prices. One herded them on a horse. She had a book about them, and they were never to be hurried or excited. It was all frightfully interesting, she thought. Besides, they paid well and there wouldn't be much money, although her mother would continue her allowance. Lloyd was putting practically all his capital in the land, and in cattle to stock it.

In spite of her request for tea, she barely touched it. She sat across from me, twisting the large star sapphire which had been her engagement ring and talking feverishly. She was certain it would be good for Lloyd. It was dry, and that would help his cough. And she had been to see her mother. She was better, but she did not approve of the scheme.

It appeared in fact that Caroline had called Norton a fool and Elinor an idiot. "Just why should you think you can get along in a place like that, when you can't get along here?" she demanded. "At least you know what you're about in the East. Cattle? What do you know about cattle? And if

77

Lloyd Norton imagines himself cutting a figure on a horse, I only wish I could see him!"

Nevertheless, Elinor thought she was secretly relieved, and this I believe was true. I know now that Henrietta had been to see her, and had told her some pertinent facts. But there were other factors. Her race was almost run, and she knew it. Truculent and aggressive as her life had been, she was looking for peace in which to end it. Then, too, there was that secret knowledge of hers, that there would be little or nothing to leave to Elinor. Perhaps the ranch would succeed, and she had the faith of her generation in the land.

She remained Caroline, however, stubborn for all her feebleness. She had told Elinor during her visit that her allowance would go on so long as she stayed with Norton, and not a moment longer. Elinor, with her face turned to a new life, had not resented it.

"I hated to leave her," she said. "But I knew she didn't want me. She never did, really. She kept sending for the nurse so I shouldn't be alone with her, and when I went back to say good-bye she pretended to be asleep. Of course, I shall be back and forth to see her."

She never did get back to see her. Not even when Caroline Somers died, or for the reading of the will which left her practically without a dollar. When she did come it was to discover that Caroline, perhaps making a tardy peace with her God, had left the house at Seaview to Henrietta and her order; and that there was little else to leave.

The second time I saw her was when I saw her off on the train. I had brought her the usual books and magazines, and there was a moment when I thought our old intimacy was to be restored. She put her hand in mine and looked directly at me.

"You can trust me, Carroll," she said. "You know that, don't you?"

"I always have, Elinor. I suppose I always will."

Then Isabel Curtis appeared and the moment was over. It was Isabel who told me, after the train had pulled out, that Leighton was still in the West and staying indefinitely.

"What keeps him there?" I asked angrily.

"I told you once. He may not like to leave anything unfinished."

I hated her for that. I realize now that she was unhappy herself, for she had more than the usual woman's intuition. She saw the makings of catastrophe where I was largely fearful for Elinor's well-being. Also I think she was lonely that day, for she asked me if I would take her somewhere that night. But I begged off, and she smiled rather cheerlessly.

"All right," she said. "Let's both go home and brood. I'm a little behind in my brooding anyhow."

I put her into a taxicab and went back to my office and my life, such as it was; walking downtown for exercise in the morning, walking home at night to Taki and an apartment which was only a place in which to eat and sleep. On the desk in my living-room was Elinor's picture, but I avoided looking at it. Taki, watching me with Oriental shrewdness, cooked me special dishes, and more than once, rather than hurt his feelings, I slipped something into a bathroom and so disposed of it.

But my mind for the next three days was with Elinor, on the train and headed West. I know something of that journey now, of her eager excitement, her determination to be through forever with Blair, her belief that she and Lloyd could build up a new life between them. On the morning of the third day, however, she looked out into barren country with a distant backdrop of blue mountains, with only here and there a muddy stream filled to flood from the melting snow on their tops, and at first it daunted her. It was not real. It looked as though it had been picked out of a motion picture and settled there. She was accustomed to the wooded East, and the only trees now were along the creek bottoms, and for mile after mile she saw only sage-covered flats and strange eroded buttes, standing bare and fantastic in the sunlight. She peered out the window and wondered how it could support any life, and almost two years later she was still wondering if it could.

But those were the early days after the war, and there were still plenty of cattle. They hung in bunches around water holes or along the creeks, or spread out grazing over the range. Now and then beside the track she saw rough log corrals and loading platforms, and the conductor told her what they were for.

"Never been out before?" he asked.

"No. But we have bought a ranch out here."

"Going to run cattle, eh?"

"Cattle and turkeys."

"Well now, that's fine," he said heartily. "Cattle and turkeys and dudes, that's about all this part of the state is good for. Sheep, too, but they're not what you might say popular."

Dude was a new word to her then. She had no idea what he meant by it, and was vaguely affronted.

In her purse was a letter from Norton. She was to get out at a water tank where the engine stopped at the top of a grade, and he would meet her there. Long before the train slid to a halt she was on the platform, staring out, but the empty country showed only a muddy strip of road, dipping here and there into a wash and precariously rising out of it again. For the first time her heart began to fail her. What could she do against a land like that? What would it do to Lloyd?

When the conductor put a kindly hand on her shoulder she was trembling. "Well, here we are," he said. "And there's your husband!"

It was Leighton. He stood smiling up at her from beside the track, debonair and cheerful, a battered Stetson hat on his fair hair and his trousers tucked into muddy boots. There was a dilapidated car nearby, and it, too, was coated with mud. He whipped off his hat.

"Sorry," he said, "but Lloyd is getting the house to rights. Have a good trip?"

"Very comfortable," she told him. "Are you staying at the ranch?"

"Only for a day or two. Don't worry!"

The train was still there, and the fatherly conductor. She kept herself in hand, watched Leighton load her bags into the car, shook hands with the conductor. Quite definitely, however, she distrusted Leighton's easy manner, and equally definitely she was afraid of him. She did not believe in his day or two, or that he had not carefully engineered their meeting. But within a mile or so he had reassured her.

"See here," he said, "let's get this straight, Nellie. I'm not hounding you. Lloyd wanted to get things fixed up a bit for you, and I stayed over to help him out. Tomorrow I'm off."

"For where? The East?"

"I'm visiting some people near Billings. That's a hundred miles away, Nellie. Isn't that far enough?"

She relaxed then. "On roads like this it should be!"

The road was incredible. It was hardly more than a track, and as they moved back through the eroded lands there were places where a skid would have dropped them 100 feet. Here and there the wire crossed it, and Leighton would get out, open a gate, drive through and then close it again. But he was amazingly at home. The brutality of the country seemed to suit him. Even then she sensed that he liked to match his strength against it.

Once he leaned back and drew a long breath. "Can you smell it?" he asked. "The sage, I mean. It's best after a rain."

By the end of an hour he had completely disarmed her, and not by intention. He was not acting. She was only incidental to his supreme content in that vast open countryside, and later on she was to put that into words. "Blair's real love is for the land," she said. "He fights it, but he loves it. He never really needs anything else."

She began to relax. She felt sure of herself, not afraid any more. His spell was over, she thought; ignorant that it was over only because he so willed it. He made no attempt to recall her. He was even silent for long stretches of the way, whipping the car about by main strength, but at peace, within and without. She began to watch for the ranch.

Always, along the way, she had been waiting for some

Promised Land. There would be a turn of the road and a green and civilized valley would lie before her. Even when Leighton opened the last gate and said, "Your wire now!" she continued to hope. But when she saw the ranch house her heart sank within her.

In the years to follow she was to see the strange beauty of that semi-arid country, always stronger than the human race which thinly populated it. She was to know it well, its violent storm rages, its bitter winters, its hail to destroy the crops, its plagues of grasshoppers to eat the grain and of disease among the cattle, and its days of gentleness and peace.

But always she felt that it defied control, was unpredictable, capricious, and sometimes deadly.

It seemed deadly to her then, ugly and hopeless. What she had expected I do not know, certainly not what she found when in a swirl of dust they drew up. There before her was a frame ranch house with a shallow porch, and behind it a miscellaneous group of ugly structures, including a barn. A clump of cottonwoods at some distance provided the only bit of real green, and beyond it lay the bad lands, broken, terrible, and majestic.

It looked like the land of despair to her, and Leighton glanced at her. "Don't show Lloyd a face like that," he said almost roughly. "You can fix the house. It's a good house."

"It's all so new to me. That's all."

And Norton, when he appeared, she found touching. He was almost boyish in his pride and fear; his pride in the ranch, his fear that she might not like it. There was a sort of humility about him when, having kissed her, he led her across that awful porch and threw open the door. "Welcome home," he said.

She had herself in hand by that time. She put her arm through his and together they went over the house. The two men had done their best, but nothing could conceal the facts; the lack of anything but the most rudimentary sanitary arrangements, the small low-ceilinged rooms, the dirty and inconvenient kitchen. Leighton had not gone in with them, and it was in the kitchen that once again she put her arms around Lloyd and told him that she was there to stay, and that they would see the whole thing through together.

His answer to that was characteristic. "It's the life for me," he said. "I only wonder why in God's name I didn't come sooner." Nothing more about her, or if it was a life of any sort for her. She had accepted it—and him—and that was enough.

Some of her furniture had already arrived and had been put in place. She carried that determined smile with her up the steep staircase and into her bedroom. There her face stiffened. She threw off her hat and went to the window. She felt utterly and completely alone; and all around her, as far as she could see, was that fantastic countryside, broken and torn into nightmare by wind and water erosion, lonely and absolutely still. As she stood there the sun slipped behind the distant mountains, and from some hillside nearby a coyote began to howl.

12

It was the end of June before I heard from her, a long letter full of detail and with the personal element entirely left out except for the postscript:

Dearest Carroll: I have been too busy to write letters, save one to Mother now and then. Also I had to have time to readjust some of my ideas—about turkeys, for one thing! I doubt if this country would support a single self-respecting one, although I may be wrong. It does support cattle, and that is our business.

Lloyd seems amazingly better, and there is no doubt that this move has been splendid for him. He is out all day, and I rarely see him until evening. Then he comes in dead tired but quite contented. He has bought quite a lot more cattle, but they are scattered about. If you have any idea that range cattle are driven into the barn at night to be milked, you will have to correct it! (We use condensed milk ourselves.)

Already we seem to be a going concern. We have six men in the bunk house. They are a democratic bunch, and when Lloyd rode off this morning one of them said, "He sure is a loose rider, Mrs. Norton."

The house begins to look much better. It was rather awful at first, but I have spent more than I should, knocking out partitions, putting on porches and painting everything white. There is a town only 20 miles away, for my shopping. My only real failure is the bathroom. That is merely a shed on the first floor with a tub in it, so far. One fills it patiently with pail after pail of water, but it does empty itself, and that is something. Eventually we intend to pump water into the house, and maybe also to get a lighting plant. However, just now it is enough that we are comfortable.

The men in the bunk house have a man to cook for them, and in the house I have a dour but efficient woman. She is not much of a cook, but Lloyd is not particular now, and is too tired at night to care anyhow. She thinks I am foolish to use my good silver and dishes, and the night I first used candles on the table she said it was silly to eat good food in the dark! But I loathe an oil lamp, Carroll; and I will live like a lady. I WILL.

There was more to it. She was worried about her mother, and she had had a letter from Isabel Curtis, more than hinting that she wanted to come out. Also Aunt Henrietta had sent her pages of advice and a few books on the contemplative life! *One good thing about all this, Carroll. The last thing one has time for is to think.* She had a good horse, not too wild, and rode a great deal. Indeed she spent most of her day in breeches, to the horror of Mrs. Alden; who was, I took it, the woman in the kitchen. *No woman out here wears breeches.* And in the fall they expected to ship some cattle and to have some money. Just now they seemed to have everything else. And she was *always affectionately, dear Carroll, Elinor.*

The postscript was short: *B. L. is in the vicinity, if you call it near to be 100 miles away. He comes occasionally, but all that is over. Please believe it, Carroll.*

I read it twice, carefully. Except for the protest that she would live like a lady, I could find nothing to indicate her real state of mind. Even she herself was never articulate about those early months when, alone but for the morose woman in the kitchen, she faced the fact that this was to be her life hereafter; that those long empty days would continue indefinitely, and with that the increasing knowledge that Norton neither actually needed her nor would let her leave him. Her sacrifice meant literally nothing to him.

Outside of that, he was more nearly normal during those first months than he had been since the war. His inferiority sense was lulled by action. The necessity for doing things provided him an escape from himself. He even put on a little weight. He rose early and retired early. If Leighton's visits were more frequent it was because he urged them.

Elinor was the housekeeper, nothing more nor less. It was to Leighton that he took his problems. Pretty serious problems at that; for he had spent money recklessly, overbought, overstocked. By the end of the summer he began to realize that.

I replied to Elinor's letter, of course. Also I sent her a lot of books, non-contemplative, for which she thanked me in July; an unimportant note in which she told me Isabel was there, but little else. Then there came a long silence. Late in August I spent two weeks at the Seaview cottage, for my father was still far from well and wanted me about. But they were painful weeks for other reasons also. Elinor was lost to me, if I had ever had her; but some of the glamour of our early days came back during the long summer days on the beach or on the water. It was useless to try to escape her there, although I knew that only the year before she had lain there, reaching full womanhood at last, ripening in the sun for someone else.

It was on the beach, toward the end of my vacation, that I had the first inkling that things were not well with her. I had taken a long swim, and was lying stretched out on the sand when I felt a shadow fall on me, and looked up to see Isabel Curtis.

"Hello, Carroll!" she said. "I thought it was you."

She sat down beside me and lighted a cigarette. She had, she said, motored over from Newport to see old Caroline, now permanently bedridden, and she had seen me from a window. "How is she?" I asked.

"Not so well. But her mind is clear enough. I had to do some pretty tall lying, and it wasn't easy."

"Lying? What about?"

She turned and faced me. "Look here, Carroll. Just what do you know about things out West? What does Elinor tell you? She didn't tell me anything, but I have eyes in my head. It's no go, if you ask me."

"I've only had one letter and a note. What do you mean, Isabel? The cattle business?"

"Cattle my eye," she said rudely. "As far as that goes I suppose it's all right, but with Blair Leighton in and out and a sort of little tin god to Lloyd—and nobody else but a bunch of cowboys and the woman in the kitchen to speak to—I'd drink myself to death if I were Elinor."

"You can't mean that she is drinking!"

"Drinking! No. Better if she would."

"Then you mean Leighton?"

"Who else? He's there too much. And—I'm fond of Lloyd, and I suppose you know it—the comparison isn't any too good. That isn't all of it, either. Lloyd is trying to coax Blair to put money in the ranch and come there. He's spent most of his money, but he still wants to expand. The thing's gone to his head. I'll give Elinor credit for fighting the idea, but he simply doesn't listen to her." And she added, while I thought this over, "Queer, isn't it, how we are always jealous of the wrong people? If it were you, he

86

would go crazy. He simply doesn't believe that his god would stoop to Elinor!"

"I suppose there's no way of heading it off?"

"Not unless someone tells him the truth. Even then he probably wouldn't believe it." She threw away her cigarette and got up. "Well, it's a mess any way you look at it," she said. "I've talked to Blair, but he only laughs at me. He's a typical younger son; gets an allowance from home and has a little capital. The life suits him down to the ground, too. I think he'll do it."

"You're sure that the other isn't over? After all, women do get over those things."

"Do they? I wonder!" She stood for a moment looking out toward the sea. "Anyhow, what *is* over? Trying to forget or trying to remember?"

The next moment she was gone, and I did not see her for several weeks. At the end of that time I met her on Fifth Avenue and she told me Leighton had bought a half interest in the ranch and was moving over in a few days. "Kismet," she said, shrugging her shoulders, and quoted from somewhere or other, *"This is the fulfillment of destiny. This is to love."*

We were both helpless, of course.

I saw her rather often after that. We drifted together, not because we had anything in common, but because we were both at a loose end. Looking back I realize that we had drifted rather further than we knew. She would wander into my little place, sometimes late in the afternoon, once or twice at night; a tall, always beautifully groomed young woman with a discontented face and tired eyes, who would as often as not lapse into silence almost as soon as she got there. We had so little in common that there were times when I racked my brains to find something to say to her, but slipped into the habit of kissing her when she came and when she left. Then she would go away, entirely composed, to whatever awaited her, a party or her bed.

It was Isabel herself who showed me where we were drifting. She was leaving one night, very late, when she smiled and said, "I really ought to stay all night, to save your reputation!"

"Not at the price of yours!"

"I have none left to lose."

She went out on that, not even looking back at me; and I felt a bit of a fool to let her go. But it was all wrong, and I knew it. The only real bond between us was that group of three people in a ranch house 2,500 miles away. I was no anchorite, God knows, but I had cared for only one woman in my life. I could not have offered Isabel even a decent affection.

Then quite suddenly my father died. Katie carried a cup of tea one afternoon to him in his library, and found him peacefully dead, with a book on his knee. It was almost the end of the world for Mother, and a shock and grief to me; but it ended Isabel's visits and all danger that we might seek any sort of fugitive comfort together. Mother moved back into the city again, and I went back home to live; to sit long hours while she recaptured, one by one, the tragic memories by which we keep our dead alive; to wander in at night to sit by her bed; and sometimes to hear her moving about long after the house was quiet and softly crying to herself.

It was a long and dreary winter. Once I happened on one of the Newport cousins, Elizabeth Mayhew. She was leaving the Ritz as I passed, and she called to me. I remember that she wore a handsome mink coat for the day was bitter.

"What do you hear from the Nortons?" she asked.

"Nothing since early fall."

She seemed to hesitate. Then she asked me if she could drop me somewhere; she wanted to talk to me. I agreed, and we went uptown together in her car. But at first I was a trifle monosyllabic. That big car, the coat, the soft fur rug over our knees, roused me to indignation, for against it I was remembering Isabel's story of the ranch; of the battered car and the general scarcity of money there. Elizabeth eyed me.

"You're not listening to me, are you?"

"I'm sorry."

"Then I'll repeat it. What's this story Isabel Curtis is telling, that Elinor is living like a—"

"Like a ranch woman? Well, I dare say she is."

"And what does that mean?"

"I suppose there are not many luxuries. Plenty of comfort, probably. Enough to eat and all that."

"And clothes?"

"Good heavens, Elizabeth! How can I know about that? She doesn't even write to me."

Her color rose somewhat, but she persisted stubbornly. "We can't let her go shabby," she said. "After all, she is a cousin. Ada and I have been talking it over, and we wondered if we sent her a box—you know her so well, Carroll. Would she take clothes? She's about my build."

"Old clothes?"

"Not old," she said impatiently. "Good clothes. They've had some wear, but they're not rags. And Ada has a fur coat. She'd like to send that."

"I think she might like a fur coat," I said. "It's very cold out there, I believe. I don't see why anyone should resent a kindness."

She looked actually grateful, and I realized that there had been a genuine impulse behind that offer. They were still unmarried, the two Mayhew girls, and close to 30 by that time; still moving within the narrow orbit of the rich: Palm Beach in winter, New York in fall and spring, Newport in the summer. Of all of them only Elinor had escaped from it, and probably there was some envy mixed with their sympathy.

"I wish you'd tell me something, Carroll. Is Blair Leighton out there too?"

"I believe he is."

She drew a long breath. "Trust Elinor for luck!" she said. Then the car stopped and I got out.

"It's all right to send the box?"

"You can try, anyhow. But I don't advise any evening clothes."

"None at all?" she asked, astonished.

"None at all," I told her.

13

A far cry perhaps, all of this, from that room in the county courthouse. Yet not so far. Even the box of clothing was to play its own part in due time, and the development of inevitable catastrophe lies as often in the small nagging events of day-by-day living as in the great ones.

I did not hear from Elinor at all during the autumn, but at Christmas I received a card from her. It was a mounted snapshot, showing a white ranch house almost lost in snow, and with a deer in the foreground warily gazing at the camera. On it she had written, *A happy Christmas, dear Carroll, and love to your father and mother.*

She did not know of my father's death. Not even the picture revealed the isolation of her new existence as that did. The card itself I hid from Mother, but now and then at night I took it out and studied it. What was the life that went on behind the blank eyes which were the windows of that house? How did they manage, those three highly civilized human beings, shut up together as they must be during that winter for days on end? Did they read? Did Elinor play her piano? Was Leighton restless and Norton irritable? And where was Elinor herself, trapped as she was between those two men, the one a healthy animal and the other a fastidious and querulous neurotic?

There was no answer to that, unless I count a noncommittal letter from Elinor which came later in the spring. She had learned of my father's death, and most of it concerned that. But she went on: *I am so glad the spring has come. The wild flowers are astonishing, and we have a meadow that is acre on acre of forget-me-not. It hurts me to ride over it. The winter was very long, and we are rather crowded. I suppose you know Blair has bought in on the ranch. Lloyd seems so much better now that he has work to do and can get out again. We have a fair crop, too, and that helps.* The rest concerned her mother. She wished she could come East to see her, but it was an expensive trip. Besides, she did not know if her mother wanted her. Her letters were so few and cold. Perhaps I could find out.

I seemed to read discouragement between the lines; as though she had lost that fine frenzy of self-abnegation of the early days, and had found nothing to take its place. The bit about Lloyd too was revealing. He was *so much better*. It was to be a long time before I knew the hell that first winter had been for at least two out of the three of them; the jeering devil in Norton riding him hard, until Elinor shut herself for days in her room and Blair took his horse and rode over the hills; or when the road permitted it drove the car into town and the local speakeasy, and drank rather more than he should.

The meals, I gathered, were the worst. Leighton, to the wrath of Mrs. Alden, insisted on an evening dinner, and presented himself for it scrubbed and freshly shaven. Elinor did her best, changed her dress, presided with such dignity as she could. But Norton would slouch in, perhaps fresh from the corral or barn, unshaven and grim.

"Damn it all, man!" Blair would say. "You smell of live-stock."

"If you don't like it, you know what you can do."

"I know what I'd like to do. Drop you in the horse trough."

Blair would laugh then, his big hearty laugh, and Elinor would breathe again. Nothing much got under his skin, and he never held a resentment. But for days Norton would be sulky and even more careless in his habits. He would quarrel with the ranch hands, and it took all Leighton could do to hold them. More than once he brought in his horse with sides bleeding from his spurs, and it would be Elinor's turn to protest.

"It's cruel, Lloyd. It's barbarous."

"He's a surly brute. He asked for it."

There was still no jealousy of Leighton, nor any reason for it. Together the two men were companionable enough. Norton, on the plea of bad nights, had moved to a room downstairs, and Blair had one adjacent. They played endless games of cribbage by the living-room fire, made rounds together daily to look over the poor stock, driven in from the range for feeding and care at the home ranch, and figured costs and possible profits for the coming season. It was only when Elinor was around that they bickered; and so she would stay upstairs as long as she dared, listening to them as they came and went, to the slam of doors, the heavy thud of their boots as they walked, the jingle of spurs taken off and hung up.

Then when they had gone she would slip downstairs, hoping only to be unnoticed so that there would be peace. Neither of them was apparently greatly interested in her. She had long ceased to be Norton's wife in more than name, and Leighton had at least enough virtue not to make love to his partner's wife. He was supposed to have a girl of sorts in the town, but she did not know.

That is Elinor's picture of their first winter. It was queer enough, considering that only a few months before she had been madly in love with one of those men, and had immolated herself to save the other. She herself seems to have felt little or nothing for either of them during those months. "I don't seem capable of feeling at all," she said. "I couldn't even think."

Oddly enough, the only ally she had found was the dour woman in the kitchen. She openly disliked both the men, but Blair she detested. When Elinor remonstrated it had no effect.

"I know his kind," she said. "Good with horses and bad with women. I've seen plenty of them."

In spite of all this, the only real scene that winter took place when the box arrived from Ada and Elizabeth Mayhew. Leighton had opened it on the porch and Norton stood by, faintly curious until he saw what was in it. Then he went white. "By God, clothes!" he said. "So your fine friends think we're objects of charity! Nail it up, Blair. It's going back."

"Don't be a fool," Leighton said. "They're Elinor's, not yours. What do you say, Elinor?"

"Certainly I shall keep them. They are sent out of kindness, not charity. And I need them. If Lloyd can remember when he has bought me any clothes, I cannot."

Before they could stop him Norton had kicked the box out into the snow, and for a moment Leighton looked as though he might kill him. He stood with the hatchet in his hand, glaring until Elinor went over to him and took it from him. Then Norton banged into the house, and the other two retrieved the box. The fur coat was in it, and she wore it the rest of the winter.

Not once during all that time had Leighton made even covert love to her, and apparently her own infatuation had died the death of daily prosaic association. Men doing hard physical labor are not given to dalliance, and if the opening of the spring thawed some of her frozen emotions, Leighton apparently remained much as he had been. True, he went rather oftener to town. Once he was gone for three days, and came back rather the worse for drink. But as the spring wore on there was a subtle change in him. She would find him watching her, and there came a warm night when she was certain she heard him coming furtively up the stairs, and had only time to lock her door before she saw the doorknob moving.

That frightened her, and afterward she always kept the door locked. But up to the time she wrote me matters were much as they had been.

"Norton was never jealous of Blair?" I asked her.

"Not then. There was no reason. Of course, jealousy implies some sort of love, and he had no love for me at all. None whatever. I used to think that I meant so little to him that he could not conceive of anyone caring for me."

However that may be, the relationship among the three began to change soon after that, and it was indirectly due to the box again. In it there had been a Chinese lounging suit of jade-colored, brocaded silk. It was before the day of pajamas for women, and certainly the things were modest enough; a full high-necked coat and a pair of wide trousers. She wore them around her room, and one night she had a headache and did not change for dinner. Leighton said nothing, but he stared at her as though he were seeing her for the first time in months; and Norton saw him.

The meal was chilly and constrained. Norton said almost nothing, but when the Alden woman had at last banged the door into the kitchen he addressed her.

"I can't decide whether this is a masquerade or whether you have simply come down in your night clothes. In either case it strikes me as rotten bad taste."

"What you mean," Blair said, "is that she looks devilish pretty. And don't worry about me. I've seen women with less on than that."

"You keep out of this," Norton said savagely. "Or get out and stay out."

But Leighton refused to be angry. "It wouldn't hurt you, Lloyd, to come to dinner sometimes in your pajamas. At least they'd be clean!" Then he sauntered out, and left the two of them together.

Norton made an effort then and kept his voice down. "I don't fool myself that this costume is for me," he said. "Or for Mrs. Alden. I'll merely say that the effort is lost on Blair. He is interested elsewhere."

She faced him across the table. "It was for neither of you," she told him proudly. "I regard what I wear as strictly my own affair. I have still some rights, you know, although I have given up most of them."

"Including the right to lock your bedroom door against me?"

"I didn't know it was you," she said, and then felt sick and dizzy when she saw his face.

"Oh! And who did you think it might be? By God, I believe you thought it was Blair!" He laughed, but he was watching her; and she felt a slow flood of color dye her face. "Blair! Well, I suppose I have to be thankful for small things. At least you locked the door. Blair! Maybe the wish was father to the thought. Maybe you hoped it was Blair. Maybe this dressing up tonight is for Blair. Blair, who thinks more of his little fingernail than he does of your whole body. By gad, I'd like to tell him."

"If you tell him I shall leave you. Make no mistake about that. I have played the game straight, Lloyd."

Then she escaped to her own room. She thought very seriously that night of carrying out her threat. Lloyd did not need or love her. He did not even like her. Most of the time he actively resented her. She turned out her lamp and sat by the open window, thinking it over. There was no sound from downstairs, none of the companionable squabbling of the winter. A coyote was barking in the hills, and from near the bunk house one of the men was playing some melancholy cowboy dirge on a harmonica. But how could she leave him? By that time Norton's capital was practically exhausted, and there would be no money until the time to ship their cattle in the fall; no money, that is, save Leighton's modest remittance and her own allowance from her mother. They were largely living on that allowance.

She felt trapped that night. More so than ever when she heard Leighton speaking softly from under her window: "That's you, Nellie?"

"Yes."

"I wouldn't worry too much about tonight. He'll get over it."

She did not reply, and he waited a moment. Then: "You looked very lovely, you know, Nellie."

She maintained her silence, and he drifted away. He had

the faculty of some big men, of moving very lightly. She hardly knew he was gone.

She was frightened, not at his tone, but at her own reaction to it. It had been tender, and all tenderness and gentleness seemed to have gone out of her life. She cried herself to sleep out of sheer terror for the future.

Whether Norton was alarmed for fear she would carry out her threat, or whether he actually regretted the night before, she did not know. He came to her the next day with an apology, and she accepted it in good faith. What is more, he began to take better care of himself. He shaved daily, and in various small ways tried to conciliate her. She met him more than halfway.

"I left some red lilies in the kitchen."

"Thanks! That was nice of you."

One day he brought home a fawn which one of the men had roped; a bit of a creature which she fed out of a bottle and which thereafter followed her like a dog. "Knew you liked pets," he said awkwardly.

"I adore it!"

They were very busy that spring. Not only with the cattle. They put in hay along the creek bottoms, repaired and built fences. One day she asked the irrigator to dig up a garden patch for her, and thereafter she worked there daily. She planted vegetables, although Mrs. Alden preferred them out of a can. Around the border she planted annuals of all sorts, and she placed hollyhocks and phlox against the house. She even planted wild cucumber vines to shade the wooden porch.

There must have been times during this heavy labor of hers—and it was heavy—when she thought back to her mother's garden at Seaview where half a dozen men kept it in order, and where Caroline herself, gloved and hatted against the sun, had fulfilled the Victorian idea of a gentlewoman's duty and had cut her own flowers for the house. If she remembered it it must have had a dreamlike quality of unreality, there with her newly spaded earth turning to dust

96

before her eyes, and with every growing thing a triumph against a nature hostile in the extreme.

But she did not often look back. She had set her course and meant to follow it. And work was the answer. Thank God for work.

She was still very lonely. They had no near neighbors, but when the spring opened up a few ranchers came to call, bringing with them their kindly work-worn wives. Times were beginning to change for the ranch women. Soon they were to have a life more closely patterned after that of the East, to have their bridge clubs, even a society column in the local newspaper. Also the dude ranches were to bring them their share of women like Elinor, women who rode in breeches as she did, who smoked cigarettes on occasion, had indolent good manners, and used a racy speech which was a vernacular of their own.

But these women who came were still isolated on their ranches. The men would talk cattle, but Elinor puzzled and daunted them. They had little or nothing in common. What was the very foundation of their existence was too new to her.

When the time came they would get up to go, and she would say, "Can't you stay a little longer? I am rather alone, you know."

They did not stay. They were responsible women, with work to do. They would stand there, uncomfortable and uneasy, feeling the appeal in her voice without recognizing it. "I wish we could, but you know what this life is. And your road isn't any too safe!"

Far less safe than they knew, that road she was following; but how could they know that, with her transformed ranch house around her, with alfalfa growing in the creek bottoms and cattle scattered over the pastures?

They did not envy her. They did not even dislike her. Both she and her manner of living were different, that was all. Even her men were different. Unlike Mrs. Alden, they preferred Blair Leighton to Lloyd, but both of them were

97

amateurs. Their own men were scarred with battle, the honorable scars of the cow country. These were interlopers, and they had seen Easterners before, coming out to battle with the country. Men who wore English boots and riding breeches for the day's work, and as often as not made good, for all their queerness. If there was any envy in them at all, it was for their own men, not for themselves.

But Elinor they could not understand, with her casual cigarette and her slim young figure in breeches and coat. When they rode in those days they wore divided skirts, and I doubt if any of them in that remote spot and in the year 1920 had ever before seen a woman smoke.

They came and went, but they never accepted her as one of themselves. When the time came and she sat in the dock of the courtroom, she could not count one real friend among them. They sat there much as they had sat on her porch, but the gulf was between them, wider and more unbridgeable than ever. Now and then as the case went on I saw her glance toward them, still with that breathless, expectant look in her face. They were women; they must understand. It was as though once more she was saying that she was rather alone, as God knows she was, and wouldn't they stay with her? And as though across the crowded courtroom they replied, "I wish we could, but you know what this life is. And your road isn't any too safe."

14

I reached the ranch early in September of that year. Some business for the firm had taken me to Helena, and I wired Norton from there. He sent me an invitation which seemed cordial enough, and late one evening I met him at Billings.

The change in him was surprising. Nothing would make him handsome or even arresting; but he was excited and voluble. They were getting ready to ship some cattle; not a lot, only 400 or 500 head, which seemed considerable beef to me. The market was fair and they would make some money, but it was a tricky business.

"In good years the market's glutted and in bad years you lose your shirt."

He did not mention Elinor, nor did I. He did, however, ask about old Caroline. "Still hanging on," he commented. "Well, we can do with what she leaves when she goes. It's make or break out here, no halfway business."

I was new to the West, and especially to that part of it. It was a long drive over dirt roads, and the summer had been long and hot. Here and there we met Indians, not the Indians of romance but stolid men in store clothes and driving buckboards. Save for their black, braided hair they might have been anything.

Norton thought little of them. "Lazy devils," he said. "Shoot the game and raid the cattle. But they raise good horses."

Well, that is a different story. Our Indians are what we have made them. I said nothing, and soon Norton lapsed into silence. But it was not a moody silence. Evidently his old jealousy of me was over. He told me incidentally that he was drinking little or nothing, and added with a grin that Leighton was doing enough for both of them. Elinor he hardly mentioned.

We were three hours on the way. The road was dry and dusty, and the country brown from summer suns. Here and there a clump of quaking aspen was already turning to golden yellow, but although I felt its impressiveness, that semi-arid landscape looked drab and monotonous to me. It seemed a queer setting for Elinor. I could not see her in it, and when at last I held her hand and looked into her face I still had a feeling of strangeness.

She had not changed, although in repose her face looked sad and her eyes haunted. She was undeniably happy to see

99

me, and I thought there were tears in her eyes. She blinked them back, however.

"Carroll!" she said. "Welcome to the N-Bar-L. And how —how Eastern you look!"

Leighton was not in sight, and Lloyd had driven the dusty car back to the barn. She was still holding my hand, and now she put it up against her cheek and held it there. "Why is it that old friends are always so dear?" she asked. Then she dropped the hand.

"How we are going to talk!" she said. "We are going to talk for days and days. But now you'd better go up and wash. I have a little coop of a guest room. I'll show it to you." She was actually about to pick up my bag when I took it from her.

I did not go down at once. The meeting had shaken me, and that guest room also. I was touched at the pains she had taken for my comfort, the flowers on a table, the books beside the bed. But I was uneasy also. Norton had seemed to me to be still unstable and feverishly excitable. His failure to enlarge on either Elinor or Leighton had also seemed ominous. And until that day I had not realized the actual isolation of the ranch.

There was not another house for miles. Even the road by which we had come ended there, although there was an uncertain track leading to some vague destination beyond. And as I stood at the window I realized what actual silence could be. It beat on my eardrums like a great noise.

I found Elinor waiting for me on the porch. She did not hear me at first, and I found her staring far away over the hills. Just so had I seen her stare at the sea long ago; a slow, thoughtful gaze, as though she measured herself against it. Now I think she measured herself against this land, for primarily her battle was with the land. Not only with the problems it brought, but with its effect on herself. Later on she was to say something of the sort.

"It was too big for me. Too strong, Carroll. It wasn't only that it cut me off. It was that it was eternal, and what was I?

100

I could imagine God looking after His hills, but not after me. That's not a defense, it's a fact."

She came to with a start when I touched her arm, and together we went over the house. She was very proud of it, but I viewed it with mixed emotions. The lighting system was in, and there was water now piped to the bathroom. I realized the amount of labor that had gone into it all, but at one point she showed me her hands. They shocked me. She had had beautiful hands. Now, although still small and shapely, they were rough and work-hardened.

"One pays a price for everything," she said. "And the water is very bad. Alkali."

That was her only complaint, and certainly she had worked wonders with the house. Except for the walls in the hall, where Stetson hats, a pair of heavy chaps, and an odd spur hung on hooks, it might have been any hall anywhere; and the living-room any living-room, except for a gun rack by the door. With the interest of a man who likes guns, I stopped and looked at those inside. There were half a dozen shotguns and rifles, all well cared for, and on the bottom of the rack lay Norton's service automatic, still in its holster.

The room itself was large—she had thrown two rooms together to make it—with an open fireplace at one end and a wide davenport near it; and of all the house this one room best represented her. It was here that she had most clearly shown her determination to carry on as best she could. Her grand piano stood in a corner, the heavy chairs were lightened by bamboo furniture, painted the color of old ivory and with bright chintz cushions, and still further to offset the colorless land outside, she had hung on the walls here and there a soft old India print. Scattered about were photographs in silver frames, along one whole side were open shelves filled with books, and on tables and on the piano were more flowers cut from her own garden.

"I told you," she said. "I will live like a lady, Carroll!"

"You didn't need to tell me that."

She let her hand rest for an instant on my arm. "No," she said. "You never needed much telling."

The next moment she was calling my attention to the wide fireplace, and saying casually that Blair and the men had built it late in the fall. It was her first mention of Leighton and she glanced at me; but I only said that it looked a workmanlike job, and let it go at that.

My room was at the back of the house, and as I cleaned up for dinner I saw Leighton riding in. He was on a big horse, and both horse and man looked tired. He dismounted heavily by the barn, unsaddled and turned his animal loose, and then came still heavily toward the house. Watching him, I thought he came unwillingly. I thought, too, that there was a vague change in the man, and not for the better. Nevertheless, he was still an astonishingly handsome animal. Perhaps I have forgotten, or perhaps the Western outfit suited him; the soft collar open at the throat, the neckerchief against the dust, the big hat. He was coatless, and although he seemed heavier than I remembered him, his stomach was still flat and his flanks narrow. Like Norton, he wore English riding-boots, much the worse for wear.

It was his expression which had changed. He looked discontented, almost surly. The good humor was gone out of his face. He looked like a man raddled with nerves or drink, or possibly both. But later I was to wonder if it had been only fatigue, for he turned up for dinner hospitably smiling.

That meal still has all the qualities of a dream for me. Elinor gravely gracious in something white, and around her in the candlelight the three men who were so closely interwoven with her life: her boyhood lover, the man she had married, and the man who was now in love with her. It was irony, if you like; for that Leighton was by this time deeply in love with her I felt certain before the meal was over. He concealed it, but it was in his eyes when he looked at her, in his voice when he spoke.

The only enigma was Elinor herself. She was rather silent. She ate little, and I felt that she was tense with anxiety that nothing should disturb the surface calm of the meal. Nothing did. The other men ate with the appetite of the outdoors, talked ranch and cattle to me, and were totally uninterested in the world they had left.

The sole sop they threw to the East was an occasional inquiry: "How's business? Still going strong?"

"It's going, but nobody knows where."

"Well, they'll still eat beef, thank God."

Or, from Leighton: "I can show you some fishing if you're keen on it. A few miles off, but as good as anything you'd get back home."

Some time during the meal Elinor's fawn came to the porch and made small tentative passes at the screen door, and the only break in our serenity was Norton's irritable comment: "For God's sake, can't you keep that animal away from the house?"

No one said anything, and at last we heard its small hard hoofs pattering across the porch and down the steps.

One thing I noticed. The two men had little to say to each other, or to Elinor. They talked to me, all three of them, and I wondered whether this was because they were long ago talked out among themselves, or whether there was some inner strain which my presence helped to relieve. The latter, I gathered, when after the meal Leighton stated that he was going to town.

"I thought you were going with Pete in the morning," Norton said.

"I'll be up. Don't worry."

He said a polite good-night to me, and some minutes later Norton and I, smoking on the porch, saw the lights of his car as it swung out into the road.

"Busiest time of the year," Norton said sourly, "and he gambles most of the night. What's more, he's got liquor cached around here somewhere, and one of the boys has been getting at it. It's the hell of a way to run a ranch."

He had little to say. His loquacity of the early afternoon was gone, and there were intervals when we sat there gazing out at the black darkness and silence beyond the porch,

103

and both of them seemed unbearable; and then I thought that death must be something like that, without form or color or sound, and only the tired mind thinking its confused disembodied thoughts.

"Is it always like this? At night?"

"Like what?"

"Quiet."

"You city fellows!" he said derisively. "Can't go anywhere unless there's a lamp-post."

But he was not unfriendly. He was not only not jealous of me any more. He was not even thinking of me. I gathered from his talk after that some deep obsession with Blair and a cold resentment against him, but I was not sure that it concerned Elinor.

It was not until after he had left me, on some errand to the bunk house, that Elinor joined me. She came out quietly, a slim white ghost, and sat down on the steps beside me. "If we closed our eyes," she said, "we could imagine that we were back in the country at home, and that the sea is out there. I often do."

"Would you like to go back, Elinor?"

"If I could turn back the years. Not as things are now."

"And how are things now?"

She did not reply at once. The little deer came up and stuck his head into her lap, and she rubbed his ears gently. "I don't know what to say to that. Nothing seems quite real. Lloyd is better. He is busy and interested, and much more normal. Lately, of course—"

"He is not so happy?"

"He has turned against Blair. At first it was nothing but Blair. Blair here, Blair there until—well, I didn't belong. That's all. I hadn't wanted this arrangement, but it was made and I did my best. Now he would like to change it, but what can we do? Blair's money is here, and he has worked hard."

"Isn't it possible that if you were not here things would settle themselves?"

She glanced quickly toward me, but I could not see her

face. "I don't think it's that. Blair is popular. He's even more popular than Lloyd with our men. I think Lloyd is jealous of that."

"It has nothing to do with you?"

"Not unless he imagines things."

"Then you are contented? With things as they are?"

She made a small movement in the dark. "Contented? What is contentment, Carroll? I am not unhappy, and I chose my life. I have to live it."

"Not necessarily," I said carefully. "You have done your bit. You say yourself that Lloyd is better. Isn't that why you came? And isn't your work done? If he doesn't need you now—"

She stirred uneasily. "Don't, Carroll. Don't tempt me. Besides, granted that Lloyd doesn't need me any more, where could I go? Mother wouldn't have me if I left him, and I'm not trained to do anything. I couldn't even support myself."

"That could be arranged," I said, none too steadily. "You aren't friendless, you know. You have me, for one thing. I haven't many virtues, but at least I am dependable."

"Dependable," she repeated. "Yes, you are that. I wonder if you know what a wonderful word that is? There are so few—"

But the next minute she heard Norton returning. She got up quickly. "It's getting cold," she said. "Let's go in, and have some lights and music."

It was a strange evening. She played, and in the intervals I talked against the silence and the dark outside. When I stopped, or the piano, they seemed to creep in through the windows, and I felt cut off from everything living and vital. Norton slept heavily in a big chair near the fire, the local paper on his knee, and outside of the three of us there was no living world, nothing. Yet I could see already that the country might have a fascination of its own. The night breeze that came through the windows was pungent and exhilarating. And finally Elinor left the piano and put a hand into mine.

"You've helped me, Carroll. I was a bit homesick tonight. That's really all." And she added slowly, "I don't even believe I could go back. This country fascinates me. Somehow I feel grown up here, as though I had never been an adult before. Then, too, I've made something here, out of nothing. I never had a chance to do that until now."

Norton stirred then in his chair, and with a quick gesture she freed her hand and moved quickly across the room to the bookshelves. "What sort of book?" she said. "Something thrilling? We haven't anything new."

I went up to bed disturbed in mind. That swift, almost stealthy movement of hers looked like a maneuver frequently rehearsed; and I could see other evenings, with Norton asleep in his chair and Leighton close beside her, talking perhaps, but beside her. And then Norton stirring and Elinor moving away, it might be to the piano, to fold up her music and say:

"That's all for tonight. My arms are tired."

I felt certain that, of the three, two at least were acting. Perhaps all of them. Leighton's urbanity was false, Elinor was acting a security she did not feel, and by the time I undressed for bed I was convinced that Norton was insanely jealous of Blair and that he was watching both him and Elinor, day and night.

There was small peace for me that night. Outside everything was still with the ancient quiet of the earth before life quickened it. But under that roof there was no quiet. Late in the night I thought I heard Elinor moving about her room, as though she, too, could not sleep.

15

The next day, the second of my stay, remains almost blank in my mind. There was a bustle over the place, I recall; extra horses being driven in for the round-up which was to begin the next morning, the chuck wagon being gone over back by the barn, and the riding in on horseback of other ranchers, youngish men in chaps—one of them on a bad-tempered horse—who would accompany the outfit and cut out their own brands. They elected to eat in the bunk house, and I saw little of them.

One incident, however, stands out with distinctness. There was a steer to be killed for the round-up, and after our early dinner that night Norton asked me to go with him to do it.

"It's up in the pasture," he said. "Maybe you'll like to see how we handle things for ourselves out here. You Eastern fellows never see beef until it's on a table!"

There was a thin contempt in his voice, but I did not care to offend him. He was in an uncertain temper, for Leighton had not appeared all day and his comment at dinner had probably been correct.

"Not here yet, eh? Nice shape he'll be in tomorrow! The bloody fool."

He had learned that this was one adjective Leighton would not tolerate, and even in his absence it gave Norton some curious satisfaction to utter it.

We rode together to the pasture, Norton carrying a rifle. The steer, a big flat-backed Hereford, was grazing quietly and paid no attention to us. But I paid little attention to the creature, then or later. There was something in Norton's manner which was vaguely disconcerting; a gaiety, a sort of blood-lust as he left his horse and loaded his gun, which

107

made me uncomfortable. I am not sentimental. I recognize that food animals are raised for food, and that death is a part of that process. But I am certain that the first really happy expression I had seen on Lloyd Norton's face since my arrival was when he whistled to the steer so that it would raise its head, and when with a bullet in its brain it sank slowly to the earth.

He looked at me and grinned. "It's a great life, Warner!"

Then his interest waned. He did not wait for the men to strip off the hide or to cut open with thin sharp knives the great carcass. He did not speak at all on the way back.

Sometime late that night I heard Leighton's car coming in, and still later high and furious voices from below. Elinor was shut in her room, but the dour woman opened her door along the back hall and called down angrily. "Stop that racket," she shouted. "I've got to get up at the crack of dawn, and I need my sleep."

They stopped, and except for a banging door there was no further noise. Help of any sort was difficult to get in that remote spot, I suppose, and probably they had already said what they had to say. Nevertheless, the air of tension and strained nerves that night merely added to the unreality of the entire situation. It was impossible to picture Elinor as definitely a part of the vulgarity of the whole business; the two men, one of them the worse for drink—quarreling loudly below, and the shrewish voice of the Alden woman shouting at them from above.

I was mildly astonished, therefore, when, waking very early the next morning, I saw Leighton and Lloyd Norton walking together amicably enough toward the barn and their saddled horses. Evidently they had some *modus vivendi,* some philosophy born of necessity which permitted them at least to work together in peace.

It was a busy scene. The chuck wagon was already moving off, driven by the round-up cook. From a corral the extra animals of the cavvy were being released, blankets and saddles were being slapped onto the backs of horses irritable from having been stabled overnight, and a half dozen or more cowboys were already mounted and ready to move.

It was to Leighton, I noticed, that the foreman rode for some order or other. Norton moved on, a morose and angular figure, and for the first time since my arrival I felt a stirring of pity for him. It was only too evident that in that subtle conflict between Leighton and himself he was already outmatched and defeated. He carried it off with a certain dignity, however, mounted and rode quietly off in the dusty wake of the running loose horses. But some little distance along the trail he stopped his horse and turned around.

Apparently he was watching to see if Leighton went back to the house. He did not, and Norton kicked his spurs into his horse and went on.

Elinor asked me at breakfast several hours later if I cared to lunch at the camp that day.

"They're rounding up about eight miles off," she said. "You might like to see it. And Mrs. Alden says that Blair has left you boots and breeches. Lloyd's are too small for you."

"Thanks. I brought my own. Yes, I'd like to do it, Elinor."

She was eating almost nothing, I saw, and in the strong morning light she looked pale and tired. Thin too, in her riding clothes; I had not realized how thin she had grown. But I saw, too, that between the Alden woman and herself there was both liking and understanding. She was not dour to Elinor.

"You eat something, Mrs. Norton. It's sinful waste of good food, the way you treat it."

She tried, took a bit of egg, a mouthful of toast, made indeed a heroic pretense at a meal. Then when Mrs. Alden left the room she put down her knife and fork. "I'm never hungry in the morning, Carroll. Don't mind me, please."

I did not see her again until it was time for us to leave. With the departure of the outfit silence had once again settled down, heavy and oppressive, broken only by some occasional sound from the kitchen. I realized then how many such days there must have been for Elinor, days when time itself stood still and life ceased to be a panorama and became a static thing. Even the day was quiet. Not a breeze rustled the leaves of the cottonwoods, and I remember the extraordinary effect on me when a jack-rabbit suddenly came to life and bounded across the road.

At 10 o'clock we went to the corral and found our horses, Elinor's a black mare and mine an ugly but powerful roan; and soon we were winding up a narrow trail with the creek below us and the ranch house small and white on the other side. From this elevation it was possible to see how the ranch lay, and we stopped to survey the country. We were in high rolling land, the hills spattered here and there with the sparse pine and spruce of that semi-arid region. Twenty miles away and clearly visible in that atmosphere lay the small town, reached by the branch line of one of the railroads and beyond it, how far I do not know, rose a majestic wall of mountains.

At a turn in the trail Elinor stopped her horse and looked out over that vast expanse. "Our metropolis, Carroll. And our mountains!"

"One is highly effective. I don't know about the other."

She drew a long breath. "I always feel less shut in when I get up here," she said. "Isn't it queer, Carroll, what life does to people? Especially to women. Who would have thought that you and I would some day be here, and that I would belong here, for the rest of my days?"

"I'm not sure you do, or will."

"But I must. Don't get any such idea in your head, Carroll. This is where I belong."

"Belong!" I said bitterly. "To whom? Or to what? You can't call this living. It's being buried alive. What possible contribution can you make, down there? Keep the peace between two quarreling men? You can't even do that."

"I think," she said, with that new gravity of hers, "that if I left they would kill each other."

"I could put up with that too," I said, and she turned her horse and rode on.

She was not angry, however. Now and then she talked over her shoulder of small unimportant things. It was a long slow climb; only here and there could we attempt even a moderate trot. But as we rose into the higher air her spirits rose also. Small and slim on her black mare, very straight in her saddle, suddenly she began to sing one of the songs we used to sing when we were out in the old yawl.

"Do you remember how your voice used to break over that?" she said, and laughed. But a moment later I saw her stealthily fumbling for her handkerchief, and knew that she was crying.

Nevertheless, we recaptured that morning something of our old boy-and-girl relationship. The barriers were down for an hour or two, her marriage, the long years of my absence during the war, the ugly triangle in which she was so hopelessly involved. And, whatever she felt about her life, there, she loved the hills and knew them well.

"I often ride here," she said. "I put a sandwich in my pocket and spend the day."

"Alone?"

"Alone, of course. But a horse is company."

I choked back some savage comment, and soon she was pointing out a timber wolf, standing at the edge of a clump of evergreens. Later on we stirred up an antelope, and I was touched at her pleasure in these small discoveries of hers.

"This is my lucky day," she said. "I must find you a bear. I must. A nice mamma bear with a cub or two."

I tried to play up to her. "I'm afraid of bears," I told her. "Especially with cubs. They are very dangerous when they have cubs. The only way to subdue them is to look them straight in the eye, and when their eyes are on their cubs, where are you?"

She laughed at that, and we were very gay the rest of the way. I remember that we resorted to an old device of our childish days and invented limericks, and one of them still sticks in my mind. It was about a cowboy named Pete who, according to her, would not travel a foot on his feet. A horse, he opined, had no sense and no mind. But the way it could go was a treat. We roared with laughter over that, I remember. Pete, it appeared, was one of the outfit, a bow-legged individual who would saddle a horse rather than walk 100 yards.

Childish, all of it. Perhaps it has no place here, in this defense of her. Yet I think it shows something too, that trouble and the vicissitudes of her life had not greatly changed her, and that underneath somewhere was still the little girl, still largely playing at being a woman. It was not until we topped the hill and looked down at the round-up camp that she lost her gaiety.

Except for the chuck wagon, the cook, and a water-boy, the camp was deserted. The men's bed-rolls in a heap at one side, an empty rope corral, and a mess tent over a stove, constituted most of it. But on an opposite slope had been gathered a bunch of cattle, and a lone rider was slowly moving about them and holding them there. As we watched a dozen or so more came lumbering in, with Blair Leighton and a cowboy at their heels.

He saw us, and without lessening his pace he turned to-ward us. It was downgrade, but he came on a long lope, and Elinor sat her horse and watched him with something enigmatic in her eyes.

"He'll break his neck some day," said the cook. "Aren't you getting down, Mrs. Norton?"

She slid out of the saddle then, but she was still watching Blair. It seemed to me that she scarcely breathed until he had reached the creek bottom, and clattering across it to the better ground beyond, brought his horse to a quick and dramatic stop beside us. He was still smiling.

"Why must you ride like that, Blair?"

"Like that? If you'd seen some of the riding I've had to do this morning! Hello, Warner. Come up for our little show, eh? Well, Norton ought to be in soon. Then we'll eat."

He took Elinor's horse, and would have taken mine. But I attended to him myself, and we turned the lot into the

112

corral. It was easy to see that he belonged to the life. He was a natural horseman, a natural follower of the wild. Much as I distrusted him—and I still did—I could not help admiring him. No bigger than I am, he was better co-ordinated. Every muscle counted, every move.

And Elinor? I began that day to wonder whether there were not two Blair Leightons, and that this was the one she still loved. For she still loved him. I had seen that in her face as he came down the hill. The other, the Blair of the squabbling, bickering winter, of the girl in a back street in town, of the cache of liquor and the all-night gambling, she detested. But she could fight him. This one left her helpless. I saw it when he dragged a blanket from his bed-roll and carried it over to her.

"Better sit on this, Nellie," he said in that caressing voice of his. "And what can I get you? Want a pillow?"

She was defenseless against him then, and he knew it. And it seemed to me that the thin elderly cook, in his soiled apron and Stetson hat, gave an ironical lift of an eyebrow in their direction.

Norton came in before long. He sat his horse loosely and badly; nothing would ever make him a horseman. He looked tired and not too amiable, but he was civil enough.

"God, what a morning," he said, mopping his face.

It was the water-boy who took his horse, Norton muttering that he never wanted to see the damned thing again. Nor did I, for he had roweled it with his spurs until it was bleeding, and I saw Leighton flick a glance at it and then at Elinor.

The meal was quiet enough, however. The rest of the outfit did not come in, and the four of us ate sitting on the ground and holding our tin plates on our knees. Both men were hungry. They ate incredible amounts of fried steak and beans from their tin plates, and washed them down with cup after cup of strong black coffee. Elinor had little to say. I asked details of the round-up and the cattle business generally, and so kept the conversation going. But there was some new antagonism between them, most marked on Norton's side, clearly comprehended on the other.

In fact, Leighton mentioned it to me when we found ourselves alone for a moment or two.

"Difficult chap, Norton," he said. "Makes it hard for me sometimes. But what am I to do? All I've got is tied up here."

"He's not made for this life. You are."

"I like it," he said slowly. "And by another year I'll have a house of my own. That is, with luck." And he added, apparently irrelevantly, "The winters are pretty long."

It was not until we were about to leave that their animosity flared, and might have had serious results.

Elinor's mare, quiet enough on the way up, had been excited by something; and Norton had insisted on saddling her. He fought her over that, and brought her out finally in no shape to be ridden.

"Better let her quiet down," Leighton advised.

"She's all right. Come on, Elinor."

I saw Leighton get up as Elinor moved toward the horse. He said nothing, but he was like an animal ready to spring. But Elinor mounted easily, and then Norton's nervous anger took control. He jerked the bridle cruelly, and the mare reared.

"Stop that, you damned fool!" Leighton roared.

But the mischief was done. The next instant the mare had broken away and was bucking straight down the slope toward the dry creek bed, and Elinor went off among the rocks there.

It had been too quick for anyone to do anything. The mare was gone, and Elinor lay quite still. The three of us pounded down the slope, followed by the cook. She had not moved, and Leighton was the first to reach her. He bent over her, and then straightened himself and looked at Norton.

"If you've killed her I'll shoot you like a dog," was what he said.

114

Then she moved and tried to sit up. "What a silly place to fall!" she said, and lay down again and closed her eyes. The air was thick with tension, for I expected the two men to grapple at any moment. It was the cook who broke it. He pushed us all away, bent down and seemingly without effort picked her up in his arms.

"No place is a good place to fall," he told her. "And you ain't hurt none. Just shook up a little. Here's Mr. Norton now. Just tell him you're all right. Nobody's fault, you know. I reckon that mare she got stung by a bee."

He put Elinor down on her feet, and she smiled holding rather dizzily to his thin arm. "Just putting up a little ride for you, Carroll," she said. "I sat the first half dozen jumps, and that's not so bad."

There were all the seeds of a tragedy there that afternoon, but it did not happen. Fortunately the water-boy had gone to the spring and there had been no onlookers; I saw the cook talking first to Blair and then to Norton, and somehow it was fixed up. Leighton apologized in my presence, and Norton grudgingly accepted it. As for Elinor, I doubt if she ever knew about it at all.

We did not stay for the calf-branding that afternoon. Elinor maintained that she was all right, but she looked pale and shaken. Anyhow she disliked the branding, the frantic cows, the calves wailing under the red-hot iron, the smell of burning hair and flesh. I watched the first one, and was glad myself to get away. Norton I thought was enjoying it, with much the same sadistic pleasure he had found in shooting the steer. Leighton took it as a matter of course. He was insensitive, like all men who lack imagination.

But he left the branding corral and was at hand to put Elinor on her horse when the time came.

"Good-bye, Nellie. Better go to bed when you get home and have a tray supper."

He was on the other side of the horse tightening her cinch, and I could not see him. But I could swear that he dropped a kiss lightly on her hand.

16

She was silent on the way down, and I myself was in two minds, irritable and uncertain what to do. It seemed impossible to go and leave her there, on the edge of that volcano. Yet to stay was to make things no better, possibly even make them worse.

Finally, near the house, I asked her bluntly, "Shall I go, Elinor? Or stay a day or two?"

"I had hoped you would stay. But why should you? It can't be very pleasant for you."

"That's not the question. I'm doing nobody any good here."

"Nor any harm, Carroll. It's between the two of them. They will have to work it out."

"Isn't it among the three of you? Elinor, you're in love with that fellow. What's the use of denying it? You would lie down and let him walk over you."

I had stopped my horse, and her mare stopped also. We had reached the turn in the trail, and she sat in her saddle, gazing out over the plain toward the mountains beyond.

"Not always," she said quietly. "Sometimes I hate him."

"How long do you think it can go on like that? Don't you suppose Lloyd knows? And Leighton himself? Do you want to precipitate a tragedy? Use your head, Elinor."

"I'm worn out with thinking about it."

"How far has it gone? I have the right to ask that. You have the right to lie about it too; but I don't think you will."

"No," she said. "I needn't lie to you. It hasn't gone anywhere, Carroll. That's the truth. I don't think it ever will." And she added with her first bitterness, "You see, he has a girl in town. He doesn't really care for me. I'm just another woman."

"But if it were not for all that?" I insisted.

"Just what do you think I am?" she asked, flushing. "I am neither wanton nor a fool. And I've told you; Blair not only knows that. He doesn't really want me, either as a mistress or as a wife. Even if he did, I won't be the one and I can't be the other."

I was not so sure of that, and the uncertainty lasted through the remainder of my stay at the ranch. He was in love with her. If that love was subordinated to his desire to maintain the *status quo* and his unwillingness to disturb a life which he was hugely enjoying, it was still there ready to leap into his eyes during the idle hours when the day's work was over.

On the surface things were better. While the outfit remained in the hills with the gradually augmenting herd, the two men rode in at evening, bathed, dressed, and ate dinner with us. Sometimes we played a rubber or two of bridge, but soon Leighton would be yawning and the game would break up. They were not openly at odds, and to an outsider looking in we must have presented an unexpected picture of civilization, set down there in the wilderness; the pleasant room, the fire—for the nights were cool, the lamps and flowers, and around a card table three men and one woman politely wrangling over a game.

I was there for a week. Long before the time was up I wanted to leave, but one and all, each in his separate way, asked me to stay. Perhaps it was Leighton who put the reason most clearly; Leighton, with his British insistence on the amenities of life.

"Too easy to sink out here," he said. "Need somebody to jack us up now and then. A man gets slack. Stick around for a few days, like a good fellow."

I stuck, although I was not much of a good fellow. Elinor was grateful, I know, and even Mrs. Alden found occasion to give me her approval.

"I'm glad you're staying," she said. "Like two wild beasts, those men have been. And she doesn't know what to do about it. If she's got any family they ought to take her

117

away, Mr. Warner. She isn't used to this life anyhow, and at best it's hard on women."

It was probably the longest speech she had ever made there. And things undoubtedly did improve. Elinor looked better and lost some of her haunted look, there was more general talk, and while Leighton drank several highballs each evening, he did not again go into town. Only Norton remained much as he had been.

"Stock raising is no business for a white man. You ship your cattle East and then what happens? Two or three fellows go up an alley and figure what's the least they can pay for them! And they've got the cattle. You can't ship them back. Rustling is an honest job, compared to them."

Or: "It's the hell of a country. Man raises wheat, and either hail gets it or grasshoppers. Then when he tries to market what's left he can't make its cost."

Over Isabel Curtis's visit he remained darkly silent. I gathered, however, that she had registered disapproval, of the ranch and the whole project, from the moment of her arrival; and that it had hurt him. There was some curious bond there which I have never understood. It may be that he had, after his own fashion, cared rather deeply for her. And that Isabel always knew that he cared.

His only comment, however, was casual and characteristic: "She hadn't been here an hour when she told me I was a fool to try this game. And when I asked her if she had ever seen a cow before, she said yes and behind too, and she didn't like either end of it." He chuckled drily. It was, so far as I can recall, the only time I heard him laugh during that week.

The days were pleasant enough, although with conditions as they were I was uneasy and not very happy. Elinor took the car and showed me the country roundabout. The town was hardly more than a hamlet, sprawling in the sun. A row of shops on its main street, dusty side lanes with a few houses, a two-story frame hotel and a courthouse and jail; that was all.

When I said that it was certainly useful but hardly beautiful, she was quick to resent it. "That's too easy to say, Carroll. What can you know about the struggle to have a town at all? You and Isabel!"

From which I gathered that Isabel had as usual spoken her mind.

Those were the best days of my stay, with Elinor firmly gripping the wheel of the unwashed car, a soft hat pulled low on her head, her eyes intent on roads that were always poor and often actually suicidal.

One such track led up the foothills toward the mountains. We had carried a lunch with us, and after leaving the car we climbed up through a small canyon to a lookout point and ate it there. Before and beneath us lay the wide flat valley bisected by the railroad, and along its lanes here and there were cattle, being slowly driven toward the track and the shipping pens. Even at that height we could hear a faint lowing as the thirsty beasts lumbered along toward rest and water. A hovering cloud of dust marked the progress of each herd, with the dim figures of men on horseback almost smothered in it.

Now and then a car, like a black ant at that distance, would meet a herd, hesitate, be lost for an indefinite time and then gradually emerge on the other side.

"Machinery versus brute force," I said. "Your mother versus the ocean."

She glanced at me, and I had to explain. She was very thoughtful after that.

We never recaptured the mood of that first morning on the trail. I think she was glad to be with me, but that was all. In every move, every gesture, every silence, she was telling me the book of the past was closed and a new one had opened. But neither of us could have foretold how shocking its contents were to be. Or that the very trail we had climbed to that lookout point was to see, before many months had passed, its strange night procession in the snow.

She was holding to me, however. She did not want me to go. On the last day when I was packing she came to the door of my room and stood watching me.

"Let me fold that coat, Carroll. You'll never do it."

"I was one of the best packers the army ever saw!"

"It will be queer without you."

"Who regrets an aching tooth, my dear?"

"Don't ache, Carroll. I'm all right."

That evening I watched the final cutting of the herd, and the beginning of the long slow drive toward the railroad. The cars were already on a siding, and there was a suppressed excitement manifest everywhere. By prearrangement Leighton was to go with the cattle, while Norton in a car was to precede him to the town and the track.

Then, the night before the start of the drive, Leighton took his car and disappeared. When I left the next day he had not returned, and Norton was wandering around the place like a maniac. He scarcely knew that I was going, and it was Elinor, pale but composed, who drove me to the town where I was to take a local train.

Neither of us mentioned Leighton and his absence. We talked of Isabel, of her mother, even of her Aunt Henrietta. She was busy sending messages to this one and that. But for most of the 20 miles she talked only from the surface of her mind. Far back in some secret part of her soul she was obsessed with him, and him only.

"You aren't listening, Elinor."

"Certainly, I am."

"Well, what shall I tell your mother? That you'll be East this winter?"

"If she wants me, and I can afford it." Then she roused herself from her absorption. "How I'm going to miss you, Carroll! And how far away it all seems!"

Her voice broke on that and, of course, I made her the usual speech of immemorial numbers of men who have loved unattainable women. I told her that it was not far, and that distance didn't matter. That if ever she needed me I would come on the wings of the morning.

"I have given you so little," she said, "and you give me so much." We were close to the town by that time, and she leaned over and kissed me rather breathlessly. "Thank you,

120

Carroll, for being you. I always know I can count on you."

"You know you can, Elinor," I said, not too steadily.

Then the train roared in, and the last I saw of her she was sitting there staring after it with an odd expression on her face. It was not, I felt, that it was taking me away. It was because that train and track were at once the barrier to her past and the only link connecting her with it. The town was on the other side of the track, and all I could see was Elinor, sitting alone in her small car, both dwarfed by that gigantic country behind them. It looked secretive as well as vast. And it looked lonely. God, how lonely they both looked!

I suppose she turned then and went back to that hell. Or did she? There was a story later of one time when she hunted Leighton out in the town and took him, still fuddled with drink, back to the ranch with her. Perhaps she did it then. Or perhaps she did it later on, after Norton's death. All I know of that autumn is that the cattle were shipped, with Leighton or without him; that there was a moderate profit on them; and that Elinor planned to come East at Christmas to see her mother.

She did not come.

17

Norton was killed early in November, in a hunting accident in the mountains. My first knowledge was from a morning paper containing the brief last minute Associated Press dispatch: *New Yorker Killed. Lloyd Norton Victim of Accident.* There were no details; merely the fact, with a bit about his life and his war record. I wired at once asking if I could do anything, or if I should come out, to receive a laconic reply from Elinor herself: *Thanks. Everything arranged. No need to come. Love. Elinor.*

121

Later editions were more explicit. Norton, accompanied by Leighton and a guide named Henry Raleigh, had started out for elk and possibly bear some days before. They had left their car at a ranch at the foot of the mountains, where Raleigh met them with saddle animals and camp equipment, and they had been in the mountains for more than a week when it happened. Apparently trapped by a heavy snow, Norton had attempted to reach a ranger's cabin near a fire station, and had slipped and sent a bullet from his gun through his heart.

That was the bare outline of the story as I had it at first from the press. Accurate as it was, the real story was far more dramatic.

The weather had been cold from the start, and game scarce. Norton had missed the one good shot of the trip and was in bad humor. On the fourth day Raleigh, an experienced mountain man, said that there was snow in the air and advised their getting out. But Norton refused. As a result they headed still farther back, toward a cabin high in the range. By night the snow started, and they attempted the next morning to get away. It was still coming down heavily, however. It caked on the horses' hoofs, half-blinded the men. They tore up blankets and tied them over the horses' feet, but by late afternoon they knew the trails below would be blocked. They turned back to the cabin.

All evening and night it sifted down. The horses had sheltered under a rim-rock nearby, but they were belly deep in drift. In the cabin they had wood and sufficient food, but Norton was in a queer state of nerves, infuriated by inaction, walking the floor, even urging Raleigh, the only one who had snowshoes, to get to the ranger's cabin and telephone their predicament into town.

Raleigh was unwilling. The fire station and cabin were only a few miles away, but the air was still thick and all landmarks were obliterated.

"Much as my life's worth, Mr. Norton," he said. "I'll go if you say so, but these early storms don't last. We may get a thaw tomorrow."

122

But there was no thaw the next day. Instead, a bitter and penetrating wind had set in. The temperature dropped, and to step out the door was to be assailed with hard frozen snow driven like shot. Even Raleigh became uneasy, and that afternoon he volunteered to try for the ranger station. He never made it, and one of the tragedies of that double catastrophe back in the mountains was the single line in the Eastern papers: *The guide's body has not been found.*

The two men left alone in the cabin stood it for three days together. Leighton apparently slept most of the time. Norton, out of tobacco and with nothing to read, went slowly crazy.

Back at the ranch Elinor waited anxiously. Not only was she too snowed in. The fence telephone line was down and all communication shut off. At first she did not worry. The men had plenty of food and Henry Raleigh knew his business. But as time went on and the snow still lay she became frightened, and on the ninth day she managed to get a man through to the town on horseback, and to notify the authorities that the party was in the mountains and possibly needed help.

It was too late. Not only had Raleigh already left, to die in the snow. Some time during the afternoon of that day, while Leighton slept in his bunk, Norton had disappeared.

"He had wanted to go, but I thought I had persuaded him it would be suicidal," Leighton was quoted as saying. "When he planned it he had said that if he got into trouble he would fire his gun. That was why he took his rifle. I don't of course, know how long he had been gone when I heard it. I had no trouble following him, or—finding him."

Norton had been heavily clad, and wore thick mittens. That might account for the tragedy. When Leighton found him he lay where he had fallen, with the gun beside him in the snow. He had been shot through the heart.

With the rescue party about to start late that evening, the chief ranger below was aroused by a telephone call.

123

Leighton, in a state of exhaustion, had reached the cabin and was calling for help.

But it required all the next day to reach him, and still longer to bring down the body. It was midnight before they reached the bit of trail where Elinor and I had lunched and stared out through the September haze. The scene was different now. At the mouth of the canyon a half dozen cars were parked, and waiting at the foot of the trail were the sheriff, the coroner, a local doctor, a handful of townspeople.

A cowboy had brought word that the rescue party was working its way down, and so they waited, the three officials, in the still falling snow. It sifted over the cars they had brought through the drifts, it obscured the light from the lanterns they held. It was a bitter night. Then at last far up above them they saw a gleam, and soon they heard the slow thud of the horses' feet. It must have been an eerie thing, that slow procession down the trail, with a pack animal carrying a body, and two men on snowshoes steadying it as they came.

Leighton rode behind it, almost asleep in his saddle from cold and exhaustion, and the rest followed: weary ranchers, a half dozen rangers in uniform, and a group of wranglers and cowboys.

At the foot of the trail the procession halted, and the body was transferred to a car. Another car took Leighton, and so they moved slowly toward the town, where Elinor was waiting for them.

By what miracle they had got a car to the ranch for her I do not know. I only know that she was there, very composed, very polite to them, almost unaware that they were there at all.

"Thank you. You have been very kind to me. And I am all right. Please don't worry."

What she wanted there in the hotel was to be left alone. She had not been alone since the news came to the ranch. It still had no reality for her. All she felt was terror; the

124

two men shut away together and Norton's hatred and jealousy precipitating a fight. She did not believe there had been an accident. But they would not leave her alone, those kindly women of the town. Theirs was the age-old conviction that women in grief must be fed and comforted; and in the end, out of sheer desperation, she locked her door and closed them out.

It hurt her, that closed door. Later when she needed them they remembered it and did not come. She had thrown back their compassion. She did not want them.

She was alone at last in the hotel bedroom. It had a bed, a pine bureau, a straight chair or two and a table by the window. There was an untouched tray of food on the table. When darkness fell she did not turn on the light. She stood by the window, watching the street below for the returning rescue party and Blair Leighton. When the room grew cold she put on Ada Mayhew's fur coat, and when she heard the first cars coming back, she merely continued to stand there and wait.

She was not thinking. She was not trying to visualize Norton dead and herself widowed. She could not look ahead and she dared not look back. She was concentrated on the moment; Leighton's return and the truth about the tragedy.

Then at last he came. She saw the cars in the street and saw him getting out of one. Two men got out with him and helped him into the hotel. He was apparently stiff with the cold, and weary from that struggle to reach the ranger station, but he was there, alive and well; and somewhere in one of those cars was her husband, dead. In that moment she hated him for being alive; for the very voice from the pavement which was demanding a drink and a bed.

She moved from the window to the door. She heard Leighton and his escort come up the stairs, and their heavy footsteps as they passed her room.

"I meant to ask—does Mrs. Norton know?"

"She's here. Yes. She knows."

"In the hotel?"

"Yes." They moved on down the narrow hallway, and a door slammed.

She was still standing inside her door when the two men left. She had hardly moved. But now she turned on her lights and sat down. He knew she was there, and soon he would come and tell her about it; quiet her fears, explain. But he never did come. Not that night, at least. She waited almost an hour, and then she unlocked her door and made her way down the hall.

The hotel was almost empty, and there was only one closed door at that end of the passage. She did not hesitate for a second. She opened it and walked in; to find Leighton heavily asleep and only half-undressed on the bed, a half-empty bottle of whisky and a glass on the floor beside him. She stood by the bed looking down at him, and a great wave of resentment and stark rage and anger swept over her like a wave. She bent over and shook him fiercely.

"Blair. *Blair*."

But he did not move, and at last she gave up the attempt to rouse him. She stood looking down at him. He was gigantic on that small bed, unlovely, unshaven. How could she ever have cared for him? Or had she ever cared for him? Hadn't she built up about him something which had no basis in truth? Perhaps women always did that; the dream more real than reality.

She did not know. She went slowly back to her room, to wait in a chair until the morning.

It was noon of the next day before he came. Then he entered without knocking, closing the door behind him, and standing just inside it.

"I suppose you know all about it, Nellie."

"I know nothing about it. That's what I am waiting to hear. What I've waited all night to hear."

He looked up at her then, really looked at her, for the first time. "Just what do you mean by that?"

"Was it an accident? That's what I mean."

"For God's sake, Nellie! You don't think I murdered him, do you?"

She looked at him. "Why not?" she said quietly. "You hated each other."

"You're hysterical. Why would I murder him? And you're wrong. I never hated him."

He told her the story then, as I have told it here. He had bathed and shaved, and he was entirely sober. Entirely convincing too, for at last she was able to breathe freely again. Lloyd was dead, but he had died as the result of his own headstrong folly. When he came over and put a hand on her shoulder she did not flinch from it.

"I'm sorry, Nellie. I needn't tell you that."

"Sorry. That's such a feeble word, Blair. He has lost his life, and it was all he had."

"I couldn't hold him. I had told him that if either of us tried to make the ranger station, I was the obvious one. That angered him. He said I seemed to think I was the only real man God ever made. Then I went to sleep, and— See here, Nellie, do you think all this is easy for me? I didn't come last night because I didn't want to face you. I couldn't."

She accepted that. He looked better, but he still showed signs of exhaustion and the long exposure to the cold. And something of her fierce resentment died when he suggested that she go to bed and get some sleep; and later on himself brought her a tray of food. He was kind, and she was grateful. If she did not love him, he was at least something friendly and familiar to which to hold.

When he had put the tray down on a chair beside her bed he bent over and kissed her on the forehead. It was in its way an acknowledgement of a new relationship between them. They were not lovers, but friends.

She felt safe that day for the first time since she had known him.

It was a week before they could travel the road back to the ranch. By that time Lloyd lay under a blanket of snow in the bare little cemetery on a hill over the town; and now, in her modest black mourning, she went home again. She was stunned rather than grieved. Her grief was for him, not for herself. But she was no longer afraid of Blair, nor suspicious of that accident in the mountains. Like the town, she recognized the brute courage and strength of the man. That solitary journey of his through the blizzard was still being applauded.

Perhaps it had its effect on her, that sheer physical courage which is the common attribute of men with feeble imaginations and strong appetites. She confused it with moral strength, and before it her defenses gradually went down. One thing was certain. On that drive back to the ranch he completely disarmed her.

"When you've recovered a bit," he told her, "we will have to talk over some plans. I suppose you will go back East again?"

"I haven't given it any thought."

"But one of us will have to go, Nellie. Haven't you thought of that?"

She did think of it, then and later, but there was no clearness in her thinking. During the next few days he was gentleness itself with her, and he took precautions which seemed almost absurd to her. He moved out to the bunk house, bag and baggage, coming in only for his meals. He managed never to be alone with her. He would not even spend his evenings in the house. Instead, he built great fires in the living-room so that she might be warm, and then went out to the roaring stove and the thick air of the other building. All this he did, not stoically but matter-of-factly and cheerfully.

But she knew that it could not go on. "Half the place belonged to him," as she said later. "He wasn't a hired hand, and it simply wasn't fair."

One day she had a talk with Mrs. Alden, and as a result Leighton came back into the house to stay. She herself expected to go East very soon. Indeed, she packed a trunk, to be ready when the time came. But there were things to be settled about the ranch, various legal proceedings in town, matters of policy. She and Blair were now partners in a going concern. And she herself was curiously undecided. One part of her was facing East, to the life and the people there; another was bound up in that snow-covered land, where peace now reigned in the house and where—why not be honest about it?—where Leighton was gradually reassuming his old supremacy.

Yet even the woman in the kitchen, still half suspicious, could have found nothing to complain about. He breakfasted early and alone. At dinner their talk was entirely impersonal. Then, if he were going out or to town, she would spend the evening in the living-room by the fire. When he stayed there she would go up early to bed.

"What are your plans, Blair, tonight?"

"I have to go to the barn. And you?"

"I'll stay up for a while and read."

Norton's room, with his belongings in it, was closed and locked away. Except for the automatic in the gun closet he might never have been there. But he was there, in spite of all that. He was a ghost between them. There were evenings when she could have sworn he was sitting in his deep chair by the fire. She would sit at her piano—she never played now when Blair was there—and feel his eyes on her, cynical and disapproving. Once or twice the impression was so strong that she actually spoke.

"Why do you hate me so?" she would ask. "What have I done? I've been faithful. I always have been faithful."

18

I know very little of the winter which followed at the ranch, except that for a brief time there was a threat of what was to come the next year. In the only letter from her which I received at that time she said there had been more snow, and no wind to blow the ridges clear; that they had driven in a good bit of the "poor" stock and were feeding it. But she said nothing of the general hardship of the winter, of the cattle scattered hither and yon all over the country; huddled in breaks and sheltered spots, and marooned and largely foodless. Or that after the snow had come intense cold, so that even the streams and water holes froze over.

I know that now. Also that Leighton came in one night to tell her savagely that if the weather did not change soon she would better take her trunk and get out.

"We'll be through," he said. "Better go while the going's good!"

"Go where?" she asked.

For by this time Caroline's letter had come: *I think you should stay for a time at least and watch your investment there. I have suffered heavy losses, and as you and Norton insisted on tying up a great deal of money there, you certainly should not turn it over entirely to someone else. After the estate is settled possibly Mr. Leighton will buy out your share.*

I have greatly reduced my establishment here, and you would not be very comfortable. Also I dislike, so long as I am ill, to complicate it further. There was more, of course. Henrietta came now and then. The stock market was behaving strangely. She herself hoped to be about again by spring.

A typical Caroline letter, important only in one thing. It closed to Elinor her only door of escape. On its receipt she had gone upstairs to her cold bedroom, heated only by a portable oil stove, and had unpacked her trunk.

The weather moderated in time. By the end of March they had fed all of their hay, nursing along such cattle as required it, but there was still feed on the ground. Inside the ranch house, however, that fantastic life still went on, although even Mrs. Alden, interrogated by the wives of the ranchers, could find no fault with it.

130

"She keeps to herself a good bit," she said. "And all she's got is in the place. She has to stay on. I don't think she trusts him any too much. I know I don't."

Through all the winter then and into the spring Elinor carried on as best she could. But she was very lonely and not a little sad. Now and then she would go into the warm kitchen and talk to the woman there, out of sheer need for companionship.

"You surely have done some queer things, Mrs. Norton. Imagine putting feathers in your hair and bowing and scraping before those people! What good did it do, anyhow?"

"My mother wanted it. I didn't care."

"Weren't you scared?"

"Frightfully scared."

As a matter of fact, it was in this same kitchen that Mrs. Alden's distrust in Leighton received further corroboration one day. She was pressing an old suit for Elinor, and had found a Paris label in it. She considered all the French immoral, and Leighton came in while she was expressing this conviction. He grinned at her, with an eye, however, on Elinor.

"You women!" he said. "Don't you know that conventional morality is merely a development of the theory of private property? That it is never important where property is held in common?"

"What's that got to do with decency?" Mrs. Alden demanded.

"Decency? What is decency?" he teased her. "What I am saying is that as soon as men began to own something, they wanted to leave it to their own. Not, in other words, to other men's bastards."

"You get out of my kitchen," said the Alden woman indignantly, "and save that sort of talk for the bunk house. They'll like it there." But the seeds of suspicion, dormant all winter in the dour woman's mind, were apparently roused to new life that day. It is probable that she never trusted either of them again.

131

With the opening of the spring things were somewhat better for Elinor. Leighton was out much of the time, and when he came back he was tired and went to bed early. She herself made her garden again, and sometimes in the evenings she and Leighton would lay out the ranch books on the dining-room table and he would explain their position to her, and his hopes. When he had leisure he would work in the breaking-corral with the men, and occasionally he would take his rod and there would be trout for dinner.

He was like a boy then. "Look at this one," he would say. "Been after him since last year. He was a wise one."

Impersonal, all of it. They might have been brother and sister, and she was lulled into a false sense of security. She stopped locking her door at night, although when the roads improved enough to let him drive into town she still lay awake, ready to leap if she heard his unsteady step on the stairs. For he drank heavily at intervals that spring, and she suspected either the same or another woman.

"It was only when he had been drinking that I was afraid of him," she said later. "At other times he seemed not to care whether I was there or not."

Beyond all this, as I have said, I know very little of that year. For Elinor it seems to have had a dreamlike quality. She was still much alone. Leighton's brief popularity after Norton's death had waned, and although she seems not to have realized it the situation at the N-Bar-L was too anomalous to encourage many visitors. Even the little deer had deserted her in the spring, wandering off perhaps in search of a mate. And then in the late spring something happened which she did not know, but which was in time to set the tongues of the countryside to wagging.

A bullet hole was found in the log wall of the cabin in the mountains where Leighton had apparently slept while Norton went out to his death in the snow.

The body of the guide, Raleigh, had not been found, and now an extensive search was to be made for it. With that practicality which is the hard common sense of a people who have had to fight for sheer survival, the object of

132

the search was not sentimental. It appears that he had left a considerable family, and there was a small life insurance at stake which could not be collected until the body was found.

Neither Elinor nor Leighton, isolated and busy with their own concerns, seems to have known about it. It began, it ended; yet in its ending it was to have results which were to affect more than one life. Never perhaps had Henry Raleigh, training his wolf hounds and begetting his family been so potent as when he lay hidden behind that pile of rocks in the mountains, a bundle of clothes, a rifle, and not much else.

The search was to start on Saturday, and early in the morning volunteers began to gather in the town. They came on horseback, each man carrying his blankets and a small supply of food; and in addition, by a road not much more than a track, wagons with further supplies had started the night before and were making a devious way up to the ranger station.

At 11 o'clock the procession rode off, and late that afternoon it reached the station. All but two men, that is; two men, one of them a brother-in-law of the dead man, who went directly to the cabin itself. It had not been occupied since the autumn tragedy. Later on, when the cattle were moved into the mountains, men would throw bed-rolls on its floor, light a cooking-fire on its deserted hearth and make a bit of home in it for a night or two. But it was still as it had been left when they reached it. The very dishes, such as they were, were still on the table. Cans of food stood on a shelf, with an empty tobacco tin. Even the blankets were still there, except the one which had been wrapped around Norton's body for the long trip down the trail.

The two men were not imaginative. Apparently they turned in at once, and slept the sleep of utter weariness until morning. It was then that one of them, wandering about for firewood for the breakfast fire, came back with a condensed milk can which had a bullet hole through the top of it.

133

"What made that hole?" he asked the other man.

"Pretty heavy slug. Somebody's been target shooting."

"At a full can of milk? Look at it. Never been opened! And with a slug that size!"

They looked at each other, but they belonged to the taciturn brotherhood of the plains. Both of them were cattle hands, accustomed to the long loneliness of their occupation. Whatever they thought, they ate their breakfast without further comment, although the milk tin sat on the table between them. Only when the meal was over did one of them get up and examine the shelf nailed to the wall. He moved the remaining tins and examined the wall behind it.

"Nice job," he said quietly. "Plugged up so nobody could hardly see it."

He got out his penknife and neatly lifted a wooden plug out of the bullet hole in the wall. There was no bullet there, however, and so he slid it back again.

"Dirty work somewhere," he said. "Not our business, I guess." He measured the height of the shelf with his eyes. "Not the bullet that got Norton anyhow. He was shot through the heart. This is too high."

They seem to have agreed mentally that it was not their business. Perhaps, too, the law was not particularly popular with them, nor had Norton ever been. Of the two men they preferred Blair. However that may be, neither of them mentioned it when they met the rest of the searching party that morning; and the discovery of Raleigh late that day and the careful carrying down of those rather ghastly fragments seems to have driven the discovery from their minds at the time.

Which one of them eventually talked I do not know. Throughout the summer, however, in bunk house and corral, the word got about. In the fall it was whispered over fires at round-up camps and in the cabooses of cattle trains. But it did not reach the ears of authority. If there were some who watched Leighton a little more closely when

134

he came to town, they gambled with him and drank his liquor much as before.

Possibly he felt it, without being certain of its cause. He was certainly irritable during those months, and I have wondered since if he did not know. If he did he lacked entirely moral courage to face it out. Instead, he resorted to escape, the escape of some woman in a by-street, of drink, and of gambling which he could not afford. On the mornings after such attempts to forget he would be haggard and truculent at breakfast.

"Why in heaven's name *fry* everything? Can't that woman do anything else?"

"I've told you. The stove is no good. We need a new one."

He would stalk through the kitchen and slam the door behind him. At such times Elinor hated him.

In the end it was mutual trouble which threw them together again.

19

I know practically nothing of the cattle business, but even in the East we learned something of that tragic year of 1920-21 which ruined nine-tenths of the stockmen: a long hot summer which burned out the grass, followed by a long cold winter and snow which lay until late in the spring. Men who had hay, or were near enough to the railroad to buy it, were in luck. Oil cake rose to fantastic prices, as did all feed. Penned by the wire into their vast pastures, cattle drifted hither and yon searching pitifully for food; and even those which had been driven into the home ranches were not much better off. So deep was the snow in places that the feed wagons could not reach them.

The fight on the N-Bar-L was for actual survival. By Christmas the road to town was practically closed, and by the middle of January it was entirely shut off. Over plain and hill the snow lay so thick that even the ridges were never clear of it. Day after day Leighton and the outfit made their way to the hungry stock, and drove in for feeding the ones which were obviously in bad shape. But as February became March their small stock of hay was exhausted, and feed was prohibitively expensive even if they could have transported it from the railroad.

There came a day when Leighton talked to Elinor about money. "We're going to be up against it properly," he told her, "unless we can buy feed. If the spring is late we're done. Can you borrow from your mother? I can get a horse through to town."

"I can ask her. I don't like to."

"Well, it's that or give up."

The greatness of the emergency had sobered him. During the past two or three months she had noticed a change in him. He seemed to have set a guard on himself. He went less and less to town, drank only occasionally and then alone. If he was watchful—of the men, of the few ranchers who came for one reason or another—she did not realize it. All she knew was that he showed an increasing dependence on her, and a new and gentler consideration. Unconsciously she had commenced to rebuild him into his former stature, and that day she faced the issue squarely. He needed her. For good or evil their lives were bound together. And she would not give up the ranch.

He watched her. "Do you want to give it up, Nellie?"

"I hate to confess a failure."

"Do you *want* to give it up, Nellie?"

"No."

He smiled. He had won. "Then you'll write?"

"I'll write," she said submissively, and he stooped and lightly kissed her. It was the first time he had touched her since the time of Norton's death. When he straightened he was still smiling.

She wrote her letter that night, a long one. Now and then old Caroline's nurse had written her briefly, but she had not heard directly from her mother for months. Her checks, signed in Caroline's shaky hand, came monthly with a brief note from Shirley Johnson:

Dear Elinor: Herewith check for the January allowance. Hope you are well. S. J. So she wrote two letters that night, one to her mother and another to Shirley, and then came the long wait for a reply. It was a week before Johnson's letter came, this time a longer one.

My dear Elinor: I am in receipt of your letter of March the 10th, and am extremely sorry to learn that you are in difficulties. As you know, I advised against the investment, which seemed to me unwise at the time.

I regret to say that I have bad news for you. Your mother put her affairs in my hands last autumn, and I discovered them to be in bad condition. For many years she has been encroaching on her capital, and also making unwise investments. In the present state of things, with a panic in the air, her condition is far from satisfactory.

Actually, and not to make too long a story of it, she has about enough to see her through to the end, and not much more. I am at present attempting to put a mortgage on the house she is in. The city house has had to go. There is a small bit of capital left, but she should have that to make her comfortable.

She has not been told. She is very weak and I am afraid has not long to live, and after all there is nothing to be done but to keep her comfortable and her mind at rest. My own suggestion is that you sell out your share of the ranch and come East as soon as possible.

Leighton read the letter, and for a moment he seemed stunned. Then once more she caught a glimpse of the man under the veneer, and she was frightened. He stormed and swore. He even accused her of willfully misleading him as to her financial status. She was insulted and furious, and there was a scene of savage bitterness. It ended by his

137

knocking over her small sewing-table and slamming out of the house.

That was the incident that was brought out at the trial: "Tell the jury what you remember of that afternoon."

And Mrs. Alden, unwilling but truthful: "I heard them quarreling, and then I heard the table go over and I went in. She was crying, and I picked up the table and put the things back in it."

"Did the defendant say anything to you at that time?"

"Well, yes. She said she would have to get away at once. That her mother was very sick and needed her."

"Is that all she said?"

"That's all she said then." She hesitated, glanced toward Elinor.

"Come, come, Mrs. Alden. What did she say after that?"

"Well, she stood at the window and saw him riding out on his horse. He went as if he had been shot out of a gun. And she said, 'He's a beast, Mrs. Alden. A cruel beast. Some day life will pay him back.'"

20

She was fairly frantic. Brought face to face with Caroline as a dying woman, her long-repressed affection was behind a part of her desperation. Added to that, of course, was her furious anger at Leighton himself. The combination was more than she could endure. Immediately on his departure she had ordered her mare saddled while she packed a small bag with clothes for the train. Later she and Mrs. Alden had themselves tied the bag to the saddle, the ranch woman weeping, Elinor cold and quiet. Her last words had been to tell Mr. Leighton that she had gone and would not be back.

I learned of that ride from Elinor later on. She belittled it, but I still think of it, along a faintly broken trail in a temperature far below zero, as one of the most courageous things I know. Her horse struggled into drifts and out again. Fresh snow began to fall, and familiar landmarks to disappear. If her horse threw her she knew she might lose him, and so she tied her reins tightly to her wrist. And she had 20 miles of this before, late that evening, she saw the lights of the town far ahead. She was barely conscious when she reached the hotel, and she fell flat when she dismounted.

She was snow-blind for three days!

It was on the second day that Leighton turned up at the hotel, to find her back in the same bare room half mad with disappointment, still furious at him, and almost entirely helpless. He walked into the room, himself in a rage, and demanded to know if she wanted the whole countryside to talk about 'them.

"You've given them a damned good chance. What do you suppose they think? That we've had a lovers' quarrel?"

"They are completely at liberty to think what they want."

"That will be plenty!"

"Why should it be?" she asked proudly. "They know here that my mother is very ill. I have wired Shirley Johnson for money to go East."

"And *that's* all over town too," he said roughly. "Don't you suppose that girl at the telegraph office has talked? So we're broke, and I let you ride here alone in a blizzard! Good God, will you never learn anything?"

"I am learning every moment you are in this room."

"I've got some decent pride."

"What about my pride?"

They were far from lovers then, and her whole story would have been different had not an interruption come. There was a rap at the door, and a telegram was handed in. She could not read it, so Leighton read it to her.

It was from her Aunt Henrietta, announcing her mother's death. She had thought she was prepared for it, but she was not. She forgot the hard later years and was a

139

child again, with her mother a mysterious figure, dominant and handsome; sitting at her desk in the tower room writing her innumerable notes, going veiled and gloved into the garden to cut flowers for the big house, in the late summer afternoon holding her court on the broad verandas. Against this background, solid and apparently indestructible, she had lived her carefree childhood, and it was through the glamour of those days that now she saw the hard old woman who had virtually cast her off.

She burst into a passion of tears, and before she knew it Leighton had taken her in his arms. She stayed there. She was tired and defeated. She was a child again, and he comforted her.

"I'm terribly in love with you, Nellie."

"Not always."

"Always. Even at my worst. I'm at my worst when I feel I can't do for you what I want to. You know that, don't you?"

She released herself finally. Some part of her still doubted him, but she needed what he offered her, tenderness and physical strength. They sat down and discussed what she should do. She could not reach the East in time for the funeral, but even he acknowledged that she would have to go. Only she must promise to come back.

"They'll try to hold you," he said. "Warner will try. I don't trust him. But there will probably be some estate—I know these lawyers—and we can use it."

He kissed her again, and that kiss definitely sealed her to him. She would come back to him as soon as she could, and they would be married. He had always loved her. He always would love her; and things would be better now. Even a little money was better than none.

I think he meant it then. Certainly she believed him. Out of pure relief he was his old gay debonair self; once more she fell under his spell. "I'll write home and tell them," he said. "They'll be glad I'm going to settle down."

"And are you?"

He took her again into his arms. "Listen, darling. Can

140

you imagine a man married to you wanting another woman? The old bad days are over, sweetheart."

She felt that they were. She was still grieved for her mother, but now it was a grief of the past rather than the present; and before her stretched long years of living, of living with Blair, of having the right to love him, of being his wife.

It was not all acting on his part. Even now I am certain that he was in love with her at that time. She still had the lure of the unattained woman for all men of his type, she had lost none of her beauty, and those long months of association had increased her hold on him. Also she had the moral courage he lacked. It was a part of her tragedy that the two men who most profoundly influenced her life both turned to her at one time or another for strength. There are women like that, and she was one of them.

There was nothing of all this in the wire she sent me that day, however. It was merely that she was coming, and would I meet her at the train. And I received it when I came back after helping carry her mother to her grave.

There was irony in that, that after all the years when she had held me as less than the dust beneath her feet I should have carried old Caroline to her last resting-place; and irony in the fact that her wire should be awaiting me on my return. I had been drafted for that service at Seaview. Now I was to be drafted again.

The funeral had been very small, hardly even select. A handful of old acquaintances and a curious group of villagers had comprised it. The war had altered everything Caroline Somers had believed in, had cut a gulf between her and the living world. The old standards were gone, and she was too old to learn new ones. Then, too, she had held her place by dominance, never by affection. Her passing grieved no one but Elinor; unless it was my mother, to whom she had been a symbol rather than a woman, but to whom all death was sad after my father's going.

"Poor soul," she said wistfully. "You never liked her, Carroll. But she stood for something that has gone."

"Stood for what?"

"Order. Decency," she said valiantly.

"And no compromise, Mother!"

"Isn't there strength in that? Is it only the young who know anything now?"

In her quiet way she had been flattered when Shirley Johnson asked me to serve as a pallbearer at the funeral. Here at last was recognition for me! I was no longer the boy, prowling around the gardens and that incredible maze, hoping for a glimpse of Elinor. I was not the lovesick youth on the pavement at Sherry's, or the Warner boy who was to get a cigarette case out of Elinor's wedding. She got out my top hat and morning clothes that day, and I found her carefully smoothing the hat with a soft pad.

"I want you to look nice, Carroll."

"Why? She won't see me."

"Other people will."

So, with Elinor's telegram waiting for me at home, I helped to bury Caroline Somers. The day was cold, with a high wind coming in from the sea. It blew the clergyman's surplice about him and sent huge rollers thundering up the beach. "Blessed are the dead who die in the Lord . . . For they rest from their labors." Henrietta touching her cross, Isabel Curtis staring with inscrutable eyes at the descending casket, the villagers appraising the elect, and one and all shivering in the wind; that was old Caroline's last hour of pomp.

A handful of us went back to the old house afterward. Henry had set out highballs and had built a fire in the long drawing-room. Isabel had come for some reason or other, and, after the others had gone we stayed by the fire out of mere gregariousness, for we had nothing to hold us together.

I had seen little of her that winter, and I saw that she was haggard and very thin. At first she had little to say. She sat in a low chair, staring at the blaze and twisting a bracelet around her wrist. I thought she looked bitter and disillusioned, if indeed she had ever had any illusions.

142

"You haven't heard from Elinor?"

"Not recently."

"She should have been here. Long ago."

"I imagine there isn't very much money."

"Oh, money!" she said, and relapsed into silence. When she broke it it was to startle me almost out of my chair. "I suppose you realize that Leighton killed Lloyd, don't you?"

"Good God, Isabel. No!"

"Think about it. Do you believe that Lloyd, who knew all about guns, was blundering through those drifts without the safety catch on his rifle? Don't be an idiot."

"But why? That's a grave accusation to make, Isabel. And I don't believe you."

But she only looked at me with lack-luster eyes and a cynical smile. "You too!" she said. "Leighton's bewitched you, as he has Elinor. Or else you're a fool. I don't think you are a fool, Carroll."

It was from that conversation that I went home to find Elinor's telegram, and to meet her a day or two later at the train. But I forgot it when I saw her. Her face was too radiant, her whole manner too confiding. She had nothing to hide, and I knew it.

She was still in black, this time for her mother, but she still had the curious distinction which never left her. Cheap and shabby as her clothing probably was, she wore it with an air. But she looked far too slender and very tired.

She kissed me like a sister. "Dear, dear Carroll," she said. "If you knew what it is to see you again!"

"Always around, like a good dog, Elinor."

She held my hand in the taxicab, as though it gave her some feeling of solidity. Indeed she looked rather lost and frightened. "I think it's the noise. I'm not used to it." And she asked me the details of her mother's death. Some of the radiance died as I told her, and she shivered.

"If she had wanted me I would have walked, if I had to. But she did not want me, Carroll. I often wonder why she did not care for me. I *did* try. Perhaps I was stupid."

She cried a little after that, but she was too honest to

143

pretend any overwhelming grief. "I'm just tired," she explained. "It has been a dreadful winter, Carroll. Dreadful. And then the journey. You see, I couldn't read. I have—strained my eyes."

At the hotel she asked me to dine with her that night, and I agreed. And it was over a table in a brightly lighted room that she told me about Leighton. Perhaps I had expected it, but I could hardly speak for a moment or two.

"Try not to think too badly of me," she said. "I am shocked and grieved about Lloyd, but you know how things were. I am sorry for him, because he is gone. But not for myself. Is that very dreadful?"

"Not dreadful at all. It is very natural. Elinor, are you determined on this marriage?"

"Determined?" She eyed me. "What do you mean by that? I am going to marry Blair, certainly."

"When?"

"Not for some time."

"This spring? This summer?" I persisted.

"This spring, probably."

"Here? In the East?"

"He can't afford to come East. We are frightfully hard up, Carroll."

"But don't you realize," I said, as patiently as I could, "that you can't go back to the ranch until you *are* married? Things were different when you were merely partners in an enterprise. Not too good, but at least different. Now you are engaged to him. You can't live in the same house with him."

"I've done it for a year and a half!"

"That's childish."

She refused to be angry. "And how conventional you are," she said. "Men are far more slaves to convention than women. Look at the clothes you wear! And where would I stay?"

I refused to be drawn into an argument about convention, however. I suggested that she stay with the Mayhews, but she refused.

144

"Very well. The Mayhews are out. What about me? My mother is living with me. She would love to have you." And when she shook her head: "What about Isabel? Why not go to her?"

But that door was closed. She had not heard from Isabel since Lloyd's death, and she thought she understood it. "I believe she has always cared for him, Carroll. And perhaps if he had married her he would have been happier. I was always wrong for him. Now he is gone, and—well, you see how it is."

I did see. Willy-nilly, she was going back to Leighton. She wanted nothing to interfere with that return of hers; no arguments from anyone, no attempts to hold her.

She still wore her traveling clothes. She had no others, she admitted. With her gloves off I saw that she had taken off her wedding and engagement rings, although she still wore her pearls. She saw me looking at her hand, and she flushed.

"I was wondering, Carroll," she said. "We—the ranch needs money badly, and Shirley says there will be almost nothing from the estate. Do you think I can sell my star sapphire, and these pearls? They must be quite valuable. Then later on I can sell the house at Seaview. It should bring something."

The jewels, however, she wanted to sell at once.

I suppose I was in a state of nerves that night anyhow, but the thought of Leighton living and flourishing on those pearls of hers somehow made my gorge rise. She could have no great sentiment for them. They had been only a part of that pride of old Caroline's which had wrecked her. They were like the black she wore, emptily symbolic. Nevertheless, they were her own, and certainly she had paid a price for them.

"Surely that's not necessary, Elinor. Are you telling me that that man—"

"That man is to be my husband, Carroll."

"I'm sorry, Elinor. I didn't mean to say that."

"And do you realize that the only money coming in now

145

for the ranch is Blair's? I have to do something. I can't be entirely a pensioner."

"Not even when you marry him?" I asked. "Most wives hardly consider themselves pensioners."

"You must remember that we got Blair into this."

But I was stubborn, and neither of us ate much as a result. She was sensitive to my disapproval, and she must have known that I was wretchedly anxious about her. Nevertheless, she did speak of Leighton again, as though she wanted me to know the facts. She told me at length, I noticed, of the complete separation of their lives in the ranch house after Lloyd's death, and that the thing had happened—"the knowledge of how they both felt"—just before she left for the East. She was almost timidly anxious that I should know that everything was all right, and that "I need not be ashamed of her." But both of us were relieved when Shirley Johnson came in, resplendent in full dress, from some dinner party or other. He was friendly, but disapproving, when she told him she meant to go back as soon as possible.

"You can't do that," he said. "You owe something to your friends and to yourself. Let Leighton run the place and pay you your share of the profit—if any. Or better still, let him buy you out."

"He cannot do that. He has only a small monthly income, from England."

"A remittance man, is he?"

"Not at all," she said sharply. "Why do all of you hate him so, Shirley?"

"Hate him? Never saw the man in my life. He sounds like a remittance man, but if he isn't, my apologies."

"I'd better tell you," she said, with her head high, "that I am going to marry him."

"Marry him! Good God!"

Nevertheless, it was Shirley who solved her immediate problem. He told her that she would have a few thousand dollars eventually from her mother's estate.

"She had never faced her financial situation," he told her, "and she never told me very much. Toward the end I urged

146

her to cut out certain bequests, but she would not. I am certain she didn't realize how she was leaving you." He hesitated, glanced across the table at her. "But I didn't want to talk business tonight. Better let it wait until tomorrow, Elinor."

"Bequests? What bequests?"

"Only one of any importance. Toward the end she grew increasingly dependent on her faith, religion, whatever you choose to call it. The result was that—I am certain no influence was brought to bear on her, Elinor, and as I say, she herself didn't realize—"

"Oh, for heaven's sake, Shirley! I'm not a child. Why don't you tell me?"

"She left the house at Seaview to your Aunt Henrietta, Elinor. For herself and her order."

It must have been a blow. In that last talk in the hotel about money undoubtedly the sale of the property by the sea had figured. Her jewels were only a stop-gap until the estate could be settled. She said nothing for a moment, and I was certain that she was wondering about the effect of the news on Leighton. But she smiled faintly when she spoke.

"I suppose I deserved that. Poor Mother! Why should she have worried about me? I had gone my way and she had gone hers. I—can I have the money at once, Shirley?"

"It's not payable for almost a year."

"But that's ridiculous, Shirley. It's now that we need it," she said sharply.

If he resented the tone or the "we," he made no comment. He sat listening gravely while she talked; the necessity of buying feed for the cattle, the probability of a catastrophe if that were not done. He told her the ways of the law were long and devious, but she hardly listened. Two thousand dollars would save them, and she must have it at once. At once.

It was I who finally agreed to advance her the money. Johnson was disapproving, and after we had seen her to the elevator he told me why.

"Maybe you don't know it," he said, "but there has been

147

some talk. Now you are sending her back, and by back I mean to Leighton. He *is* a remittance man; I've looked him up. He's got an allowance provided he stays out of England. Why in heaven's name couldn't you let well enough alone?"

"She'll marry him anyhow. The thing to do is to relieve her of her worries."

He looked at me shrewdly. "Why don't you marry her yourself, Warner? She deserves something better than what she's going to get."

"Because she is in love with him. Maybe you and I can't understand that, but she can. She knows him too. She has no illusions. It's apparently something she can't control."

"Nonsense! People get into that condition because they want to; not because they have to."

I have thought that over since then. Is it true? Or is that too easy, too simple? Romantic love may grow in that fashion, but what about those infatuations which obsess some men and so many women? Women who have gone straight all their lives, and who suddenly throw away all they have valued for the sake of a man they know is unworthy? It is like a madness, and as unreasonable.

I know now that Elinor in her hotel room that night was asking herself much the same question. The two of us together had managed to shake that new confidence of hers, and with distance she saw Blair for what he was. One side of him was gross and cruel, and nothing could change him. But there was another Blair, and she cried herself to sleep that night because he was so far away.

21

She stayed in New York for a month while old Caroline's will was probated and other details settled. Some time during that month she went out to Long Island and saw Henrietta; a calm Henrietta, asking few questions and offering no apologies.

"We are very poor, Elinor. The house is an answer to prayer."

Whether Elinor agreed with her or not, the meeting was entirely friendly. They sat together in the small reception room, with its rows of books, its smells of cooked food and the faint pungent odor of incense, and some echo of that earlier time must have been in Elinor's ears. Henrietta's voice saying, "One fights these things. Not alone, of course." And Elinor's passionate retort: "Do you think I haven't fought? I don't want to be in love with Blair. . . . It's not rational."

When Elinor told of her engagement Henrietta made only one comment: "You are very faithful, Elinor. It has lasted a long time."

"I was faithful to Lloyd, while he lived."

"And you think he will make you happy?"

Elinor stirred. "It isn't a question of happiness. It's something quite different. I can't explain it to you, Aunt Henrietta."

Henrietta looked down at her thin hands, lying quietly in her lap. "Perhaps you don't need to," she said simply.

After that there was no more real talk between them. Henrietta must show her a new cow in the barn, even eventually the plans for Seaview. She meant to add a small chapel to it, she said; Mortimer was overseeing the building, and the old boathouse was being done over as a priests' house, where visiting clergymen could be put up comfortably overnight.

It was Friday, and later on she ate in the refectory the meager luncheon of that day. Henrietta was fasting and ate little or nothing. After it a lay sister drove her to the train, and she sat there thinking back over the day. Was she faithful, or was she only weak? Why had she said it was not a question of happiness? Surely it must be that or nothing.

Never before had the word entered her mind in connection with Leighton; and I think that that day for the first time she realized that her approaching marriage might bring her many things; fulfillment, even ecstasy, but serenity and happiness would not be among them.

I know comparatively little of the remainder of this visit of hers; except that she was buying her trousseau. I went to the door of her hotel room one day on some errand or other, and I saw that she had laid out on the bed small heaps of undergarments. She flung a dressing-gown over them, but she was slightly breathless.

"I needed everything," she told me. "I feel frightfully extravagant."

Then I saw that Isabel Curtis was in the room. She was sitting with her back to the window, smoking a cigarette, and she gave me a malicious smile. Evidently Elinor had not confided in her, but she suspected the truth. "Looks like a trousseau, doesn't it?" she drawled. "Come in, Carroll, a few undies won't hurt you. I've been trying to persuade Elinor to go abroad with me. My party. But she's headed West, and in a hurry."

Elinor only smiled faintly. "I must get back," she said. "After all, it is my home. And my life," she added.

"You've said it." This was Isabel. "It's your life. Well, we learn by the trial-and-error method, don't we?"

"I don't know what you mean by that."

"Don't you?" And she quoted, watching Elinor, "Where thinkest thou he is now? Does he walk? Or is he on his horse? O happy horse!"

150

Yes, she knew well enough, did Isabel. I even think that in her indolent way she was definitely trying to save Elinor from that marriage. She had never hated her. What hatred she had, and it was plenty, was focused on Leighton.

She laughed at Elinor's heightened color, and got up to go. "I'm off," she said. "Coming, Carroll?"

We left together, but she had nothing much to say. Looking back I am convinced that some time during the month she had obtained from Elinor the full details as Elinor knew them of Lloyd Norton's death. Perhaps it was that day. Away from Elinor, there was a set look about her face that I did not like. I was relieved to learn that, Elinor or no Elinor, she still intended to go abroad for an indefinite stay.

"I'd better go," she said. "I'd only make trouble if I stayed."

After that I saw Elinor whenever I could; which was not often. She was occupied with the estate, with her buying, even with attempts to repair the damage to her hands, her skin and hair. I know that she saw the Mayhew girls, who had heard rumors and were avid with the curiosity of virginal women as to the situation, although I fancy they went unsatisfied. And once at least she made the long excursion to her mother's grave and laid flowers on it. I know that because she told me later that she went to the beach and stood there in the cold, trying to bring back some of the earlier memories. "But they wouldn't come, Carroll. I didn't seem at all the same person."

Always, however, from all of this she hurried back to her hotel for the daily letter from Leighton; letters at first discouraged and urgent, telling her that the snow was still lying deep over the country, that the cattle were beginning to drop and not get up again, and once that he had been out with a revolver to shoot some which were obviously finished. He needed both hay and oil cake, but even if he got them it was still a question whether they could be transported.

Queer love letters. When the time came to prepare her

151

defense Shirley Johnson found them in the secret compartment of her desk and went over them carefully. They were hardly love letters at all, although they ended with a personal phrase or two: *It will not be long, darling, until we are together again.* Or: *This house without you is impossible. All my love, dearest, always and ever.* But even they showed that the man's real love was the ranch. Even she must have known it, blind as she was. It was written all through them.

There was only one which was cheerful and even gay. That was sent after she had wired him that she had obtained the $2,000. *What a girl you are, sweetheart! So you got the money, and if this damned snow will only let up we will be on easy street. I cannot tell you what it means to me. Yesterday out of sheer exuberance I went out and shot a deer. There will be venison when you get back, darling. (Only don't ask the game warden to dinner!)*

Last night I went up to your room. Do you know that I have never been in it before? Such a pretty room, and so like you! But cold and empty without you. It is such a lonely room, darling. I met Mrs. Alden on the way down, and she gave me quite a dreadful look.

I am sending this by airmail. If you could wire part of the money it would save a lot of time, and if you yourself could come by wire it would save me a lot of heartache. Blair.

It was the Leighton of that letter to whom she went back. Less than a month after I met her I was seeing her off again, but this time I was not alone. Isabel and the Mayhews were there, and Shirley Johnson. The women were excited, like spectators on the edges of their chairs at a play. Johnson and I were inclined to be silent. And Elinor? She was radiantly happy. I did not know about the letter in her bag, to be read and reread on the way West, but I knew that she was lost to me. I never expected to see her again.

I went home that night and locked away the framed snapshot of her on the raft, with my war medal behind it. Two memories, both painful, and one as completely finished as the other. Some time after midnight my mother came in. She had thrown a black dressing-gown over her nightdress, and I remember that she looked wan and uneasy. "Aren't you going to bed, Carroll?"

"Just as soon as I tuck you up. I had some papers to look over."

"She's gone, I suppose?"

"Elinor? Yes, she left today."

She looked at me timidly. With her hair down she looked absurdly young, and I saw that she wanted to say something comforting. She could not quite bring herself to do it, however. "Perhaps you'd sleep if I made you a sandwich," was what she said. "It takes the blood out of the brain, or something. I—I wish she hadn't gone back there, Carroll. It seems so far."

"It's as far as hell and back, Mother."

She drew a long breath. "I don't understand it," she said. "I always thought she was in love with you. If only you would forget her, Carroll. There are so many nice girls."

"Millions of them, all waiting for me!" I agreed. "But it's food I crave just now, Mother, not women. Was that sandwich a bluff or did you mean it?"

She went obediently, and although I ate what she brought I dare say I did not fool her. When I had tucked her in bed she reached up and put her arms around me, drawing me down to her. "I would like to have a grandchild, Carroll," she whispered.

"Mother! What an immoral suggestion! I must get a wife first."

That made her laugh a little, but she was still insistent. "Why doesn't Elinor marry you, Carroll? She is free now."

"Because I'm a lawyer, darling. Lawyers are nice. They make good husbands and they produce notable grandchildren. But they are not romantic. They are not gods on horseback."

"Then it *is* that Englishman!" she said surprisingly, and asked me to put out the light.

I have been thinking of my mother as I have written all this. It seems to me that while the dramas of life center around the younger women, it is the older ones who face its tragedy. She was still young, barely 50, and going through the double strain of her widowhood and the climacteric. She was not one of those women who can substitute one interest for another, and my father's death had left her only one, myself.

Now I was frustrating the only hope she had, to live again the vicarious life of her grandchildren. I remember that I lay awake for a long time, wondering whether I should not look about for some nice clear-eyed girl and try to marry her.

This is Elinor's story, however, not mine. As I gather it together I realize how little of it directly concerns me at all, or how small a part I know first-hand. For much of it from now on I shall have to use what came out in the trial or in the talks which took place during the trial, in hotel bedrooms and the speakeasy across the street; or wherever two or three cowpunchers were gathered out on the range. From such odd sources I must build this case for the defense. But I know more or less in detail about that return of hers.

Leighton met her at the train and took her home; although he was glad to see her, he was not exuberant. Conditions were bad and getting worse. There was still snow on the ground, and dying cattle everywhere. Part of the money had gone for feed, but the cattle were too weak to drive in and still no carts could reach them in the pastures.

He was hardly a lover then, and something of her radiant happiness froze in her. Only at their own gate did he stop and draw her to him. "But I have you," he said. "At least we will be together, darling."

He was at his best that night, gentle and tender. He built a great fire and then made her play for him. If there was a ghost in that room she at least was not aware of it. The old enchantment was back, stronger than ever for their separation. They talked of their marriage, and after Mrs. Alden had gone to bed she brought down bits of her trousseau. Why not? They were for him. She would cheerfully have died for him then as he sat, big and blond and carefully restrained, stroking softly her little bits of finery.

It would have been easy to have made a false move that night; easy to frighten her. One passionate gesture and she would have been on guard. He never made it. He knew her fastidiousness, and so he soothed her instead. She was his wife and he adored her. He would never hurt her; and she who had been hurt so often and so long, believed him. In a day or two—maybe tomorrow—he would go into town and get the license. In the meantime—

She went upstairs in that happy confidence.

I wonder if I can make her clear, this woman I have called Elinor Norton, moving about in her cold bedroom that night? Her starved love-life and her infatuation, both at war with old Caroline's rigid code and her own early training that sin was sin. She was no Isabel Curtis, lightly following an impulse and emerging apparently unscarred. In her own group in the East were dozens of young women, married and unmarried, whose whole attitude toward such matters was completely casual. She had never belonged to them.

Did she even know that he was coming up? I think not. Probably she moved about the room putting away that armload of small intimate garments. Perhaps she stood for a time at her window, looking out. It was cold outside, but it is not difficult to imagine that once more she could hear his caressing voice as he spoke to her cautiously from beneath it, more than a year before: "You looked very lovely, you know, Nellie."

She did not give herself lightly, that I know. When some time later she heard his step on the staircase she made a move to turn the key. But she did not turn it. When he opened the door she was standing in the center of the room, looking at him with the frightened eyes of a small child. Even then she might have sent him away, but he was skillful. He put his arms around her very gently.

155

"My wife," he said. "My lovely wife."

She never forgot that, in the days to come. To her that relationship was a marriage, nothing less. When she could finally face the facts, it was to assert to herself that she was his wife, at least in common law.

For he did not get the license, the next day or the next. At first she understood. The emergency was great, and he was working hard to save what he could. Late in the day he would come in, exhausted and red-eyed from snow and exposure, to eat heavily and often in moody silence, and later on to fall asleep in Lloyd's chair by the fire. It might have been Lloyd himself then, breathing stertorously, his mouth slightly open. But later on he would waken, rested and cheerful again, and become once more her lover and her husband.

She laid it to the pressure of their emergency that he had ceased talking about their marriage, and she did not hurry him. More snow had fallen; indeed, it lay until early in May. Then there came a day when the road opened again and he went to town to see the local banker and attempt to add to their mortgage. She asked him that day to see about the license, and was alarmed when he said nothing.

"You will, Blair, won't you? This can't go on. I'm your wife in fact; I want to be your wife in law."

"Why worry?" he said. "And why hurry? If I can get this damned situation cleared up, I'll have time to think of other things."

"There are no other things for me but this. I can't go on indefinitely, Blair."

"Oh, for God's sake, Elinor. I have other things to worry about just now." Then he saw her face and lightly kissed her. "Well, well," he said. "So she wants to be made an honest woman, does she? Well, so she shall!"

Nevertheless, he came back that night with neither the loan nor the license. It was the beginning of the panic of that year, and banks were tightening up their credit, especially country banks, suffering from the over-expansion of farmers during the war years when Europe was out of production. There was no such thing as a chattel mortgage to be had. No money could be raised on cattle, and a part of that check of Elinor's had gone for a payment on the ranch itself.

He came back sullen and aloof, and she guessed that he had been drinking. But she gathered up her courage. "And the license, Blair?"

"What license?"

"You know perfectly well."

"Good God! Are you at that again? Do you know that we may lose this place? Has it occurred to you that our cattle are gone or going, and that I can't raise a dollar to buy any more?"

"I still think that I am more important even than cattle."

"I wonder!" he said brutally. "You've lived snug and warm all your life. Your kind of woman always finds some man to work for her, but I'm damned if I'll stand any nagging."

Then Mrs. Alden came in from the kitchen, and he pulled himself together. When they were alone again he apologized. "Sorry, Nellie," he said. "Of course, I'll fix it up; only don't drive me too hard just now. I'm in the devil of a hole. That can wait."

He did not come up the staircase that night, and she was frightened. She saw her peril too late, for she could not force him to marry her. She knew then that all she had was a physical hold over him, and if that ended she was lost.

She had other anxieties too. Mrs. Alden, she felt, was suspicious, and even the men in the bunk house. Like all Westerners, they sublimated good women and sharply defined them from bad ones. There was no halfway ground, no no-man's-land between virtue and sin. She felt that they had placed her among the bad ones.

Alone in her room she faced her situation. She sat in front of her dressing-table and drew the lamp close. By its light she examined herself desperately; her face, her neck and arms. Mrs. Alden, coming in, discovered her there and found her rather pitiful. She saw that Elinor had put on

157

the gown she had intended for her wedding night, one of white silk and lace. She was shivering in it, for the room was cold; but she had brushed her dark hair until it shone, and when Mrs. Alden went in she was feverishly rubbing some sort of cream into her hands.

But evidently he did not come up at all that night. The dour Scotch woman, opening her door back along the upper hall, saw her much later. She was standing at the top of the stairs; standing still and listening, and there was no sound from below.

She must have slept very little. On toward morning Mrs. Alden saw a streak of lamplight under her door. And she must have sought comfort, all other having failed her, after old Caroline's fashion. The next day Mrs. Alden found her prayer book beside her bed.

It is from the same source that I reconstruct the next morning, and something of the following spring. On that morning, it seems, she went down the stairs with her head high, a careful bit of make-up on her face and wearing one of the simpler dresses she had bought for her trousseau. He did not even see it. He seemed indeed hardly to see her. He ate in a hurry, put on his chaps and gloves in the hall and went out.

She was too spirited to give up, however. She followed him through the kitchen to the door. "Blair."

"Yes. I'm in a hurry. What is it?"

"Nothing. Nothing important. I'll see you at noon." She was determinedly smiling. No tears now, no appeals. Play the game, woo him, win him. She had to win him. When she closed the door behind him she was still smiling.

Only Mrs. Alden noticed the dress. "That's a pretty thing," she said. "You look like a young girl in it."

"But I feel so old, Mrs. Alden. As old as all the women in the world."

The next month or two must have been nothing less than torture to her. The cattle country was taking stock of its losses, now that spring had come. Men who had been millionaires the fall before were trying to raise money on

158

what they had left, and failing. Leighton spent much of his time in town, drinking when he could get liquor and gambling when he had money. Not once did he refer to their marriage, and by that time she was afraid to do so; literally afraid. He had changed. His courage was gone. That streak of weakness in him was beginning to show itself once more. He was even changing physically. He was coarsening, adding weight around his body, and there were times when his features were swollen, so that the face he showed her across the table was like some grotesque copy of his own.

She saw all this, but she was helpless. A protest from her brought only anger or, even worse, denial. She was confident, too, that he had returned to the woman in the town. She was making no effort now to win him back to her. She was glad to be left alone. But he would have to marry her. On that she was determined. Reared as she had been, there was no other answer to her problem.

One night she heard him come in late, and after a brief interval heard him stumbling uncertainly up the stairs. She leaped out of her bed to lock the door. Then, her hand on the key, she hesitated. She did not even dare to lock him out.

22

That winter and spring tragedy in the stock country did one thing to her, however; although she did not know it. The countryside, obsessed with its own tragedy, forgot the tale of the milk can and the bullet hole in the cabin wall. It was facing its own probems gallantly, but it was ruined and it knew it.

And then there happened one of those unimportant occurrences which seem trivial at the time, but have momentous results. Mrs. Alden came in one day to tell Elinor that her daughter was sick, and that she would have to leave. Elinor replaced her with the daughter of a coal miner, a gangling girl of 18, and for a week Mrs. Alden taught her what she could. Then one day she was ready to go, and she came in before she left, still dour of face but red of eye, and confronted Elinor squarely.

"I'm not one to talk, Mrs. Norton," she said. "I guess you know that. But I've got good eyes and a pair of ears. If Mr. Leighton isn't ready to marry you now he never will be. I know men and I know that man. And you're still young. Better go back to your people, before it's too late."

They faced each other, those two women, and it was Elinor's eyes which fell. "I can't force him to marry me, Mrs. Alden. And I have no people."

"Then heaven help you, for he never will."

With that she went out, and so far as I know Elinor never saw her again until months later when she appeared on the stand, an unwilling witness against her.

Elinor went on as best she could. The gangling girl was inexperienced in some things, and as old as sin in others. Also she was given to sly visits to the bunk house, to an unceasing espionage on both the man and the woman in the main building, and later on to strange half-shy attempts to attract Leighton's attention. I can see her now; a tall thin creature with a bush of red hair, a weak mouth and a high shrill laugh. Unkempt and untidy at first too, so that Elinor had to instruct her even in personal cleanliness. Her name was Sally Ulman.

All this was late in June. The brief hot summer of the semi-arid country had come. Except for the emptiness of the great pastures and the bleaching bones of dead cattle, there was nothing to indicate the blight which lay over the land. Elinor worked like a ranch woman now. Her garden had become important, since it supplied food; not only for the house, but for the bunk house. She had a few chickens. In the creek was a family of young ducks; they waddled to her like a line of puppies when they heard her voice. And in the kitchen she had Sally, won at last to the gospel of

160

regular bathing and fresh white dresses to work in, and eyeing Leighton furtively as he went in and out.

Elinor was busy now, most of the time. There were fewer days when, in her boyish riding breeches, she took her mare out for a canter; and once when she did she was badly thrown. The mare shied suddenly at an unburied carcass, and Elinor was in bed for a week.

It was this accident, possibly, which brought about Leighton's first voluntary mention of marriage in all that time. It was the first night she came down to dinner, and she came in that gay Chinese suit of Elizabeth Mayhew's. He looked at her, and then ran a finger over the delicate planes of her face.

"You're thin, Nellie. What's the matter?"

She managed to smile at him. "Why spoil a nice evening?"

He said nothing more until they had finished their meal, and the girl in the kitchen was washing dishes and singing shrilly. When he reverted to it she was sitting in her old place on the porch step, looking out into the twilight. All around her stretched that monstrous country, like a land God had forgot, and she must have felt rather like that land; as though God had shaped and then forgotten her.

"Now then," he said. "Let's have it. What's the trouble?"

"Do I need to tell you, Blair? I suppose I'm thin because I'm not very happy. You have made me feel like a common thing. I feel like—Sally!"

He was more like himself that night than he had been for months. Then, too, there was the further sum to be paid to Elinor in the fall. Already he had plans for her money. He must have remembered all this, for he took it quietly, even explained. He had been selfish, but she was not to hold it against him. He had always considered her his wife. In a sense she was his wife; a common-law wife.

"What is a common-law wife?"

"A wife in fact. I acknowledge you as my wife. That's all."

"But you never have."

"Then I will, my dear. Unless you prefer the other sort bell, book, and preacher. Or isn't that the method for driving away devils?" He had coaxed her into cheerfulness. They laughed together, and until late they sat there in the dark, making plans.

"You're marrying a poor man, my darling."

"What have I? Nothing. I am living on your bounty now. Where would we be without your monthly income?"

I have wondered about that night. What did he really think, sitting there with his arms around her? About her small inheritance? Or was he simply following his usual impulse with women, to win them by empty promises or to quiet them with words? Or was that letter from England even then in his pocket? Did he know, as he sat there, that he could never marry her?

He is dead, and he cannot defend himself. But I think he was choosing the easiest way out of a situation. He was entirely satisfied with his life as it was. Perhaps he had really found himself in that country, as he never had before. He was still hopeful, for all of the spring debacle, and physical activity was the very breath of life to him.

"We'll put this place on its feet yet," he told her. "I've learned a lot. If Lloyd hadn't insisted on over-expanding last year—"

It was the first time he had mentioned Norton openly since his death. It startled her.

Nevertheless, she had those few hours of happiness. They lasted, to be exact, until 11 o'clock the next morning. Then she saw him coming in on his horse, riding slowly for him, and she met him in the hall. He was taking off his spurs, and his face was sober.

"I've been down for the mail," he said.

"*You* went for the mail?" She was surprised, but not suspicious. The mail was usually brought up from the box at the gate by whoever happened to be passing. "I hope there is no bad news?"

"Nothing very good. I've had a letter from home."

162

"Is it your father?"

"It's my father all right," he said. "But it's not what you think. He's still alive."

They went together into the living-room, and there he gave her the letter. It had no envelope, but she did not notice that; and what she read was a brief and almost legal notice from his father that in case of his marriage to an American, any American, his monthly remittance from England would cease at once.

I have seen that letter. Behind it lies God knows what old prejudice and more recent resentment against this country and its people. Our tardiness in entering the war perhaps played its part. But underlying it all is a lack of faith in Blair himself, a conviction that, left alone, he was bound to make a mess of his life.

Elinor read it and reread it incredulously.

"But it can't be, Blair! Not in this day and age."

"Can't it? You don't know my father."

She was stunned. "What am I to do?" she asked helplessly. "I can't go on and I can't go back. He's making me a wicked woman."

He tried to take her in his arms then, but she jerked herself free. Perhaps she knew intuitively that his disappointment was assumed. Certainly she had suffered a psychic shock of the first order.

"I wish I had never seen you," she said, "I've paid for every bit of happiness I've had with you. And he is wicked as well as cruel, your father. You are both cruel. You don't really care about this, do you? It lets you out. You can't marry me now, can you?" And then some further intuition came to her. "How long have you had this letter, Blair? Did you have it before I began to live with you?"

He denied it, absolutely and in toto. She asked for the envelope, but he said he had thrown it away. And he ended with an argument she found hard to answer.

"Listen, my darling, I admit all you say. I know my father and you do not. But he is an old man. He won't live forever, or even very long; and I'll have something when

163

he goes. Can't we go along as we are for a bit? After all, this is between us. If it is all right with us, if you love me and I love you—"

"Do you love me? Or isn't it something different, Blair?"

"Don't ask me things like that," he said impatiently. "Men don't analyze what they feel. I want you. Isn't that enough?"

"How do you want me? As a mistress? Is that all love is, to a man?"

He did not answer her, and now at last she was trapped. She knew it, and she was frantic. She shut herself in her bedroom, refusing to eat, and later on she saw the girl Sally on her way to the corral with the news. She did not care. It was too late to care. For the first time she felt herself what Norton had called Isabel Curtis at the dock. "That strumpet!" he had said. She felt like a strumpet.

Late in the afternoon, Leighton being out, she walked the mile to the gate and the post-box there. But she found no envelope.

She commenced a long letter to me that night. In it she told me the whole story. She made no defense, but she did ask my help: *Your moral support, Carroll. You can think so much more clearly than I can. You see, if I felt that Blair already had this letter when our relations first became what they are, I should feel like killing him. Or myself. But I cannot be sure. He says he did not, and to save my self-respect and my reason I must believe him.*

Don't misunderstand me. It is not a matter of money with me. I would starve rather than be where I am. And you can't help me by sending me a check to come East. I shall never leave him until I am his legal wife. I can't. You see that, don't you? Perhaps if someone went to England and talked to his father it would help. I have wondered today if Isabel, who is there now, could have given someone a wrong impression of me. That's not Christian, but—

She never finished it, and later on Sally Ulman was to find it locked away among her belongings, and to identify it in court.

"Do you recognize this letter?"

"Yes, sir."

"Is this the letter you handed to the district attorney shortly after Mrs. Norton's arrest?"

"Yes, sir."

"Will you tell the jury where and how you found it?"

"It was locked in her desk. When she was arrested she left her keys, so I—well, I just opened the desk and poked around." She glanced unhappily at Elinor. "But I didn't give it to the district attorney. I just told somebody about it, and—"

That then was the picture as it was in the summer of 1921; with old Caroline dead in state in her stone mausoleum, and lying closer to Howard Somers than she had lain for many a long day; with Lloyd Norton alone on that bare hill of his, with the sagebrush just beyond the wall and the mountains standing sentinel; with my father gone and Mother making her pitiful little journeys to his grave, to stand for a moment facing a great emptiness in the world, and then coming home to lie alone and awake in her old-fashioned bed.

And with that damning letter of Elinor's lying locked away in her desk, to be used against her later on.

Of the living, only four of us remained to carry on, step by step, to the inevitable end: Isabel Curtis, still suspicious and revengeful, Elinor, Leighton, and myself. Rather, there were five, for I must not forget Sally Ulman, already beginning to copy Elinor's speech and manner, already buying rouge and lipstick and even a pair of imitation pearl earrings; and as amoral as the animals in the fields about the ranch.

"I put some saddle soap on your boots, Mr. Leighton."

"Thanks, Sally. Learning a lot, aren't you?"

He was noticing her now. Not a great deal, but he saw that she was not unattractive. One day he sharply told the men to keep her away from the bunkhouse.

23

I knew nothing, of course, of all this. For months I had considered the marriage as an accomplished fact. I had even accepted it, but with the philosophy with which a man accepts such matters. I did not contemplate suicide. I ate and drank and went about my business as usual, and I worked harder than usual at the office. I remember that we made a good bit of money that spring and summer. Already business was beginning to squirm under the income tax, and to hunt for legal methods of evading it.

There must have been rumors floating about even then about Elinor, but they did not reach my ears. The Mayhews were at Newport, but Mother had refused to go back to the Seaview cottage and I did not urge it. And Isabel Curtis was still abroad.

Then, with the shock of a man waking from a drugged sleep, early in August I received a short letter from Elinor, enclosing a small check for the interest on the loan I had made to her. She had insisted on that, and I had realized that it saved her pride and had agreed.

I had hoped to reduce the loan, Carroll dear, but I suppose you know how conditions are out here. Blair is working hard and expects to save the ranch; even a moderately good year would do it. Just now, however, it takes all his income to carry on, and as you know, I have nothing.

The check was on a local bank, and it was signed *Elinor Norton!*

It had come in the morning mail, and I took my hat and left the office. I walked for hours, trying to map out some course of action, but all of them seemed futile and more than one actually absurd. My own impulse was to go out at once and confront Leighton, but the picture of a discarded lover interfering under such conditions was pure comedy.

Late that afternoon I went to see Shirley Johnson, and his matter-of-factness cooled me somewhat.

"What can you do, Warner?" he inquired. "She'll leave him eventually, and have learned a damned good lesson. Besides, you don't know that she's living with him. She may be stubborn like her mother, but she's her mother's child in other ways too."

I asked him if he would be willing to go out and see for himself, but he shook his head.

"During a long life," he said, "I have learned one thing, and learned it well. Never interfere between a man and a woman. Between a man and his property, or a man and the law—but a man and a woman, never."

But he added, before I left, that there was no reason why I should not go out and see for myself.

"You've had business that way before," he said. "You can drop in on them and form your own judgment." He smiled across his desk. "Probably you'll find a pair of love birds, and who are you and I to ask whether the situation is regular or extralegal? But in case she needs help you'll know it."

That night I told my mother that business called me West again, and the next day I was on the train. I was in no pleasant humor. I loathed my errand, and coupled with that was an almost insane fury at Leighton. Again and again I remembered Elinor's face as she had started West, with her small trousseau in a bag at her feet and the look of expectant happiness in her eyes; and at such times I could have killed him. Yet if it were not for the tragedy which followed I could smile now at the complete anticlimax of that visit of mine.

I had wired ahead to Elinor, but it was Leighton who met me at the train. I had left the express at Billings and had taken the branch line, and he was waiting on the platform when the train drew in. He held out his hand, friendly and cheerful. "This is a bit of luck," he said. "Elinor is enchanted. I left her in a state of delirium!"

167

The man was changed. Probably he looked better than during the winter, but he was still too heavy. He had marks of the drinker also; the fine veins showing in his face, the congested eyes. He was sober enough that day, however, and I admit that he largely disarmed me as we drove back to the ranch. He spoke of Elinor as casually as he spoke of local conditions, and he even mentioned the postponement of their marriage.

"I have insisted on putting it off," he said. "Of course, with any sort of winter— But I have her to think of. If this thing doesn't go she ought not to be tied to me. It's a hard and lonely life for a woman, at the best. The way things are now—"

Perhaps his sincerity was a marvel of acting. It may not have been. Perhaps Elinor was right and there were two men in him. One of them that day may have meant to marry her eventually, although he had no liking for marriage; the other was already glancing at Sally Ulman, and appraising her youth and frank sensuality.

The real shock came when I saw Elinor. She was thinner than I had ever seen her, drawn far too fine. Her eyes, always lovely, had lost their luster and seemed sunken. She was waiting on the porch, and the pitiless setting sun showed new fine lines around her mouth. At first apparently she could not speak to me.

"I told you, Elinor. Always around, like a good faithful old dog!"

That gave her time, and she managed to smile. "Always good and always faithful."

Then I saw Sally Ulman. She came out onto the porch to get a small bag of mine, and over Elinor's shoulder she gave me a quick glance. Then she grinned at me.

I found her in my room upstairs when I reached it. She said something about hanging up my clothes, and when I said I needed no help she still stood in the doorway. "Come a long ways, haven't you?"

"Rather a long journey, yes."

"If there's anything I can get you—"

168

"Nothing. Thanks very much."

She took herself away finally, going reluctantly, and I thought I heard her giggling as she clattered down the stairs.

Elinor had tea for me when I came down. There in the house, out of the sun, she looked better. But she was very quiet. I had not expected her to welcome my visit. She must have known why I had come. But now I realized that she was actually in fear of it, as though in some way my coming had added to her anxieties. Her faint smile was gone. Even in the shade of the room she looked haunted.

"You look civilized, Carroll."

"I *am* civilized."

"Are you? I wonder. Are any of us really civilized, or isn't it something we just put on and take off?"

But she was talking against time. Determined as I was to get to the root of the business, she gave me no opportunity. Leighton did not appear, and we drank our tea without him. Rather, Elinor had tea and I had a highball. Whisky and soda were on the tray, as though by custom. Her defenses were up, however. Unlike Leighton, she did not refer to her postponed marriage.

She asked the usual questions about my mother, about Isabel. Isabel, it appeared, had written from Europe, asking if she might come out on her return. "I don't know what to do about it. Blair doesn't want her."

"You ought to have the right to ask whoever you want, Elinor. Certainly half the place is yours, if not more."

"More? I don't understand you."

"You put some extra money into it this spring, didn't you?"

"Against Blair's monthly check. Don't forget that."

She got up abruptly and showed me some flowers on the piano. "Aren't they lovely, Carroll? The blue is wild pentstemon. I used to have a dress of that color."

"Do you still play, Elinor?"

"Not often. I'm tired at night. There is a good bit to do. And"—she laughed rather cheerlessly—"my hands are so rough."

After that we wandered out. The two years had made a change in the place. It had a run-down look. Posts were sagging, manure had accumulated in and back of the barn. There were even no flowers growing in her garden, or around the house. "We are rather short-handed," she said, and let it go at that.

Even the house had changed. It had lost that first brightness. It needed paint. And inside I had noticed that, while it was orderly enough, it lacked the small touches of two years before. It had begun to look like all the other ranch houses of busy and tired women, with only utility considered and beauty forgotten. Yet that night at dinner, for all the slovenly serving of the red-headed girl, things were rather better. Leighton was urbane and agreeable. If anyone remembered Norton's empty place, it was not mentioned. I happened, however, to ask for the little deer, and saw Elinor's eyes fill with tears.

Leighton laughed his big laugh. "He left us," he said. "Went out hunting a lady friend and never came back. Well, who can blame him? It's the way of the world." His eyes were on hers, as if in a sort of challenge; but she did not look at him.

Only the red-headed girl giggled.

He left us after dinner on some excuse or other, and it was on the porch after the meal that she came very close to being honest with me. Close, but not close enough. She said, "I wrote you a long letter in the spring, Carroll."

"A letter? I never got it."

"I never sent it."

"Why not?"

She did not answer that. She sat staring out over the hills for some time before she spoke. Then unexpectedly she asked me if I believed in God.

"I suppose I do. There must be something stronger than we are."

"Is your God a cruel God, or a kind one?"

"I haven't thought much about it. If He is, He is just."

"Just! Who wants justice? It is cold and hard. Surely God means more than that."

I was as self-conscious as all men when it came to discussing such matters. I tried to tell her my feeling that in the end each man builds his own God, or his own conception of God; and that even exact justice would take into account our own weaknesses.

But she hardly listened. "I suppose one lives, or escapes," she said. "Aunt Henrietta escaped, of course; but she lived first. It must be very peaceful, that life. She is never afraid. I'm afraid so often, Carroll. How is one good? What is goodness anyhow?"

"I suppose," I said, "that to be good is to be kind, Elinor. Compassion is the great virtue, isn't it?"

But she heard Leighton coming back, and her whole attitude changed. "Platitudinous, Carroll!" she said. " 'Be good, sweet maid, and let who will be clever!' Hello, Blair. Carroll and I have been talking about God."

"And what," said Leighton, "is Carroll's opinion of God?" He had brought out whisky and soda, and he was followed by Sally with a tray of glasses. I could not see the girl, but I could smell the cheap scent she used.

I had not been there 24 hours before I realized, not only that Elinor did not mean to discuss Leighton and herself, but that there was to be no return to the life of two years before. She suggested no excursions together, planned no rides. For one thing, she was busy. The girl in the kitchen was inefficient, and all of Elinor's mornings and part of the afternoons were occupied. But also it was clear that she had decided not to confide in me. Whether or not Leighton had insisted on this I do not know. I do know that he saw to it that we were almost never alone together.

I spent long days in the saddle with him; or motoring into the Reservation, where they still had a small herd, and in the evenings he seldom left us. Never at least for long enough to break down the barrier which time and distance had built between us. And on those excursions he

171

puzzled me. I remember that once he spoke about the prejudice of an older England against Americans. Again he queried me exhaustively about the small portion of old Caroline's estate which Elinor would receive the following winter.

"I dare say one could break that will, Warner. I mean, after all, undue influence and all that. The house should be Elinor's."

"I doubt if Elinor would contest it."

But one day he told me in detail of Norton's death. Perhaps that was natural. He must have known of my interest. It was his manner which left me dubious. It was too detailed, as though he had rehearsed it to himself too often; and I remembered Isabel and her suspicion. He was concealing something. What he was telling was the truth, I felt, but not all the truth. . . .

As if to make up for what it had done the year before, the summer was a good one. Valleys were filled with grass, so that the horses rode waist-deep in it. Leighton saw only the grass and the lack of cattle to fatten on it; but I found the land gentler than I had remembered it.

Nevertheless, he loved it. There was no question about that. "Great country, Warner. Fish in the creeks and game everywhere. I'll be glad when the ducks start to come in." He was thinking about putting in some wheat in the fall.

He was not always loquacious. There were days when he rode in silence, with his reins loose and his head bent as if in thought; and other days when he went without me, and invented instead an errand for me into town, so that I should not be alone with Elinor. For he never trusted me, I know that now. He was not jealous, God knows. He was afraid that I would bring up the issue between them, or between myself and him.

I was still uncertain of their relationship. That it had changed I was certain, but how? If they had been living as man and wife, there was nothing to indicate it. But I was not entirely blind. They might meet as casually as partners in a business enterprise, their physical apartness might seem

172

as complete as their widely separated bedrooms, the good-night kiss with which he left her might be as chastely affec-tionate as it looked to be. Yet the change was there, not so much in evidence as in lack of it. He did not draw out her chair at dinner, as once he had done; nor rise when she en-tered the room. There were times, too, when he ignored her presence entirely, not through intention, but as one ignores something long familiar. Small matters perhaps, but they made me itch to knock him down, and they caused me the loss of many a night's sleep. Nights when I lay awake listen-ing to the silence which was like a great noise outside, and staring into the darkness which I thought must be like death itself; without form or color or sound, and only the tired mind thinking its confused disembodied thoughts.

Only once or twice did I get Elinor to her piano, and then except for Norton's absence it might have been two years before. There was the small wall of darkness outside the windows, the same feeling of being cut off from everything warm and living and vital. Only now it was Leighton who slept in Norton's chair by the fireplace, his mouth slightly open, his breathing heavy and stertorous.

When he roused she left the piano and took up some sew-ing. I can still see her sitting there under the lamp, her sewing table at her elbow, and the light streaming down on her small bent head.

"Why did you stop, Nellie?"

"You don't care for music. Anyhow I was playing badly. My fingers are stiff."

She was, I saw, mending an undergarment of his. Some-how it made my blood boil.

24

The days dragged on. I was unwilling to stay and reluctant to go. I had no idea that I was a welcome guest to either of them. To Leighton I represented danger in some form or other; to Elinor I represented a past and a solidity which she wanted to forget. Yet I felt that for some reason she was not willing to let me go. When I suggested it she always objected.

"Just another day or two, Carroll. I may not see you again for so long."

"You don't really want me," I replied to that one day. "You want me to stay for some reason of your own. Isn't that true?"

"You sound like Blair! Can't I want an old friend, without some ulterior purpose?"

"Certainly. Only in this case you have a purpose. Leighton doesn't want me here. I don't blame him. Why should he? And what good am I to you? I'm not even an old friend, to remind you of things. You want to forget them! I don't want to be brutal, but you'd be better off here without me—unless you will come East with me."

Her eyes went blank. "I'm not going back, Carroll. That's final."

"You still intend to marry him?"

"Certainly."

"And you are still in love with him, Elinor?"

She did not answer that. She went once more into the details of their problem, as though that explained something; of the winter and spring, of Leighton's intention to plant wheat in the fall when she "came into her money." She talked feverishly, for her, as though against time. Wheat might be better than cattle, but it took money. They would have to buy farm machinery, seed wheat, labor. It would be dry farming, for they could not afford to irrigate. Besides, the creek was uncertain. It went dry during a drought. With dry farming they might get 14 bushels to the acre, or even more. They were getting that on the Reservation, close by. Of course, they could try sheep. Sheep had two crops, wool and lambs; but the overwhelming sentiment of the neighborhood was against sheep. They would run cattle too, of course.

I listened. She was talking only with the surface of her mind, while underneath I knew that it was busy elsewhere. That was nothing new. During my entire stay I had realized her profound preoccupation, her absorption in her own thoughts. I had seen her at the table, gazing absently out a window; and Leighton's jibing voice, not so unlike Norton's.

"Well, do I hear a reply? Or do I not?"

"I'm sorry. I was thinking, Blair."

"Thinking! And what about, my dear?"

She would look at him then, long and steadily. But she never explained.

That day I finally broke into her dissertation, and did it bluntly. "I know all that, Elinor. I've had it from Leighton ever since I came. You say you are going to marry him. That's all right if you care enough for him. But do you? You've made one mistake. You can't afford to make another."

She tried to smile. "What was it Isabel said that day? That we learn by the trial and error method?"

That was too much for me. I slammed out of the room, saddled a horse at the corral, and rode hard until time for dinner. For the first time it occurred to me that she wanted me there, not for myself, but because it made things easier for her; and I know now that this was true. Just how much drinking Leighton did at night after I had gone to bed I do not know, but he did not go to town while I was there. There were none of those returns of his that she so dreaded, the uncertain movements below, and finally the stealthy

175

stumbling up the steep staircase, with Sally Ulman's quick ears listening behind her door and her sly visits the next day to the bunkhouse with her information.

I was helpless, but I could see that it was plain hell for her, all of it; the subtle change in the manner of the men toward her, the subdued laughter, as if at some bawdy joke, the affront to her dignity and even her decency. I know now that more than once she had gone to the gun case in the living-room and taken out Norton's old service automatic. Only to put it back again, however. She was not afraid of death, but suicide to her was sin. She had sinned enough.

Except for two incidents, that was my visit to the ranch the summer of 1921. Each of them—Elinor and Leighton —was preoccupied, but for widely different reasons, and each of them clung to me as a means of escape from something I did not understand. In one way I was totally unimportant. In another I must have been vital. Yet anyone looking in at us during an evening meal during that time would have seen a carefully laid table and three ultra-civilized people around it. Perhaps the red-haired girl leaned too close to Leighton as she served him, perhaps the talk was forced at times; but it was quiet, the casual exchange of people sure of themselves and of each other.

"I saw some quail today, Elinor."

"Really? I wonder if I could put some in the chicken runs."

Or: "I see the market's down again, Warner."

"Yes. I suppose we had to expect something of the sort. If only it doesn't go too far it may be healthy."

The first incident merely puzzled me at the time. Leighton had come in from the corral and was having a highball in the living-room. Elinor was sewing beside a window, and I was reading my mail, which had just been brought up from a box by the gate. Suddenly Elinor lifted her head and glanced out.

"That's funny," she said. "Who are all these men riding in, Blair?"

Glass in hand he strode to the window, and I can still see

176

his big hulking figure, stooping slightly to peer out. I went to a window myself, to see eight men on horseback cantering up the road, and to realize that all of them were armed. Elinor had risen, still staring.

"It looks like a posse of some sort," she said.

When I turned Leighton had disappeared. At first I thought he had gone to meet the men, but when I opened the front door he was not there. The riders had not dismounted. One of them asked for Leighton, and said they were after a band of cattle rustlers who had made off with a small herd and were supposed to be in the hills somewhere.

But Leighton was not in the house, nor at the barn. Even now I do not know where he hid during that brief attempt to find him. Brief, because the posse was in a hurry. In a few minutes they were riding on in a cloud of dust, having left with Elinor their itinerary and a request that Leighton follow them. I remember that she stood with a set face looking after them, and that soon after that we heard a horse racing past the house and knew that he was on his way.

He did not show up until the next day at noon. Then, dirty and exhausted, he came slowly back. They had found the cattle but not the thieves, and he himself was going to bathe, shave, and get some sleep. Not to me but to her later he made an explanation which apparently satisfied her. This was that on seeing the posse he had guessed its purpose, had taken a saddled horse from the barn and had ridden out to rope the fastest animal he had.

It had one merit. It was the truth; but once again it was not the whole truth. His first impulse undoubtedly had been headlong flight. Then, from some hilltop or other he had seen the men riding away and had realized that he was safe. To do him justice once more, he had done yeoman service that night. He knew that broken country, and it was he who located the stolen cattle, hidden in a break in the hills.

The second incident came close on the heels of the first. I was to leave the next day. My visit had done no harm that I could see, but certainly little good. Elinor was desperately unhappy, but stubbornly determined to stay and marry him; Leighton was driven by some devil which even his urbanity could not always conceal; and I was still uncertain as to the relationship between them. I was no watchdog, standing guard over Elinor's door at night.

Then, the night before I left, something occurred which made me wonder if that unhappiness of hers might not be only jealousy; and that, not without reason, of the girl Sally Ulman.

I had ridden out alone after dinner, and it was dark when, after turning out my horse, I made my way back to the house. In the distance I could hear Elinor at her piano. She was playing the *Liebestod*, Isolde's love-death song, and I stopped on the path to listen. Then I saw Leighton. He was in the kitchen, and through the lighted window I watched him lean down, turn up the face of the girl who stood close to him and kiss her.

It was no new thing to her. I saw that. She smiled up at him, and the next moment he had her in his arms. It was then that my long-repressed indignation made me do a ridiculous thing. I was beyond control, and I walked into the kitchen and confronted them both.

"I just want to say, Leighton, that I happened to be outside just now."

"Yes? And what business is that of mine? Or of yours?"

"Sometimes I wonder if you have a shred of decency left in you."

He stiffened. "If you were not my guest, I'd knock you down for that."

"I'm not your guest at this minute. And I'd like to see you try it."

It would certainly have resulted in an unholy brawl, for there was murder in me and a berserk rage in him. The red-haired girl had opened her mouth to scream, and I was backing against a table to shove it out of the way. Then suddenly the music ceased, and with that the girl flung out of the kitchen door.

When Elinor appeared I was taking off my spurs, and

178

Leighton had gone to the ice box for some ice. If she suspected anything she did not show it, and as Leighton disappeared after that for the night, on the surface at least the quarrel died.

The whole incident was preposterous, of course. If the man wanted to kiss that red-headed slut, why not have let him alone? I was not the protector of her virtue, even if it came to a question of that. I have recorded it only because, while it shows the ragged state of my own nerves, it also misled me into the belief that Elinor's unhappiness might be due to that cause.

I left the next day without seeing Leighton. He had been off at the crack of dawn, and it was a subdued and frightened Sally who brought in my early breakfast.

"I hope you won't tell Mrs. Norton," she said. "It was only a bit of fun, Mr. Warner."

"Pretty dangerous fun," I told her. "My advice to you is to get out, and as soon as you can."

"I will," she agreed. "I'll go tomorrow."

But she did not leave. She was immoral rather than vicious, but she was weak. Weak as water, and pretty seriously in love with Leighton after her own fashion, even then.

When train time came and Leighton had not appeared Elinor made his apologies for him. They were invented, of course. I knew he had left no message for me. But what else could she do?"

"He said he would try to get back, Carroll."

"That's all right. I didn't come here to see him, anyhow."

"You don't really mind, do you?"

"It would suit me down to the ground if I never saw him again," I told her brutally.

I made a final appeal to her then; to think twice before she married him, or, if she was determined on it, to marry him at once. "It's all wrong, Elinor. People will talk, are probably talking now. Do you realize that no one has been here to see you since I came?"

179

"My clergyman comes," she said proudly.

"Why doesn't he come and marry you?"

"How deliberately cruel you can be!" she said, and turning abruptly left the room.

I had kept myself carefully out of it during our talk. Ignorant as I was of the real situation, I knew she had determinedly put me out of her life. And I would have gone East without further effort had she not herself forced my hand later on the same day.

Once again she drove me to the train, but this was a different Elinor from the one the year before; less sure of herself, not even so beautiful. The planes of her face were still lovely, but her eyes were shadowed and there was a pinched look about her, as though she slept too little and ate too little. She was quieter too, and I, who would have given my life to have taken her out of that hell, found little or nothing to say.

It was not until the railroad was in sight that quite suddenly she stopped the car. "I must talk to you," she said. "I must talk or I think I shall die. Carroll, do you still care for me at all?"

"Care for you? Why am I here? It's too late to stop caring now, even if I wanted to."

"Please keep on caring, Carroll dear. Hold on to me. Don't let me slip. You see, in some queer way I still hold onto you. You understand that, don't you?"

But that was too much for me. I found myself begging her to get on the train with me. To marry me, or if not, begging her to let me give her a home until she had found herself. I pleaded my long devotion and the frustration of my life, and I even repeated what my mother had said, that she wanted to see her grandchildren before she went. That touched her; her lips quivered, but she was still obstinate, although she was tender in her refusal.

"I can't. Some day you will understand."

"I'm afraid I understand too much."

She sat very still, sliding her small roughened hands over the edge of the wheel. "I don't think you do, Carroll; and

I can't explain it to you. If you care for me you must believe that I am doing what seems to me to be best. And—trust me."

"Trust you! It's Leighton I don't trust. How do you know he will ever marry you?"

"Because he *must* marry me, Carroll."

There it was at last. She had not meant to tell me, I know. Some impulse of the honesty that was a part of her came to the surface in the last moment or two before our separation. Perhaps, too, an instinct to protect me from herself, to show me the ugly fact and thus set me free. Indeed, she said as much.

"Now you know. Now you can go and live your own life, Carroll, dear."

I reached over and took one of her hands. I could not have spoken.

"Live your life," she repeated. "Marry. Have children. You are that sort of man. And now please kiss me, Carroll. Kiss me good-bye. And don't come back, darling. Don't ever come back. I can't bear it."

I held her for a moment after I had kissed her. She was shaking. Then I let her go.

"There is only one thing that really matters in all this," I said carefully. "That is, if you still care for him, if the old infatuation still holds. If it does not—"

And then I think she lied to me, lied deliberately to save my soul. "It still holds," she said, and the next moment she was crying in my arms.

Afterward she told me about the letter from Leighton's father. She had not meant to, I think. It hurt her pride, and besides that it meant an indefinite continuance of that anomalous position of hers. But the story infuriated me. "The thing's impossible," I said. "It can't go on indefinitely, Elinor. What are you going to do? Wait until the father dies?"

"Wait until we can manage without his money, I suppose."

It was hopeless. I could not move her a hair's breadth,

181

and at last she started the car again. This time she did not wait for me to board the train. She turned the car and started back at once. As for me, I stood on that cinder path beside the track and hesitated. Why go at all? Why not go back and face Leighton again? Demand that he marry her at once or let her go; knock him down, kill him if I had to, but free her from him for good and all?

But the train was waiting. A porter had already picked up my bags, and the conductor was eying me curiously. Partly through indecision, partly through the dislike of most men of appearing ridiculous, I got on the train. I could still see her small car as we moved out.

It was after my return that I got the letter from her asking me not to go back. I had written asking if she needed money until the fall, and this was my reply.

25

It must have been shortly after that that he asked her to sell her pearls. She refused, and he apparently accepted her decision; but she no longer trusted him, even in small matters. More than once she saw him looking at them, and at last she took them and hid them.

That shows, I think, how far things had gone with them. He was less and less her lover. Indeed, I am not certain that he was her lover at all during that time. She seems never to have suspected the Ulman girl, but she knew very clearly that she had lost him.

Nevertheless, she did not weaken; sooner or later he would have to marry her. Her entire self-respect demanded that; old Caroline's creed, her own code. She expected no happiness with him, but probably she never had. Also he was drinking again at intervals, and he was brutal when he

182

drank; but he no longer went to town at those times. It is possible that that story of the cabin had been revived again, and that his old cronies had abandoned him. Whatever the reason, now he drank largely alone and in secret; and more than once she would go downstairs toward morning to find him sprawling and asleep in Norton's big chair, and to get him to bed as best she could.

Then, early in September, he reverted to the pearls again. "I've got to raise money somewhere. And what use are they to you? You never wear them."

"They were my mother's. I will sell anything else, but I can't sell them, Blair."

He was insistent. It would be January before she received that modest balance of old Caroline's estate. In the interval he had plans of his own; plans for plowing the flat valleys, for buying farm machinery and seed wheat. There was no use raising wheat in a small way. Better do it right and do it at once.

"Anything else, Blair. But not the pearls."

Evidently he thought that over, for the next day he came to her again. "You said you would sell anything else. Is that right?"

"I've said that. I haven't very much."

"You still have your engagement ring, haven't you? Why not sell that? This is your place as well as mine, although I'm carrying it. And a damned hard job it is. Maybe one of the Mayhew girls would buy it."

She stared at him, standing big and insensitive before her. It meant nothing to him that, with things as they were between them, he should suggest that he use the proceeds of the sale of that ring for his own purposes.

"It's all wrong, Blair. I don't like it."

"Do you think I like coming to a woman for money?"

"But—Lloyd's ring?"

"What difference can it make to him?"

In the end she agreed, although she felt a trifle sick as she went upstairs to get it. It was in the secret compartment of her desk, along with my heart-shaped locket and her pearls. Old Caroline's pearls, Lloyd's ring, and my locket—it was the story of her life before Leighton came into it. She stood looking down at them, and at the small bundle of Leighton's letters. It must have seemed very little to have retrieved out of all that living.

He was waiting for her when she carried the ring down, and it was he who wrapped and sealed the package. But she would not let him send it to the Mayhews, and that same afternoon he drove into town and sent it by registered mail to an Eastern jeweler for appraisal and sale.

She had learned something, however; the next day she drove into town, rented a box at the bank and placed her necklace in it. She did not tell Leighton about it.

She had driven Sally in for a day off, and Sally held the box. As I have said, she had no suspicion of Sally then, and she thought nothing of it when the girl asked to be left off at the hairdresser's; a Sally in absurdly high heels now, with enormous imitation pearl earrings, and in her purse the rouge and lipstick for use after Elinor was out of sight.

"I know you like me to look nice, Mrs. Norton."

"I do indeed, Sally." After that Elinor went to the bank, rented a box and placed her pearls in it.

It could not all have been like that, of course. There must have been peaceful intervals when Leighton was his gentlemanly best; evenings when he came in, weary from long days in the saddle, and showed her that gentler and better side of him which certainly existed; when he went to her like a tired boy, and she became once more not only his wife but his mother. Something must have led her to believe in his ultimate good faith. She was a proud woman, and hope of some sort must have bolstered her pride that summer and early fall.

"How about a little music, Nellie dear?"

"What would you like?"

"Let's have some Chopin. Not everyone can play Chopin. You can."

He could do it. I have heard him, with that damnable caress in his voice which few women could resist. But he

184

would not listen to her music. It would contribute to his sense of well-being that she sat there at her piano, playing for him. Perhaps also to a sort of macabre sense of humor that was in him somewhere; that Elinor should be playing for him, that the hot-eyed girl in the kitchen was waiting in the hope that he would pass through. Eventually he would drop to sleep in Norton's big chair by the hearth. . . .

There is a certain irony, in view of those evenings, in the fact that the one woman on whom he had never had the slightest effect was the one who eventually brought about his downfall and indirectly his death. That was Isabel Curtis. She called me up late in August, on her return from Europe. "This is just hail and farewell," she said. "I'm hitting New York like a tennis ball and bouncing off. I'm going West again."

I was dismayed. I did not want her sharp eyes on that situation. "Where?" I asked. "The West is wide."

"So it is," she retorted in her staccato voice. "It is also the place where the sun sets. Isn't nature wonderful?" But she added, "I'm going to the Leightons'. I've just wired Elinor Leighton."

"You wired to Elinor *Leighton?*"

"I did. Why not?"

"Nothing," I said. "I suppose she'll get it; but she is not Elinor Leighton. She is Elinor Norton."

There was an interval before she spoke again.

"The dirty dog!" was what she said.

It was in such a mood that she went West; for she did go, almost at once. As I write this I am thinking about Isabel. She is curious, almost unique as compared with the other women I know. There is no doubt that she had cared deeply for Lloyd Norton to the day of his death, but she was entirely without jealousy. There was no jealousy in her, of Elinor or of anyone else. I have known men like that, men who could take things or let them go, but few women. She had let Norton go deliberately rather than coldly, and had gone on caring for him, amused and scornful of herself for doing so. When he died she did not sit still and mourn. She shot to Europe and played hard there. To forget the unhappy was at once her creed and her religion.

But not to forgive, and she was still uncertain as to how Norton had died. Uncertain and suspicious.

Nevertheless, she met Leighton airily enough on her arrival. "Hello, Blair. Still remembering that handsome is as handsome does?"

"Hello, Isabel. Do we kiss or do we not? I've forgotten."

"We do not! And when we do we don't forget. Not people like you and me, Blair Leighton."

What she found at the ranch I do not know in detail. Much of it was what I myself had seen. Unlike me, she seems to have suspected the girl Sally from the start, and Leighton's secret drinking was never any secret from her. And she had not been in the house five minutes before she realized that Elinor was miserably unhappy; nor two days before she ran Leighton to earth as to their marriage.

"What's the reason? Are you trying to ruin her reputation?"

"I thought that word was not in your bright lexicon!"

But he did finally tell her about the situation, and she demanded to see the letter before she would believe him. She read it through and then handed it back.

"Personally," she said, "I think you forged it! But if Elinor believes it, that's her business. The only question is, to what extent has she believed it?"

"What do you mean?"

"You know what I mean. How far has she gone, on the strength of it?"

He told her then that she had an unpleasant sort of mind —not putting it as gently as that—and she merely grinned at him over her eternal cigarette. "Compared with yours," she said calmly, "I have the mind of a peri at the gates of Paradise."

They remained largely amicable. Both were worldly and skilled in that type of sparring. He even liked to show off before her, swaggering out to mount his vicious uncertain

186

horses, rolling cigarettes for her, cowboy fashion. She was unimpressed. One day she told him to get rid of Sally.

"Why? Send the poor girl back to that hades, out of heaven?"

"You call this heaven? It's hell on earth for Elinor, and that red-headed wench is crazy about you. I thought you had better taste."

Even that failed to disturb his equanimity; but one day he found her examining the guns in the gun case, and he told her furiously to let them alone.

Elinor must have been bewildered between them. There were days when their bickering could not be concealed, and other days when they all three rode together, companionably enough. Isabel was playing her cards cleverly, however. She never went too far with him. She could cajole him into good humor always with a bit of flattery.

"Much as I disapprove of you, you *can* ride, Blair."

"Praise from you, fair Isabel, is praise indeed."

Elinor's star sapphire had been sold; for a quarter of its value, but at least for cash in hand. Already he was deep in his wheat project, reading catalogues of farm machinery at night, making small crude maps of the ranch and drawing in red ink the areas he meant to plow under. Then, too, certain other fears of his had been allayed. The terror which had driven him into the fields the day the posse came was largely in abeyance. And by nature he was an optimist. Men of his type invariably are optimists. They lack the imagination of the brooder. Also he preferred being happy and comfortable, and worry annoyed him.

"Stay a while, Isabel. Nell's almost a human being while you're here."

"I intend to stay!"

She had no plan, so far as I know, unless it was to hear something from the men of the outfit. Certainly she spent a great deal of her time at the corral. She would sit on a bench in the sun outside the barn, and talk to the men as they moved about on their high heels, or sat making their everlasting repairs to leather and equipment. Tall and slim in her riding breeches, she told them Rabelaisian stories, sang them risqué little songs in French and then translated them with a gleam of malice in her eyes.

They took no advantage of all that. She was like a man with them, rode as well as they did, was tireless in the saddle, practiced throwing a rope until she won their applause. But she learned nothing from them. Any mention of Norton by her was met with a silence and a shift of subject. She was too keen not to find that significant.

That was the situation when Leighton decided to round-up, somewhere about the middle of September. They had nothing to ship, but there was a tally to be made and calves to be branded. Also an extra man or two to be hired: they had been short-handed since the spring.

I suppose there was the same bustle of preparation as the year before; the same chuck wagon, the same cook, the same cloud of dust as the cavvy was driven up into the hills. Probably the same camp site too, with its rope corral and the men's bed-rolls scattered about. But there was a new element this time.

It may or may not have been by accident that one of the men taken on was that brother-in-law of Henry Raleigh's. I think myself that it was by accident. I saw him at the trial, a tall, weather-beaten man named Sutton, mild-mannered and quiet. But it took only 24 hours for Isabel up in the hills to learn who he was, and to send down for a bed-roll and decide to camp with the men.

Nothing happened during the next two days. She rose with the rest at four in the morning, ate a hasty breakfast in the dark, and saddled her own horse. From then until ten, when she came in for food, she worked as hard as any man, riding through brush and breaks, into washes and out again, and at last helping to bunch and drive the cattle in.

She stuck as close to Sutton as she could, but he was taciturn and intent on the business of the day. Then one night after the others had turned in she saw him by the light of a match, sitting off by himself and smoking. She lost no time with any preliminaries. She went over, sat down beside him and herself lighted a cigarette.

"I've been wanting to talk to you, Sutton."

"So I gathered," he said drily.

"Then you're ready to talk?"

"Depends on what it's about."

"It's about—Mr. Norton's death."

He said nothing to that, and she was wise enough to keep quiet herself.

"What about his death?"

"That's what I'm asking you. I'm not here to make trouble, but I've got to know. You see, I was fond of him. At one time I meant to marry him. And you know something. I have felt all along that you do."

He denied it at first, but she was determined and skeptical. "If you don't tell me someone else will. I don't suppose you are the only one who knows it."

Even then he refused to commit himself. All he would say after much coercion was that it had looked funny to him to see that someone up there had put a heavy slug through an unopened can of milk.

"Where was that? In the cabin?"

"There's a hole in the cabin wall. The can was outside, on the ground. Might have been on the shelf when the gun was fired; I don't know."

"You mean a bullet hole?"

"It looked like it."

Then he closed up again, and she went thoughtfully back to bed. She was still puzzled. A slug through a full can of milk, and a bullet hole in a wall! That meant something, but what? Had Norton been shot in the cabin and then carried to where he was found?

She puzzled over that during the remainder of her visit. It was well on into September by that time. The days were still warm, but already the nights were cold. She awakened one morning to see a thin powdering of white on the distant mountains, and the quaking aspens along the creek bank were turning to fluttering gold. To see a deer near the house, and that Elinor was coaxing it to let her approach it. Almost it did; then it leaped back and bounded away on its small rubber feet, and when Elinor turned, Isabel saw that she was crying.

That decided her. She had some queer streak of sentiment in her, and the scene with the deer in its bleak autumnal setting seems to have epitomized Elinor's loneliness, as well as her helplessness against Leighton. Leighton who, Isabel now firmly believed, had killed Lloyd Norton. That Elinor should marry the man who had killed her husband was fantastic and horrible; and some time during the evening she begged Elinor to go back East with her.

Elinor refused, pointblank. "My place is here, Isabel dear. My money is here, you know. Besides, how would I live?"

"That's easily fixed."

"At your expense? No. I'm grateful, but I really don't want to go. Whom have I there now? The Mayhew girls, of course; but they never liked me much."

"You have Carroll Warner. You can't say that about him."

Elinor had flushed at that, but she was adamant to any suggestion that she leave the ranch, and Isabel finally abandoned the idea.

The next day she took the step which was to bring about the end. She borrowed Elinor's car on some excuse or other, and drove to the town and the sheriff's office.

26

I know little about Elinor during those weeks of Isabel's visit, an Elinor shut up most of the day in the house alone with the Ulman girl, and at least once going to plant some flowers on Norton's grave, with that strange sense of duty to the dead which is often a sort of apology to them.

I do know, however, in detail of Isabel's visit to the sheriff. He was a kindly man, and when she had told him that she thought there was some mystery about Norton's death he looked troubled.

"I hate to bring any more worry on the little lady out there," he said. "She's had aplenty. There's been some talk, but nothing you could get ahold of, so to speak."

"Maybe this is more than talk, sheriff. Would a heavy slug through a full can of milk mean anything to you?"

He sat up in his chair. "What's that? Through a full can of milk?"

"That's what I hear."

"Where'd you hear it?"

"From Raleigh's brother-in-law. He seems to think that the shot was fired in the cabin. At least there is a bullet hole in the wall."

"Where'd he find the can?"

"Somewhere outside."

He sat back again, relaxed. "Well, that doesn't mean anything. Lots of folks have used that cabin. And guns go off every now and then when you don't expect them to. I put a bullet through the heel of my wife's shoe here some time ago. Just about paralyzed her leg!"

Nevertheless, being the man he was, he took a horse and went up alone into the mountains the next day. He found no milk can, but he did find the bullet hole, neatly plugged, over the shelf. The bullet hole was nothing, but the fact that it was plugged looked queer to him. He had gone alone, and he was still alone when the day following he got into his car, the same car in which he had plowed through the drifts on the night Norton's body was brought down, and drove slowly and thoughtfully to the ranch.

He had no case. Indeed, there was no case. All he meant to do was a bit of shrewd interrogating. Back in a desk in his office, in a match-box for safe-keeping, was the bullet which had killed Norton, and tucked away in his mind were

191

innumerable instances of the strange things that happen when two men are shut away together, and in danger to boot.

"All I wanted," he told me later, "was the facts. I knew Norton and I didn't like him. Always thought he was a hospital case, far as that goes. But I was pretty well convinced by that time that he didn't die where he was found. Matter of fact it always had looked fishy to me. What I thought was that maybe he'd pulled a gun on Leighton in that cabin, and that Leighton had killed him in self-defense. I still think that's what happened."

However that may be, and it was very close to the truth, he went to the ranch the next day. Isabel, possibly alarmed at what she had done but more probably easing herself out of a difficult situation, was on her way to the train at the time; and it was not the least of the sheriff's worries that the two cars passed on the road. And that Elinor smiled and waved to him.

"I didn't like it much," he told me. "And when the little lady waved to me I just about quit and turned back. But I didn't expect any real trouble. I was sure there was a story behind it, and what I wanted was the story. But he got scared. He had a yellow streak in him somewhere, and he tried to bluff it out."

What he had intended was to see Sutton first. That proved impossible. When he got there he found most of the outfit throwing horses to remove their shoes for the winter, and Leighton in a leather coat overseeing the work.

"He was certainly a fine figure of a man," was the sheriff's comment. "He'd got a little portly; he looked big as all outdoors that day. But he was sure a fine-looking fellow."

Leighton was apparently not suspicious. "Hello, sheriff. Cold day, isn't it? What are you looking for? Bootleg?"

The outfit grinned, but the sheriff knew the men and he sensed a sort of tension among them. It relaxed when he said he was after an Indian accused of shooting some cattle, but Sutton had already put down his tools and disappeared

192

into the barn. It was Sutton he wanted to see. Leighton, however, gave him no opportunity.

"Come back to the house and have a drink."

"Well, if you're sure it's pre-war!"

They took the short cut through the kitchen. The girl there was singing shrilly, but she stopped when she saw the sheriff.

"Bring some glasses, Sally."

"Yes, sir." She stared after them as they went forward. Later on she was to say that Leighton looked queer that day as he passed her; but I do not believe it. I believe that the first inkling he had that everything was not all right was when, coming back from his room with the liquor, he found the sheriff in front of the gun case.

"Nice lot of guns you have here."

"Yes. Some of them were Norton's, of course."

"Just which were Norton's, Mr. Leighton?"

Leighton put down the bottle and stared at him. The ruddy color faded from his face. But he managed to laugh. "So that's it!" he said. "I take it this is an official visit."

"Well, yes and no. I'm not aiming to make trouble, you understand. But there's been considerable talk, and the way to fix that is to nail it now, once and for all. I've been up to that cabin, Leighton. Went yesterday. Now if you'll just tell me what actually happened up there—"

"Tell you! I've told you all I know."

"Not all, Mr. Leighton. You didn't tell me or anybody else about that bullet hole in the wall, and why you plugged it up." He had no knowledge, of course, that it was Leighton who had done that. "Taking a long shot," he called it later. But Leighton's reaction was sudden and ugly. For a moment the sheriff thought he was going to attack him. Then he laughed again shortly and poured himself a drink.

"Almost time for election, sheriff, isn't it! Trying to get busy, aren't you?" Then his voice changed. "What are you trying to prove anyhow? How many people have used that cabin in the last twenty years?"

"Only one person's been shot up there, that I remember."

He began to bluster then, to talk of persecution. He knew there had been talk. He was no fool. But the whole thing was ridiculous. They had never liked him out there. They had resented him, and Norton too. Made them outsiders. Besides, if he had wanted to kill Norton, why choose a time when it was an even chance whether either of them would survive or not? If this was an arrest, then for God's sake go to it. He—the sheriff—would be laughed out of the county if he tried it.

The sheriff was shocked. He had meant nothing of the sort, he said. There was no arrest or anything of the kind intended. He was certain that everything could be cleared up by a little talk. Now if they could have that it would be simpler, because otherwise—

"Otherwise what?" Leighton demanded.

"Otherwise I'll have to ask you for those guns of yours. I'm not demanding them, y'understand. Maybe I could, but—"

"I doubt it. I'm not an American citizen."

"Well, they're American guns," said the sheriff. "And if you're not a citizen you're probably not entitled to a license to have them! Come, come, Mr. Leighton. You don't want Mrs. Norton coming back and finding me here, do you?"

Leighton said nothing. He poured himself another glass of neat whisky and drank it, and the sheriff eyed him.

"We've got a saying out here, Mr. Leighton: 'One drink's plenty, two is too many, and three's not enough.' There's a lot of truth in that. Besides, if you're going to tell me that story—"

"What story?" said Leighton truculently.

Some time earlier the Ulman girl had brought in the glasses, had listened and then scuttled out again. Now the sheriff called to her.

"Get Sam Sutton and bring him in here," he told her; and she went on a run.

I do not know what happened during that three-cornered conference which followed in Elinor's living-room. The

Ulman girl has told that she listened outside, and that Leighton had little or nothing to say but drank steadily while Sutton told his story. He had grown ugly and belligerent with liquor apparently, and at one time he evidently made a pass of some sort at Sutton. She heard the sheriff shout to him to stop it, and Sutton's voice: "Let him alone, sheriff. If he wants trouble he can have it."

There was a chair overturned, and then silence. It was after that that she heard Sutton and the sheriff at the gun case, and later they appeared, each with an armful of guns. They packed them into the back of the sheriff's car, and later on she saw Sutton throwing in his duffle bag and his saddle. The two men drove away then, and quiet settled down over the house.

There was no sound from Leighton or the living-room at that time, but she was vaguely terrified. She went upstairs to her bedroom and locked herself in. She was still there, listening behind the door, when he decided that escape was the only course left open to him; and when he commenced —first quietly and then like a madman—to search for Elinor's pearls.

It was to this, to a Leighton desperate through fear and a house in chaos, that Elinor came back that day. She had put Isabel on the train, and bought a few essentials in the town. She drove around to the kitchen and left them there. Then, out of sheer relief that Isabel had gone and that she need do no more acting before her, she went out into the garden and gathered a few flowers for the house.

It was in the garden that she remembered a letter from Henrietta, which she had found in the box, and she put down the flowers and read it there.

You cannot imagine what people are saying, Elinor. I myself do not believe it. I cannot. But it is always best, Elinor, to avoid not only evil itself, but the appearance of evil.

It is for that reason that I suggest that you come to us here at once. You will be welcome. After all, it is your old home. But you cannot go on as I hear you are doing. For

almost two years you have lived in that house with a man
you should have married—expected to marry—months ago.
I cannot conceive what has happened, or why your plans
have miscarried. Whatever the reason, however, it is essen-
tial that you come back here until something has been de-
cided between you.

But I must make myself clear. You must not only leave
the ranch and all it stands for, but bring with you the hum-
ble and contrite heart which is the only acceptable condi-
tion of salvation. I know your pride, Elinor, but this is no
time for pride.

I have often thought about that letter of Henrietta's. She
wrote it, I have no doubt, in old Caroline's tower room
and sitting at old Caroline's desk. They were not so unlike
after all, those two sisters-in-law.

She still had the letter in her hand when she entered the
house. The letter and a bunch of dahlias.

27

There can be no great story without a great character,
and in this defense I have not sublimated the woman I
have called Elinor Norton. She had elements of greatness in
her, endurance and pride and a sort of heroic patience. She
had courage too. But she was still only in her late 20's, still
beautiful, and still incredulous that life could do to her what
it had done.

Perhaps what I have shown is not Elinor Norton at all,
but a sort of puppet, around whom—as around so many
women—revolved the weaknesses and passions and infideli-
ties of men. She was never a puppet. She was simply a bewildered woman unceasingly puzzled and anxious; and she

was still holding to her belief in a God who alternately comforted and alarmed her. I know now that she had taken to going to church, slipping away on Sunday to early service at the small Episcopal chapel; and that Leighton considered this amusing.

"Feel better now? Sins all forgiven?"

"I know there *is* forgiveness for sin, Blair."

"In that case, why worry?"

She never retorted. Those words of Henrietta's, that one did not make the fight alone, had stuck in her memory. But for what she prayed I do not know.

I do know that there were times now when she realized that Leighton would never marry her; and that at such times she had considered Henrietta and her order as her one possible way out. Perhaps in faith and good works there would be an end to pain. Then, too, Henrietta was already in the house at Seaview, and she had an almost childish nostalgia for it. But she made no move. There was a deadly lethargy in her during those last weeks.

If I had suspected anything of this I should have taken some action, but I knew nothing. There had been no letter from Isabel Curtis. I myself moved unhappily in my own small orbit, trying to reconcile the Elinor I had known and loved with the one whom, in her own words, Blair Leighton must marry, and attempting to forget them both. Even more definitely than if she had married him I had lost her, for I had lost a dream as well as a hope.

My mother noticed the change in me. "Aren't you growing very hard?" she asked me, apropos of something or other.

"Hard? Am I?"

"You are so intolerant, Carroll."

"Not to you!"

She preached me a little sermon then. My father had had many things to disillusion him, but he had kept his understanding and his compassion. "When you understand people you are sorry for them."

"Not always."

"But most of the time, Carroll. You have to know why they do what they do. There is always a reason."

Did she know? I think she did. Perhaps she had missed Elinor's picture from my desk, and certainly there was enough talk going about. She may even have overheard a conversation over the telephone one evening when Ada Mayhew called me up to demand to know if it was true, and cut short my labored explanation.

"All I can say is that it is disgraceful, Carroll. What if she does marry him now? It's too late."

"Perhaps if you knew the situation—"

"It's the situation I am talking about. Of course, you were always all for her, but how you can stick this is more than I can understand."

Talk there was. Even Shirley Johnson had come to me with a protest. But I doubt if Elinor knew anything about it until she read Henrietta's letter on that last and dreadful day.

I must have seen Henrietta at or about the time she wrote it. The cottage had not been opened that summer, and I had gone down as usual to see if it was properly ready for the winter. I saw her, but she did not see me. The alterations at the big house were still under way, and I found her on the beach where I had once seen old Caroline. She, too, was gazing at the sea. The wind blew her black habit and outlined her thin tall figure, and although metaphorically she held a cross where Caroline had clutched a stick, it seemed to me that there was a certain resemblance between them; an intrepidity and an iron will common to them both.

But her customary composure was gone. There was impatience in the way she stood, in the very gesture with which she caught her veil against the wind.

Mortimer, coming along the beach just then, had chuckled.

"Queer doings, Mr. Carroll," he said. "It's hard to think of a lot of nuns in the big house, isn't it? Prayers and incense instead of parties and liquor. D'you remember the day Miss Elinor was married, and the young squirt who swam to the raft in a top hat?"

"I do. He was killed in the war, Mortimer."

"Well now, think of that! You can't tell about folks, can you?" He eyed me. "How's Miss Elinor these days?"

"She's well, I believe."

He drew a long breath, and looked out over the sea. "Yes, things are queer," he said. "Your father gone and her at the big house. And now Miss Elinor a widow and living out among the cowboys! Well, I'd better be getting on. That sister there may have retired from the world, but she hasn't lost her eyesight!"

He moved along, chuckling. . . .

Just what part Henrietta's letter played in the tragedy, no one can say. All I know is that Elinor read it in her unkempt garden, and that she had it in her hand when she walked into the house and found Leighton glowering at her from a doorway. Beyond him was the utmost confusion; in the living-room rugs were turned back, the top of the piano had been lifted, the cushions had been taken from the chairs, and even her sewing-table had been ransacked.

"You've been the hell of a time getting back," was his greeting.

She stared at him. He was not drunk by that time, but she saw that he had been drinking. "I don't understand. What has happened? What are you looking for?"

"What do you think I've been looking for? What have you done with that necklace of yours?"

"It is in the bank," she said, as steadily as she could.

"In the bank! You *would* do that," he said furiously. But he saw that he was frightening her, and he made an effort at self-control. "Listen, Nellie," he said more reasonably. "My father is dead, and I'll have to raise some money in a hurry."

"You mean that you are going back to England?"

"Not to stay," he said. "You know me better than that, Nellie. But, of course, I've got to go back, at once."

He made a movement toward her, but she backed away.

"You will not go before you marry me," she told him, her face set. "There can be no such hurry."

"Oh, for God's sake, can't that wait? I've got a dozen things to do. Can't you get hold of those pearls somehow?"

"Not until morning."

She was still looking at him. He was badly shaken. His hands were unsteady, and he continued to talk in a sort of suppressed excitement. He could borrow money on the necklace in New York, and he would return it to her at once. He would have money now, before very long. Not a great deal, but some.

"Blair," she said quietly, "do you really mean to marry me at all? Have you ever meant to? What do you feel toward me? Am I your wife, even your common-law wife? Or am I only your mistress?"

"Why put names to things? You're always doing that." But he needed her help and needed it badly. He went to her and put his arms around her. "What do names matter, sweetheart? Of course, I'll marry you, since you think it's important."

"Since *I* think it's important!"

"Darling, a few words by a preacher just don't make sense to me. But I'll do it, of course."

"Before you go?"

"Yes," he agreed, after a momentary hesitation.

And then he actually bargained with her. Not in so many words. What he said was that in the morning they would get the necklace, and then the ceremony would take place; and she agreed.

Some of his panic had died. He still had a day or two of safety, and he knew it. The guns and the bullet in its matchbox would have to be sent somewhere for examination, and it would take perhaps a week before a report came in.

Elinor, however, suspected nothing. She felt peaceful, if not happy. She even sang a little to herself as she set methodically about straightening the disorder. He had left her, and she could hear him in his room next door, slamming drawers, throwing things about, getting ready to pack. She was only puzzled when, moving about, she happened to see that the guns were gone out of the case and only Norton's automatic lying there. She went to the door of his room.

"Where are the guns, Blair?"

He looked startled. "The guns? What guns?"

"You're not listening to what I am saying!" she said. "The guns out of the wall case, of course."

"I forgot. I sent them into town to be put in order." He added something about the hunting season, and she was still entirely unsuspicious. There must have been something helpless and unhappy in him that day which roused the mother in her; something which she mistook for grief at his father's death. She went over to him and put her arms around him; a protective gesture which he misunderstood, for he caught her to him with the first passion he had shown in months.

"Darling! Nellie darling!" he said.

She released herself, smiling. She still had to play the game. She had almost won, but not quite. "I'm really sorry about your father, Blair. When did you hear?"

"Today. By cable."

It did not occur to her to ask any further details. She left him packing feverishly, and going back finished her straightening of the living-room. Later on she remembered her flowers, still lying in the hall, and went back to the kitchen to get water for them. She was only mildly surprised to find that Sally had not yet started the dinner, and that the kitchen was empty. But Sally had her own methods, and finally Elinor went upstairs and into her own room.

She frowned when she saw it. Leighton had ransacked it from desk to closet, had even thrown back the mattress on her bed. The drawers of her desk had been drawn out, and the secret compartment was wide open. She was seriously affronted by that invasion of her privacy, and even frightened. For the first time she recognized something of the desperation of that search, and a faint alarm rang in the back of her mind. She put it from her, however, put the room in order and even got out from her closet the dress she meant to be married in. She carried it to a window and examined it. It showed wear, but it would have to do, and with it over her arm she went downstairs again to the kitchen. She could at least heat an iron and press it.

In a sense it was journey's end for her, that excursion down the steep staircase with her wedding dress over her arm. She knew that, although she never guessed what the end would be. To her it was simply the finish of a long struggle to rehabilitate herself. Her love for Leighton was gone, and there remained only occasional pity for the man and this hard resolve of hers. She refused to think beyond the next day, even then.

28

The Ulman girl was in the kitchen by that time. She was building up the fire, and she started when she heard Elinor.

"Aren't you late, Sally?"

"Yes'm. I'm sorry. I didn't feel very well."

And in truth the girl looked sick. She was still pale with fright and still watchful. Her eyes slid from Elinor to the door and back again. She had the instinct of her kind to avoid trouble, and that day she looked like a trapped animal.

Elinor saw it, although she did not understand. "Would you like to go back to bed, Sally? I'll cook the dinner."

"I guess I might as well stay here." Then her curiosity overcame her fear. "Guess Mr. Leighton was looking for something. I could hear him."

"Yes. It's all right now, Sally."

"I'm glad to hear it. What with that fuss with the sheriff, and everything—"

Elinor stopped, an iron in mid-air. "The sheriff? Was he here?"

"I'll say he was!" said the girl. "He and Mr. Leighton had some words. Then the sheriff took Sutton back to town with him."

Elinor put the iron back on the stove. She felt sick and dizzy. Sutton—that was Raleigh's brother-in-law. And the guns were gone from the gun case. There was no escaping that association of ideas, and all the latent suspicions of a year before came to the surface and confronted her. She managed, however, to keep her voice steady and quiet.

"You can call me when the irons are hot, Sally."

"Yes'm."

She still held her wedding dress, a dark blue silk of some sort. Now she laid it over the back of a chair and left the room. But she did not go at once to Leighton. Her knees were shaking. She sat down for a moment in the living-room, now dominated entirely by that empty gun case. Not empty entirely, for it still contained Norton's automatic. She must have noted subconsciously that it was still there. The rest of the room was gone; her piano with the vase of flowers on it, the India prints on the wall, the faded chintz on the chairs. She sat staring at the case, and listening to Leighton's movements in the room beyond. Then at last she got up again, and Leighton looking up from strapping a suitcase saw her swaying in the doorway, her face colorless and her eyes blank.

"Blair," she said. "I must know or I'll go mad. Did you shoot Lloyd?"

He straightened. "I think you *are* mad. Who's been talking around here?"

"Does that matter? Isn't it too late for all that? Why was the sheriff here? Why did he take away those guns?"

He made a furious movement. "If that slut in the kitchen—"

"Blair, I want you to look at me. Did you kill Lloyd?"

"Don't be a fool."

"If I thought you had, and then had lived with me as you have, I would—"

"What? Kill me?"

"Kill myself, Blair."

"You wouldn't do anything like that, Nellie?" He went toward her, caught her by the shoulders. "Not my Nellie. Not my wife!"

"Your wife? Do you think I can marry you, after this?"

"After what?"

"Blair, don't you see that with every evasion you are telling me the truth. You did kill Lloyd."

"I never meant to kill him," he said suddenly. And with that she collapsed on the floor.

When she came to she was lying on his bed and he was sitting beside her, fully sober. "God, Nellie, you gave me a fright!"

"Tell me about it," she said, almost in a whisper.

He did tell her. Much of it, I think, was the truth, the usual story of two men shut away together; the usual small disagreements leading to larger ones. Norton had been definitely going off balance for long enough before, and on that last day some action of Leighton's had apparently sent him over the edge. Perhaps that was when he had said, "You seem to think you are the only real man God ever made." However that may be, according to Leighton's story he had picked up his rifle and fired, but the bullet had missed, hitting the milk tin and the wall. Leighton had jumped at him, but he had got hold of a second gun.

"Then I got mine," he said. "It had to be one of us, Nellie. I only meant to disable him. But he jumped at me, and—well, you asked for it. Now you've got it."

There must have been more; the carrying out of the body and the frantic journey through the snow with it to where it was found; the setting of the stage there, with the snow still falling heavily to cover his tracks; and still later the attempt to plug the hole made by Lloyd's bullet. He did not tell her that, however.

"Why didn't you tell at the time?" she asked weakly.

"And be hanged for my pains!"

"Why not have told me? Why let me go on as I have, believing a lie and living one? Can't you see what this does to me, Blair? What it makes me?"

"It's going to make you my wife tomorrow."

She closed her eyes and tried to think that out, but she could not think. What was she now? What would she be if she married him?

"If I do marry you, Blair, you will be faithful, won't you? I've had so much. I can't bear any more."

"Faithful! I'll be so faithful that you'll be sick of having me around."

"You have been faithful, since—since last spring, haven't you?"

"I have indeed, Nellie dear," he assured her softly.

The girl in the kitchen might have laughed at that, but Elinor accepted it. She did not love him, but that caress in his voice still had its power over her. She believed him, and her next words were to urge him not to run away. It looked cowardly, she said; as though he had something to be afraid of. After all, it was not too late to tell the truth. A killing done in self-defense was not a murder. Why go at all? Why not stay and face it down? Go in at once and see the sheriff. Then, if he felt that he must go to England, it would not look like flight.

Apparently he agreed at last to do just that. Neither of them had had any food, and he did not wait for it. Lying there on his bed she heard him go back through the kitchen, speak a word or two to the girl there, and go on out to get his car. He had seemed more cheerful when he left her. Perhaps her reception of his story had heartened him. Probably when he drove out that night he meant to see the sheriff at once, but somewhere along the road the yellow streak in him reasserted itself. Elinor had given him courage, but along the way he must have lost it. He never saw the sheriff at all, nor attempted to see him.

After a time Elinor crawled off the bed and went up the stairs again. She was still confused. Of Leighton's proper course there was no doubt, and he had started to follow it. But what about herself? Could she marry him now? Shut in her cold room she debated the question. She knew the two men. She began to rebuild the scene in the cabin, with Norton desperate and Leighton alternately sleeping and patronizing him into anger. What had he told Lloyd in some moment of anger? That she had been desperately in love with him? It must have been something like that to drive Norton forward with a gun.

True or not, the thought drove her almost crazy. She took to walking the floor and when Sally called her for dinner an hour or so later she sent her away.

"I have a headache, Sally."

"And Mr. Leighton?"

"He won't be here. I'm sorry."

At 11 o'clock she was still in her room, waiting for him to come back. To pass the time and to steady her nerves she got out a pair of silk stockings and mended them for the ceremony the next day. Her dress was still in the kitchen, but she did not go down for it. Instead, she sat and sewed while she waited. The work quieted her somewhat, and she began to make excuses for Leighton in her mind; to be sorry for him and for his weakness. She thought of that long ride of his through the darkness, with apprehension and fear for companions, and of the next day when at last he would and could regularize her position. But when 11 o'clock came and he had not returned she put away her sewing and went down to the telephone. She could not bear the suspense any longer.

She called the sheriff's house, and he himself answered: "Mr. Leighton? Why, no, he hasn't been here."

"You haven't seen him at all?"

The sheriff hesitated. "Well, yes'm. I've seen him. He's down at Murray's, playing pool."

Something broke in her then; the strength of purpose which had upheld her for so long was gone. She wandered into the living-room where the automatic, blue and sinister, lay in the wall case. She stopped and stood in front of it, but she did not touch it. From there she went on into Leighton's room, cluttered with his trunk, his boots, the entire disorder of his preparation for flight. She had no plan. She was not even thinking coherently; but her instinct for order set her automatically to straightening it somewhat. She smoothed the bed, picked up a soiled towel. In front of the stove ready for burning he had thrown a heap of rubbish, discarded ties, papers and what not, and she stooped and gathered them together. It was then that she saw the cable, and still bending over, she read it. It said, *Father died peacefully last night,* and its date was two months before.

Then at long last she saw the man as he was and not as she had built him. Every scrap of illusion fell away, and he stood naked among his lies, his evasions, and even his possible crime. He could have married her two months before, but he had not. He had waited until he needed her help, and then had shamefully bargained with her. He had made of her a soiled and lost creature, and it had meant nothing to him. Less than nothing.

There was not only anger in her. In fact, I doubt if she felt anger. If she did there was terror too. A terror that he would try to come to her that night; would come stumbling up the stairs and to her door once more. Sooner than that she would kill herself. Yet I believe she hardly realized that she had taken the automatic until she was upstairs in her room again, with the door closed. Then she found it in her hand, and she laid it carefully on the bureau.

He was not to come in. The key to her door had been lost. She could not lock it. But he was not to come in, that night or ever.

The weapon fascinated her. She stood in front of it and looked into her mirror. How easy it would be to put it to one's head and then never to know anything more. As simple as that, as easy. She took it off the safety catch, picked the thing up, put it down again. Leighton playing pool in town, his father dead for two months, his bags packed for escape. Lloyd dead under that mound in the cemetery, and Leighton playing pool in town. Queer things came back to her: my own face as she had seen it in that crowd on the pavement outside of Sherry's, her mother watching while she was being dressed for her court presentation, and her mother again, a sick woman in a bed reading a prayer book.

She was still standing. She seemed to have been standing there for hours. The lamp in the upper hall had burned out, and it was in darkness. Over everything was complete and deadly silence, so that she could hear the blood racing in her own ears. And then far away she heard the rumble of Leighton's car.

She knew when he entered the house that he had been drinking heavily. Long experience had taught her that. She heard him clumsily making his way through the living-room to his bedroom, and for a time she thought she was safe. Then she heard him again and knew that he would soon be stumbling up to her.

She blew out her lamp at once, and stood on guard in her dark doorway. She was hardly aware that she had the gun in her hand until she found it there. There was a faint light from below, and in it she saw him emerge into the lower hall and begin with infinite stealth to climb the stairs. Just so, probably, had he come during the early months of their association, but she had never watched it before. It filled her with loathing as well as fear.

But to her utter incredulity, when he reached the top he did not turn toward her room at all. He moved, still cautiously, along the back passage to the room where Sally slept, and she heard him tapping at the door.

"Sally!" he said in a whisper. "Sally, are you asleep?"

Then some instinct made him turn his head, and he saw her standing there, frozen into immobility. And it was then that he made his final, bungling error. He turned around and stumbled toward her. "Darling!" he said thickly, and held out his arms to her.

He was not more than four feet from her when she raised the gun. "Don't come any closer! Don't touch me!"

"Listen, Elinor—"

208

"Don't touch me!" she screamed. And when he still came on she fired. She saw him sag to his knees, and drop. More, to begin that slow and terrible roll of his down the stairs. When the girl Sally came running out she was still standing there, staring. Then she raised the gun to her own head, and the girl snatched it from her.

29

"And now, gentlemen of the jury, we have completed our case. We have shown the motive for this crime; that this defendant was facing abandonment by this man with whom she had lived as his wife, although no civil or religious ceremony had been performed. We have also shown, not only the motive for this crime, but the fact that it was coldly premeditated; you have seen the letter in which such an act was clearly indicated.

"This premeditation extended still further, gentlemen of the jury. The defense has not denied that earlier in the evening of that last and fatal day this defendant carried up to her room the automatic with which the murder—for it was murder—was committed; nor has it impeached the testimony of Sally Ulman, practically an eyewitness to the crime, that she still held this weapon while her victim's body was slipping down the staircase.

"And how was she found, at that late hour? She was still fully dressed at that time. She had not retired. She was waiting, gun in hand, for the return of this man she intended to kill. . . .

"During the course of this trial the greatest possible effort has been made to arouse sympathy for this defendant, but the facts remain as we have shown them. We have established the case we set out to prove, which is much more

209

than that of the State versus Elinor Norton; it is of the sanctity of human life itself. To this end civilization makes its laws, which we are here to carry out."

The prosecuting attorney stopped here for effect, cleared his throat. He had been talking for two hours.

"And now the state rests its case with you, secure that you will see that the law is fulfilled." . . .

They had never allowed her to take the stand. Witness after witness had been called, the vast machinery of publicity carried on, the press and people had waited for her story. But she was not allowed to tell it.

There were moments during that long trial when she would look up with something of her old eagerness, as though she must speak in spite of them all, and set them right. Not in her own defense, but in the interest of truth. Once or twice I saw her half rise from her chair.

But mostly she was very still, her hands folded in her lap, her eyes taking in little or nothing of the scene. Only during Sally Ulman's testimony had she seemed to be actually conscious of what was going on; and Sally's revelation of her own relations with Leighton brought a faint color to her face.

As the days passed she grew increasingly pale and quiet. The look of patience and of waiting became accentuated. She was always carefully dressed, in those clothes sent by the Mayhews. In them she looked absurdly young, and once again I marveled that she bore so few scars; that such passionate love, such violence of fear and later of despair could have left so few marks on her.

But all through the trial her aloofness persisted, as though this strange thing which was happening to her was not greatly important to her. She wanted me to know the truth, and perhaps a few others; but what was vital to her had nothing to do with the trial. It lay in that buried story beween herself and Lloyd and Blair Leighton.

So all day, day after day, she sat in that courtroom. At night she was taken back to her cell, the room with its bed,

210

its table and its two chairs. It was warm and not uncomfortable, and the matron was still kind.

"And how did you sleep last night?"

"I slept a little, thank you."

"Maybe I'd better ask the doctor for a bromide."

"Please don't bother. I'm quite all right."

She was very calm on the last day. Shirley Johnson had centered all his efforts on a plea of self-defense, and she listened to him as quietly as she had listened to the others. Once or twice she closed her eyes, as when he said, "What was she to do? This man had killed her husband. He had admitted it to her. Every instinct of decency in her, everything she had been taught and believed, recoiled at his attempt to enter her bedroom that night after she had learned the truth. Rather than have that happen she was prepared to kill herself. It was for that purpose that she took the gun to her room. But when after she had warned him, he still came on, when in a drunken fury he attempted to take the automatic from her hand—"

It was then that she closed her eyes. What did she see? Leighton sagging to his knees, and then commencing that long roll down the steep staircase? Something of the sort, I imagine, or perhaps something very different: those evenings when he was in his gentler mood and coming to her for comfort like a boy to his mother; or that night under her window when he had called softly to her, "You looked very lovely, you know, Nellie."

She had two Leightons to remember: one of them the slim tall man who rode a horse like a young god, and the other a heavy, swollen and gross figure, looking at her out of bloodshot eyes and preparing to abandon her.

But as I have said she was very calm on the last day, very poised. At least once during the closing speech for the prosecution she looked directly at me, and across the crowded room she seemed to be sending a message to me. As though she said, *Please don't worry so, Carroll. I'm quite all right.*

But was she all right? What would they do to her, this

211

jury which was moving out with grave faces and troubled eyes? What did they know of her, after all?

I could hardly stand as I rose to my feet.

The crowd dispersed; the reporters broke for the speak-easy across the street, or for the poker game in that bedroom at the hotel. Shirley Johnson remained at the courthouse; he was tired and not too hopeful, and I stayed with him. Elinor had been taken back to the jail, for it was commonly agreed that the jury would be out all night, if not longer. I shall never forget that evening and the night which followed it. At midnight we learned that a sealed verdict had been returned, and Shirley Johnson made a gesture and ordered some sandwiches and coffee. But I could not eat. I took a walk instead along the hard frozen roads. Although it was midwinter by that time, no snow had fallen, and I remember the abruptness with which the town ended and the empty country began. There was a cold moon, and against it the mountains made a broken and sinister skyline. There was no sound except the thud of my feet on the hard ground, and when I stopped I could hear the silence as I heard it at the ranch long before.

That entire walk was an inarticulate prayer for her; that they had understood a little and had pity on her. And that her God be, as she had once asked, a little more than just.

But even I did not hope for acquittal. When I got back it was to find that Johnson had gone to bed, and to meet a reporter with the story that she had got a ten-year sentence. "And damned lucky to have got off with that," he said.

Almost I knocked him down.

I do not remember much as to the rest of the night. I did not go to bed. I had the same sort of room as that in which Elinor had waited for the return of Norton's body, and I spent the night in much the same fashion. The street below was deserted. Toward dawn a farm truck went through, loaded with milk cans for the railroad; and some time later a pinto pony, saddled and bridled, ambled into view, raised its nose and sniffed, and then set off on some objective or other. I must have smoked incessantly, and I certainly walked the floor; for at one time an infuriated voice shouted at me from the next room through the wall.

"For God's sake, stop that and go to bed."

I must have bathed and shaved, even eaten a breakfast of sorts. But nothing is clear to me until once again I sat in the courtroom, and they were bringing Elinor in.

Save that she was very white, she looked much as usual. She still wore those clothes of the Mayhews', with the shoes rather too large, the small black hat, the black suit with its white silk blouse. She still held her head high, and she still had that look of patient expectancy, as though she waited for something. What it was I did not know; not freedom, God knows, nor happiness. Perhaps, as I have said, it was for an end of waiting, or even for some ultimate sort of peace, whether that peace was to be the peace of death or of something different; or escape from the pain of living and loving.

As I say, I do not know even now. It is inherent in this story of hers, the story which was never brought out at the trial. All I know is that once again she glanced at me with reassurance before she took her place.

And then the incredible thing happened. The jury acquitted her. There was no ten-year sentence, there was no sentence at all. In two words they set her free, and I can still see the look of bewilderment on her face. God help me, she had not wanted acquittal! Not death. She had not wanted death. It was escape she had looked for, and they had denied it to her; to be shut away from life, to pay her price and perhaps achieve peace—that had been her hope. I saw it written in her face.

It was erased in a moment. The reporters broke for the telegraph office, the camera men set off their flashes. Then the crowd surged toward her, and something aloof and frozen in her seemed to relax before its friendly handclasps. They had understood, after all, those worn women and weather-beaten men. Many of the women were crying, and she looked very small and still puzzled among them. Why should they be friendly? She had done this thing. She had never denied it.

But she met them all with a gallant smile, took their hands, thanked them. The gulf was still there, but for a little while it was bridged.

At long last Johnson and I got her back to the hotel. She was very quiet on the way, and she asked to be left alone for a time. We left her there, and went into a conference during the interval as to her future. Johnson was confident that she would want to go East at once, but I was not so certain.

"Why not?" he demanded. "She can't go back to that house."

"I think she can and will."

"But why? Of all the desolate spots on earth for a woman to be alone in—"

I could not tell him what I felt; that somewhere back in that empty country she would want to work out her own problem, and that eventually she would work it out there. Nowhere else.

"We have to remember," I said, "that she has had a terrific psychic shock."

"All the more reason for her trying to forget it!"

"She can't forget it. She has to find an answer, Johnson. Maybe you and I don't understand that, but she does."

"And what *is* the answer?"

"God knows. I don't."

As I had expected, that was what she brought out when we went back to her. She was drawing on her gloves, and she wore Ada Mayhew's fur coat.

"I'm ready," she said.

"For what?"

"I'm going back to the ranch," she said with her head high. "I must go there, Shirley. I must get things straight. Not the ranch; straight with myself. And where else do I belong now? From now on I am not—like other people."

"Don't be a stubborn fool," Johnson said sharply. "That sort of talk gets you nowhere. Nor that sort of thinking." Then his voice softened. "Listen, Elinor, you've been brave up to this minute. Amazingly brave. Don't weaken now."

She looked at him. "Brave? What are you thinking, Shirley? That I may kill myself? I will never do that. I wouldn't hurt you so, after all you have done. Or Carroll. I couldn't hurt Carroll. Don't be afraid. I promise you both."

There was nothing to do after that but to take her back, and we did it during the afternoon. She was very gentle with us both, but still aloof, and it was only too clear that quite definitely she had set herself apart; not only from her old world, but from the world in general.

30

We left for the East the next day, Johnson and I. There was nothing we could do and little we could say. Physically she was as comfortable as we could make her. Mrs. Alden had gone back, and the house was clean and warm. There were still two or three men in the bunk house, and she had by that time received her mother's estate. She had enough money to last her for some time. But it was hard to leave her there, with everything in the house reminding her, day and night, of those two ghosts of hers. I myself never mounted the staircase without seeing Leighton's heavy body rolling down it; or looked at the chair by the fire without seeing Norton in it asleep and with his mouth open.

On the surface all was well. There was a fire in the living-room, the place shone with cleanliness. And Mrs. Alden hustled around, determinedly cheerful for once, busy and capable. She had been at the door when we arrived, and had taken Elinor into her arms without a word at first. Then:

"Well, well!" she said, "and you're half frozen at that. Now just let me tuck you into bed and bring you a cup of hot tea. I've got the kettle boiling."

That night, however, Johnson, sitting in the living-room, suddenly got up and went to the window.

"How many winters of this has she had?"

I counted and told him, and he swore under his breath. "When I think of her as a girl, and then listen to this silence and look out there at nothing—"

"Don't!"

"She won't kill herself," he said. "She'll go crazy. That's all."

I went out after he had gone to bed. In Norton's room, that was, although he did not know it. The creek was frozen solid, and beyond and above it was the trail into the hills. There was about everything that sense of life caught in motion and frozen into rigidity which I had noticed before; and once again I had the feeling that death must be something like that, without color and without form, and only the tired mind thinking its confused disembodied thoughts.

I saw when I turned back that Elinor's lamp was still lighted in her room.

We left, as I have said, the next day, Johnson to his office and his neglected practice, and I to a pneumonia and a nervous crash which, combined, almost finished me. During my long convalescence, however, I had time to think, and I realized that Elinor was farther from me than she had ever been. I realized other things as well. My mother was aging; my father's death had done that to her, and at any time she might go on, without seeing her grandchildren. Now and then I found her watching me, apparently trying to say something, then abandoning the idea. I had a definite sense of guilt.

216

"What is it, Mother?"

"Nothing. Do you want another pillow?"

I believe she would have accepted Isabel, although she did not like her. But I could not forgive Isabel. She came to see me one day, after I was up and in a chair, and characteristically brought up the subject immediately.

"You still blame me, don't you, Carroll?"

"Who am I to blame anybody?"

"I suppose, if it hadn't been for that, I might have a chance with you."

"You don't really want me, Isabel."

"Don't I? Well, I suppose not."

She looked away, and I knew what she was seeing: a low mound in a little cemetery on a hill, with the sagebrush growing just beyond the wall and the mountains behind it, looking down over the lives and deaths of a pigmy world. But she had brought me a bunch of flowers, and I think she had come with some idea that out of our common wreckage we might build something together.

"Two halves don't always make a whole, Isabel."

"No."

But this is not my story. As a matter of fact, I had meant to end it with Elinor's acquittal. It was to be merely my speech for the defense; the story which is never brought out at any trial, the relentless piling of event on event until they reach an inevitable climax. But as I have carried it on it has become evident that, in fairness to Elinor, I must go further. Her problem was still not solved, yet somehow if she were to live she must solve it.

Nevertheless, the solution she finally selected almost stunned me by its finality.

Perhaps I should have suspected it from the start: There was that heap of religious and contemplative books sent by Henrietta, and waiting at the ranch house when she went back there. And there had been a correspondence during the trial which continued all through the following year. But it had never occurred to me that this would be the answer Elinor would find.

She had gone through the year bravely. She did not write, and had asked me not to do so.

"You understand, don't you, Carroll? Not for a time anyhow. I shall be thinking of you; but I have to adjust myself, and I can do that better alone."

Now and then I had a note from Mrs. Alden, written in her cramped and unaccustomed hand: *She's doing pretty well and looks better. Pete's got a good calf crop and will ship some this fall. Wish she would not stay alone so much, but she wants it that way.*

Or, as in another: *Sometimes I think she lives on here to punish herself for what she did. She acts that way. I try to tell her she did what any other woman would do the way things were; but she don't see it that way. One queer thing, she won't let me talk about you, Mr. Warner.*

Even Mrs. Alden was evidently ignorant of what was in her mind, for nowhere does she mention it. And I myself might not have known until it was done had I not seen Elizabeth Mayhew. That was in the early summer of 1923, and Elinor had been alone at the ranch for almost a year and a half.

I met Elizabeth on the street one day, and she told me that Elinor was about to join Sister Henrietta's order. "And a good thing too," she said briskly. "What else can she do?"

"Is she there now?" I asked sharply.

She eyed me. "So I hear. You'd better let her alone, Carroll. It's the best answer for you both."

Then she went on, smug in her virtue, conscious that her comfortable life was still hers to live: Palm Beach, Newport, New York, bridge, cars, clothes, Europe now and then. I was savage against her as I left her.

And so I learned that Elinor was back home again, bringing with her, I supposed, that humble and contrite heart Henrietta had insisted on. Even sleeping in her old room again, but with a difference now; with only the necessities to furnish it, and a wooden crucifix on the wall. Of all the strange things that life had done to her, I imagine that was

218

not the least of them; to hear at evening the soft voices of the sisters at Compline, to see a brisk young clergyman in a flat hat coming up from the old boathouse, or to find Henrietta at her desk in the tower room where old Caroline had carried on her endless correspondence, or occupying that bedroom from which she had sent Elinor back to Lloyd Norton. I hope Henrietta prayed for her soul, for I could not.

I was bitter beyond words. Bitter even at Elinor, that she should choose what to me was death in life; and that without a sign to me she could throw back in my face the devotion of a lifetime. I made up my mind that night to have one more interview with her and to attempt to dissuade her. If that failed I would marry Isabel Curtis.

With the morning came reason, of course. I did not care for Isabel. For 15 years—20 perhaps—I had cared for only one woman. Now I was too old to change. As I shaved that morning I saw that I was going gray over the ears. Even in the early 30's men have lost the facile emotions of youth, cannot so easily love for a night or for a lifetime.

But that one talk with Elinor I would have.

I do not know what I expected to find. Probably that they had already cut off her lovely hair and dressed her in cumbrous black. I had a horror of finding her like that. But the fact was entirely different.

I reached Seaview by an early train that day. It was still early in the season, but the harbor was bright with sun and full of boats, large and small. Not only was the war over, but the panic also. Now evidently we were forgetting them both. Big and little, the white yachts floated on the blue sea, promising escape and pleasure, and speaking of a gay young world that I seemed to have forgotten.

I remember feeling incredibly old when I saw them.

I had wired Mortimer that I was coming, and he met me at the train with his ancient car. It was not until he had given me the usual small talk of the beach and the village that he gave me a quick look and said:

"What's this about Miss Elinor joining those nuns?"

"It may be true. I don't know."

"Well, what's the idea anyhow? Just because she had that trouble out West? Good riddance to bad rubbish, I say."

"It was a great tragedy to her, Mortimer."

"Well, maybe. But she's too young and too good-looking to bury herself like that. And what good does it do anyhow?"

I had no answer to that, and it was later that I asked him if he had seen her.

"I have. She walks on the beach a good bit at night. Mostly by herself. Must say she looks all right. Kinda quiet. That's all I notice."

I put in the day as best I could. Once or twice I saw a black-robed figure near the big house or on the beach, and my heart seemed to turn over. But it was not Elinor. Nevertheless, things had changed. Once Mortimer appeared at my elbow to point out a young clergyman in a shovel hat, making his way toward the boathouse.

"That's the priest, or whatever they call him," he said. "Look's queer to me, but he's not a bad sort. Celibate, he calls himself, and I guess maybe he is. Well, every man to his own way of thinking. Or not thinking!" he added with a chuckle, and moved away.

Of Elinor herself there was no sign that day, and at dusk when she still had not appeared I determined to hunt her out at the big house. To face down Henrietta and her whole sisterhood if necessary to save her from what I felt was a living death for her. Not for all women. To many it brought peace and compensation. But to Elinor I knew it meant escape and little else. It was a subterfuge, and I knew it.

As it turned out I did not go to the house at all, for just after dusk I found her sitting on the beach alone. Like Caroline, like Henrietta, she was gazing out over the water, and she was so still that at first I thought she had not heard me.

220

Then she turned and looked up at me. She gave me no formal greeting whatever.

"Come and sit with me, Carroll," she said. "I had forgotten there was such peace and healing in the sea."

I sat down, and she gave me her hand.

"Has it healed you, Carroll? I have made you suffer so much. And do you hate me for it?"

"Hate you? You are just what you always have been, Elinor. Maybe you have never been away, and we have dreamed the rest."

"Perhaps. I feel as though I have lived in a nightmare, and have just wakened from it, Carroll."

"To what? To life?"

"To good works," she said, and smiled. "I suppose you know, don't you? And they do a great deal of good." She paused, and when I said nothing: "What else can I do, Carroll? And I must pay somehow."

"Pay for what?"

"For my life."

"*With* your life?"

"There is such a thing as service."

"What sort of service? Do you have to retire from the world to find it and serve it? You were always honest, Elinor. Why not admit that this is an escape, a weak subterfuge? You are not religious, you—"

"I believe in God," she said quickly.

"So do I. But I don't go into a monastery to prove to myself that I do."

"It's not a hasty decision, Carroll. Please believe that. It simply seems the best thing to do."

"I can think of a better one. You can marry me, Elinor."

She shook her head. "Never." And she added, rather wistfully, "Can't you let me have my peace, Carroll? It is all I have. I must hold on to it."

We were silent for a long time. Then she said, "Do you remember, long ago, how we sat here together on the beach and cried together?"

221

"Don't. For God's sake, Elinor!"

"And then we danced, in the moonlight. What children we were, Carroll! You said then that I would have to live my own life, and not the life someone planned for me. Well, I did, and see where I am."

"You are here, and I am still beside you, Elinor," I said steadily.

"I am so tired, Carroll. And so—soiled."

"What about my life? I have lived it too; like any man. But I have always loved you."

"And I have always loved you. Don't misunderstand, Carroll. It doesn't change anything. I just wanted you to know."

She left me abruptly on that and I did not attempt to follow her. I remained on the beach alone for a long time after she had gone. I had very little hope. There had been a finality in her voice that showed me where I stood; even her confession had been final.

I saw her the next day. She and the brisk young priest were slowly pacing the beach and talking gravely together. I hated him with a furious hatred that day. I could not fight him, or the peace he offered her. All I could offer her was life, and she had had enough of that. I misjudged him, however. I was surprised that evening to find him on the front veranda, asking to talk to me, and to find him observing me shrewdly through nearsighted eyes.

"I wonder," he said, "if you can give me a little time? It's rather quiet where I live. We could go there. It's over the old boathouse."

"I know that," I said, not too amiably. But I agreed to go, and it was not until we were settled there that he came to the subject in his mind, and that without preamble.

"I have been talking to Mrs. Norton," he said. "She has —well, she has told me a great deal." And he added abruptly, "She has no business entering a sisterhood, any sisterhood."

"I agree with you. But why not?"

"There are a number of reasons. Please understand that her past has nothing to do with them. She would not be happy. She has no real flair for the religious life. And she is doing it as a penance." He smiled faintly. "We are not punitive, you know. Repentance for sin, yes. Punishment for sin, no. That is vengeance. Why should we punish her? That is not in our hands."

He lighted a cigarette and leaned back in his chair, eying me. "There is another thing," he said carefully. "Some of us can live the celibate life. It is not always easy, but it can be done. In that case we substitute other things, other interests, for the love life. But they must be very real, those interests, very vital. Otherwise we fail."

"And you think that she—"

"I happen to know that she is very deeply in love with you. I have told her that that automatically unfits her."

"But what am I to do about it? She won't marry me."

"Are you sure of that?" he asked. "I am not, and—good heavens, man! Hasn't she a right to live? Why don't you take her and make her happy? Surely there's enough misery in the world."

I sat very still. We were on the broad porch of the boat-house. Below us lapped the sea, the same sea that old Caroline had defied; and I thought with a certain irony that if her shade hovered near, it would shudder at the heresy of that gospel of happiness. The young clergyman, too, was gazing out over the water.

"You see," he said quietly, "if I believe in anything, I must believe that human misery is man's mistake, not God's."

I did not find her on the beach that night, and once more I made my old circuit around the big house, the vegetable garden, the pond, the maze and finally the beach again. When at last I reached the cottage it was to find her sitting on the steps of the porch, much as she had sat at the ranch. Only now there was the sea instead of the barren hills.

I took her in my arms, and she relaxed there, relaxed as

223

I think she had not done in years; and so we sat together, this woman I have called Elinor Norton, and myself. To those who know her story her identity will be clear, and I have written it for them.

It is the story of my wife.